OUTSIDE AGENCY

OUTSIDE AGENCY

CONOR
DALY

Kensington Publishing Corp.

http://www.kensingtonbooks.com

KENSINGTON BOOKS are published by

Kensington Publishing Corp.
850 Third Avenue
New York, NY 10022

LIBRARY OF CONGRESS CARD CATALOG NUMBER: 96-079079
ISBN 1-57566-162-4

First Printing: May, 1997

Printed in the United States of America

To Barbara and Ben,
Agent, mentor, friends.

An "outside agency" is any agency not part
of the match or, in stroke play, not part
of a competitor's side, and includes a
referee, a marker, an observer, or a fore-
caddie employed by the Committee. Neither
wind nor water is an outside agency.

The Rules of Golf
Section II, Paragraph 22

OUTSIDE AGENCY

CHAPTER ONE

I faded in like a lousy black and white television. Small flat screen, dark images wavering behind a shimmering curtain of dirty snow, voices swirling out of persistent static.

"Here. Over here."

"Step around, around."

"Get him outta there. Hey, get the hell outta there."

"Goddam. Look at that."

The screen sharpened, resolving into a narrow slit between two eyelids. The CBS eye swollen with a shiner. The voices receded as different sectors of my body signalled their positions to my brain. My chin rested on something springy and soft, like thick rough lining a fairway. My left arm stretched out above me, palm up, fingers clutching at air. My right bent awkwardly beneath my chest, wrist angling up to pinch my windpipe. I gagged, making hardly a ripple in the static. The slit detached itself from my eye and drifted off into darkness. Losing it, I thought. Hold on, hold on. My brain barked frantic commands: roll your head,

move your hand, unstick your arm. But nothing sparked in
the muscles.

"He still alive?"

Cold fingers burrowed under my collar and pressed my
neck.

"Got a pulse."

The touch ignited pain. Dull throbs sharpened to white-
hot points driving deep into the ball of skull bone behind
my ear.

"Roll him over, quick."

The entire world shifted. My eyes banged inside their
sockets. Pain radiated from behind my ear, circled my head
like longitude lines, and crashed back together at my opposite
temple. A hand pinched my cheeks, puckering my lips into
a fish mouth.

"Guy's got a mess of blood in there."

Fingers plunged past my teeth, poked around, tugged at
my tongue. I coughed. Air rushed down my throat and flooded
my burning lungs. Thank you, I said in my brain, thank you.
The message trailed off before the static swept over me like
a blanket. Beneath my spine, the grass felt carpet-soft and
pool-table flat. Several times I tried to sit up, actually con-
ceived each distinct muscular movement needed to lift my
torso vertical. But then waves of pain broke across the surface
of my skull, and the static consumed me again.

"Get that over there. He's over there."

Wheels squeaked beside me. A leathery, rubbery smell
weaved into my nose. Hands, too many to count, worked
underneath me, gently folded my arms across my chest.

"On three."

The hands tightened, lifted me, dropped me onto the

leather. I rolled out from cool shade into hot sun. One eyelid loosened. A man hovered above me, his white smock melting into the sky.

"Never thought it'd feel like this," I muttered.

"What you say?"

"Never thought it'd . . . feel like . . . this. . . ."

"Feel like what?"

"Getting hit by a golf ball."

I recognized the inside of an ambulance. I could hear the radio chatter, smell the pungent medicinal smells. I could feel the thrum of the tires on the pavement as tight turns pressed me against the stretcher's straps. I blinked out, then blinked on again, as the stretcher flew on its gurney and banged through doors.

The air above me filled with faces. Fingers pricked, probed, and palpated. Lights shined in my eyes. Jargon zipped back and forth, the words clumping together and stretching apart like a badly warped cassette tape. A few stuck: *concussion, stabilize, suture, tests*. Then the static returned. The voices faded, the probes melted away.

I spiralled down into the old office of Inglisi & Lenahan. A terrific rumble, like the wash of a jumbo jet, shook the building to its foundation. I sat in the conference room, wrestling a pen that skipped crazily across a legal pad. Behind me, plaster trickled from the ceiling in thin powdery streams. The rumble stopped. A single bead of sweat, the size of a cat's eye marble, rolled down my nose and plopped onto the table glass. A rush of wind blew the pages from the pad and sucked books from the shelves. Footsteps pounded the corridor. The conference room doorway darkened, and Judge Inglisi walked in, a svelte 250 in tie-dyed shirt and faded jeans. A Paul McCartney haircut, circa 1964, sat skewed on his head, but I knew intuitively it wasn't a wig.

"I'm back. I've quit the bench." He hopped on a chair, which morphed into a throne with gilt arms and burgundy cushions. "One more thing, I married Georgina."

Georgina appeared on his knee, a lush mane of curly black hair cascading to her waist. She swept a lock behind her ear, revealing a golf ball dangling from a chain.

"Twenty years was too long to wait," she said, more in sarcasm than apology or explanation.

"But it was just—" The absurdity of my answer choked me.

"Ten?" the Judge said, and they both guffawed.

Suddenly, I rose up through the roof and watched the building shrink through wisps of clouds. The Judge's jumbo jet nosed up to the back door. Tiny people criss-crossed the village green between Merchant Street and the Milton Town Hall. I waved, shouted good-bye, but no one paid any mind.

The landscape blurred, then sharpened into a map. I arced giddily over a pink North Carolina, a yellow South Carolina, an orange Georgia, then descended toward a green Florida, and into a large house with a glass wall facing a golf course studded with sparkling blue lakes. Music played; people I knew to be friends jammed the rooms. And moving among them was a woman I couldn't quite lay my eyes on as she beckoned me through the party.

Silence woke me. My head was turned left and slightly down, which aimed my line of sight at a tube connected to my wrist with a needle. I followed the tube to an IV bag hooked to the top of an aluminum stanchion. My eyeballs ached, as they did in the aftermath of a migraine. My mouth tasted like metal, stuffed with a tongue four sizes too big.

I tried turning to my right, where I sensed a window. My head exploded with pain. My arms shot up in reaction, ripping out the IV tube.

"Goddam!" I hissed between my teeth.

A buzzer sounded out in the hallway, and a nurse rushed in. She was skinny, with a sunburn set off by frosted hair. Skittish as a cat, the way she eyed me while reattaching the IV.

"A golf ball hit me, right?" The words oozed slowly around my tongue, an octave lower than usual. "Who did it? Someone playing behind me?"

She snipped the tape, patted down the ends, dropped the bandage scissors into her pocket.

"You can tell me," I said. "I'm not going to sue the bastard."

"I really don't know. I'll page the doctor."

Either I nodded off or the doctor materialized out of thin air because the next thing I knew a young guy in a green smock ripped a Velcro collar off my arm.

"I'm Dr. Ellis, Mr. Lenahan." He wore wire-rimmed glasses and a five o'clock shadow on an otherwise well-scrubbed face. "How are you doing?"

I grunted.

"Well, you've stabilized enough for us to run some tests." He shined a penlight into each pupil. "Do you remember what happened to you?"

"Golf ball hit me."

"Do you remember it specifically, or are you just guessing?"

"Guessing, I guess."

"That's expected." Ellis snapped off the penlight. "What is the last thing you remember?"

The last thing I remembered—definitely remembered before compressing into that old TV—was standing on the seventeenth tee at the Bay Hill Club in Orlando and measuring my score against the leader board.

"And before that?" he said.

"Finishing at—" I was going to say Doral. But that was impossible; the Doral tournament was over two weeks ago. "I'm a bit fuzzy."

"Memory loss is common with head trauma," he said. "That's why we run tests. Open wide."

I let my jaw hang limp, and he probed my mouth with a tongue depressor the size of a surfboard.

"You're lucky. You had so much blood in your mouth and throat, you could have suffocated."

"What from?" I said, after he tossed the stick into a wall receptacle.

"Your tongue."

"I cut it?"

"You bit it," said Dr. Ellis. "We stitched it up as best we could. How does it feel?"

"Big."

"The swelling will go down eventually. I hope you like milk shakes. They may be all you can handle for a time."

The nurse pushed a wheelchair hard against the bedside, and they both helped me in. I rolled into X-ray, where a tech propped my chin on a vinyl cushion and scanned my skull from ten different directions. After that, the nurse wheeled me back to my room.

"What time is it?" I said.

"Almost midnight." She answered the next question without me asking. "Thursday. Dr. Ellis will have the CAT scan results in the morning."

I asked whether this hospital was a noted center for the treatment of golf ball injuries. She smiled wanly and left the room.

Not afflicted with a case of total amnesia, I concentrated on the name, rank, and serial number aspects of my life and hoped that something clicked. Kieran Lenahan, former lawyer, now a golf pro. The PGA Tour always landed in Florida around the first of March and worked its way north for four successive weeks: the Doral Open in Miami, the Honda Classic in Ft Lauderdale, the Bay Hill Classic in Orlando, and the Tournament Players Championship at the Sawgrass Players Club, just outside Jacksonville.

I added Thursday to my independent memory of standing on Bay Hill's seventeenth tee. The weekly PGA tournaments begin on Thursdays, so I must have played in Bay Hill's opening round. Several minutes of intense concentration fashioned the vague sense of arguing with my caddie over the read of a putt on the sixteenth green. After that, nothing.

I passed the rest of the night in a kaleidoscope of dreams. Some returned me to the same house party, where the strange woman still eluded me. Others showed me finishing my round at Bay Hill, undistinguished yet without incident. Mercifully, none featured the Judge.

Shortly after dawn, a nursing student disconnected the IV and brought in breakfast with nary a milkshake on the tray.

"Has anyone asked about me?" I said. "Anyone from the Tour?"

She shook her head.

I let the bran flakes turn soggy in the milk and chewed carefully on the good side of my mouth. Professional golf isn't a bean ball war. A player literally knocking another player out of a tournament is a singular occurrence. And no one from the Tour called? No one sat outside waiting for word of my condition? Maybe I would sue the bastard.

Sometime about ten, another nurse brought me a blue plastic satchel filled with my personal belongings and a clipboard thick with insurance forms and discharge papers.

"Insurance allows one night for head trauma not accompanied by contusions or lacerations," she said.

"What about my tongue?"

"That doesn't count." She checked boxes on the forms and told me where to scratch my name on a bunch of signature lines. I emptied the plastic satchel onto the bed. My watch and wallet tumbled out, followed by gray slacks and a red shirt. I discreetly stepped into the slacks, slipped the dressing gown off my shoulders, and carefully poked my head through the shirt collar. The tails dropped halfway to my knees, and the short sleeves swallowed my elbows.

"It's from our goodwill bin," said the nurse. "Yours is too dirty to wear. We tried our best to match color, style, and size."

Oh well, I didn't expect to find myself on national television anytime soon. I tucked the shirt into my pants and pulled a pair of sneakers from the satchel.

"I guess my golf shoes are dirty, too?" I said.

The nurse ignored me.

No wheelchair this time, and I found walking to be a distinctly interesting experience. The terrazzo corridor appeared smooth and level to the eye, but my feet never landed the same way twice. I reached Ellis' office and dove for the nearest chair. The inside of my head felt like a lava lamp.

"You had a bad concussion," said Ellis. He switched on a shadowbox behind his desk and shoved two X-ray plates into place. "You were struck behind and slightly below the right ear. The shock waves travelled around your skull and refocused at approximately the left temple, which leaves the impression there were two points of impact. Fortunately, the CAT scan shows no hematoma or edema. That means bleeding or swelling."

I knew that.

"You will likely feel odd for the next few days," he said. "Headaches, dizziness. You might find it difficult to concentrate. You might feel depressed, apathetic, anxious."

"I'm used to that. I play golf for a living."

Ellis forced a chuckle and slid a sample bottle of pills across the desk. "Take these every four hours. They treat only the symptoms, not the concussion itself." He scribbled onto a prescription pad. "If the symptoms persist after the pills run out, fill this."

I folded the prescription into my wallet.

"What about my memory?"

"It can return as easily as turning on a light switch, or it may remain impacted like a wisdom tooth," said Ellis. "More likely, you will experience something in between. Think of memory as a system of tubes with marbles running through. The concussion jammed some of the marbles in a section of the tube, and others are now piled up behind them. A few may start rolling, and then a few more, and then the rest."

Ellis shut off the shadowbox and steepled his hands in front of his face.

"Mr. Lenahan, what do you remember about your injury?" he said.

"As I told you, Doc, I just remember standing on the seventeenth tee at Bay Hill. Oh, and I do remember arguing with my caddie. Whoever hit me must be embarrassed as hell. Bad enough to hit such a wild shot. But to conk someone, and a fellow player at that."

"You didn't get hit by a golf ball," said Ellis.

"I didn't?"

"No. And you finished your round. In fact, according to this morning's paper, you shot a seventy-four."

This might sound like lunacy, but my immediate reaction was not surprise or even curiosity about what type of blow to the skull landed me in the hospital. My immediate reaction, albeit sluggish with post-concussion syndrome, was that I was still in the tournament. One of the few things I did remember was a 12:01 starting time for Friday's round. I checked my watch. Less than an hour.

"Can I get a ride to Bay Hill?" I said.

"I'm afraid that's not possible," said Ellis.

"Why not? Will my head fall off if I take a swing?"

"No, it's more complicated than that." Ellis paused, obviously to collect himself. "Mr. Lenahan, you are in Gainesville."

"That's crazy." Gainesville was two hours north of Orlando.

"It's true. This is Shands Teaching Hospital."

"Was I choppered here? I mean helicoptered or Medivaced, or whatever you call it?"

"No. Local EMS brought you in about five yesterday afternoon."

"What the hell is going on?" I said.

"You don't remember anything?" said Ellis. "You don't remember coming to Gainesville?"

"Why the hell would I come to Gainesville?"

"I'm sorry. I don't know."

"Well, if a golf ball didn't hit me, what did?"

Ellis buffed his glasses on his smock and hooked them back around his ears.

"I would say a blunt instrument, possibly a blackjack. That's all I can say. A Detective McGriff is waiting for you in the lobby. He can answer all your questions."

CHAPTER
TWO

The elevator felt like the first drop on a roller coaster. I shuffled into the lobby and tried to orient myself, while various bodily fluids sloshed inside me. Reception desk here, potted plants there, gift shop way over there, front doors straight ahead. No obvious detectives. I angled toward reception, where a tall black man in gray slacks and a blue golf shirt chatted easily with two lady volunteers.

"You're Kieran Lenahan," he said.

I nodded. How the hell did he know?

"Detective Curtis McGriff, Gainesville Police." His handshake rocked me. "Sorry. Didn't Dr. Ellis tell you to expect me?"

"He did. He said you could tell me what happened."

"Oh yeah, I'm a regular answer man." McGriff saluted the ladies and tapped my arm. "Come on, I expect we'll have us a nice little chat on the way."

"Where to?"

"You'll see."

Outside the protective tint of the electric doors, the sunlight was blinding. Puffy clouds scudded beneath an intense blue sky. McGriff held the door of a big unmarked Ford, while I eased in. The interior smelled like a sickening mix of peppermint and stale tobacco. An air freshener shaped like an evergreen dangled from a knob over the open mouth of an ashtray brimming with butts and ashes. I rolled down the window and leaned outside, preferring blast furnace heat to asphyxia.

"Night man's the smoker," said McGriff, settling in and pushing the ashtray closed with a knuckle. Acne scars dotted his neck, and a thin beard ran along his jawline. Tiny glasses lent him a studious air. He locked his seatbelt and didn't throw the Ford into gear until I locked mine. We hung a right out the hospital entrance onto a four-lane highway lined by typical Florida sprawl of shopping malls and apartment complexes.

"You don't much remember what happened," he said.

"Ellis tell you that?"

"Ellis told me nothing. I wanted to question you when you came to, but Ellis kicked me out. No, I expect you had a concussion, and both retrograde and post-traumatic amnesia are normal sequelae of a concussion." McGriff laughed at my expression. "*The Merck Manual.* I read up on head trauma back at the station. Doctors talk to you nicer when you speak their language."

"But Ellis threw you out anyway."

"*Some* doctors," he said. "Am I right about the amnesia?"

"I've got them both, retrograde and post-traumatic," I said.

"How much?"

"More than I want," I said. "Like for instance, I don't remember coming to Gainesville."

"You definitely came to Gainesville. That's a fact. Drove here yourself."

"Where's my car?"

"Impounded," he said. "What do you remember from before?"

"It's spotty. I remember standing on the seventeenth tee at Bay Hill. Before that, I remember finishing at Doral. That was almost two weeks ago. In between, zip."

"And after?"

"Waking up in the hospital, close to midnight."

"Anything in between?"

"Sensory perceptions," I said. "Dreams."

"What kind of perceptions?"

"A golf course. A crowd surrounding me. An ambulance ride. Faces. Until I spoke to Ellis this morning, I thought I'd gotten hit by a golf ball."

"Anyone you recognize in those faces?"

"No. Strangers."

"What about the dreams?" said McGriff.

"Career choices. Alternative pasts. Personal anxieties."

We passed a couple of traffic lights in silence. McGriff drove with his right hand on the wheel, his left elbow lodged on the windowsill, while his left hand preened his peach fuzz. Now and then he switched hands and fiddled with something on the dash, giving me the once over with the corner of his eye.

"Do you know a woman named Cindy Moran?" he said.

For a split second, the dream seeped back into memory. The house, the party, the unseen woman. Just as quickly, it dried up.

"No," I said.

"We found the two of you together," said McGriff.

"Great. Does she know what happened?"

"Hard to say," said McGriff. "She's dead."

The revelation didn't stun me. Maybe it was my post-concussion apathy.

We found you and a dead woman.

Oh that's nice, Detective, can you tell me what day it is?

Maybe I already "knew" this. Maybe I read the skittishness of the night nurse and the vagueness of Dr. Ellis and fashioned this terrible scenario in some silent corner of the subconscious. Maybe I knew Cindy Moran died because I'd seen it happen.

"Here we are now," said McGriff. "Right up here on the left."

I never could figure where people dug up the cutesy names for apartment complexes. The Camelot Apartments looked less like a royal edifice on the River Cam than a collection of burghers' homes in downtown London. Eight L-shaped buildings, each two stories high, flanked a central courtyard. The lower floors were faced with red brick, the uppers with white stucco inlaid with dark timbers. Casement windows added a medieval dash. But no knights clanked about in armor, and no damsels trailed pastel gauze from tall conical hats.

I felt McGriff's eyes on me as he tooled through the parking lot and nosed into a space alongside a dumpster.

"We found your car parked right here," he said. "It's an assigned space, and its owner went out at approximately three in the afternoon."

He suggested I walk around the car; maybe I'd see something to jog my memory. I played along. The pavement was old and cracked, lumpy with potholes overfilled with fresh blacktop. A torn cigarette box lay at the foot of the dumpster, along with a crushed lid to a baby food jar and a lemon rind.

"Nothing," I said.

I followed McGriff down a flagstone path, through an archway, and into the courtyard. Azaleas were in full bloom. Spanish moss hung from a live oak tree. Patches of stiff grass sparkled under spray hissing from buried sprinkler heads. A few people were about, mostly student types. Rock music blared through an open window. A woman in a bikini watered a jungle of plants on a small balcony. A long-haired guy shackled a mountain bike to a wooden balustrade.

"Anything click?" said McGriff.

"Sure. A vision of paradise."

We rounded a bend. Two junipers flanked the entrance to a ground level apartment with a big "X" of yellow tape across the door. McGriff unstuck the tape, fumbled with a set of keys, and unlocked the deadbolt.

"You ready?" he said.

I nodded. He pushed open the door.

The apartment was nothing special. Worn wall-to-wall carpeting somewhere on the spectrum between canary and mustard, chairs and a couch upholstered in lime-green vinyl, pressboard coffee table and matching bookcase. A TV cable coiled out of the baseboard, heading nowhere. Floor tiles curled up in the corners of a tiny kitchenette.

The living room suddenly started to spin. I grabbed for the arm of the sofa, missed, and crashed onto the cushions. Dizziness rolled over me. Veins pounded in my forehead. I closed my eyes and cupped my hands over the sockets.

McGriff pried my hands off, slapped my cheeks. The spinning slowed to a wobble, and finally settled onto an even keel.

"Lenahan, you all right, man?"

"Yeah, fine."

"You didn't just—"

"No, I didn't just remember anything. A dizzy spell, that's all." I squeezed the bottle of pills out of my pocket. "Any glasses over there? I need water."

McGriff opened every cabinet in the kitchenette. All were completely bare.

"Some homemaker," he said.

"Screw it." I worked up some saliva, pitched my head back, and swallowed hard. The pill blazed a trail of sand down my throat.

McGriff let me sit awhile. Water trickled somewhere, the kind of sound that makes you want to piss. He disappeared into the bathroom, jiggled something, and came back wiping his hands.

"Goddam running toilets annoy the hell out of me," he said. "You ready to move yet?"

I struggled to my feet, waited to catch up with myself, and gingerly followed him down a short hallway.

For a second, the strips of tape on the bedroom carpet formed some strange type of aircraft. I blinked my eyes, and the perspective shifted into the outline of a human body spreadeagled on the floor. I edged along the wall, not wanting to disturb anything in the room or to violate the figure's airspace. The bedroom hit the same level of apartment decor as the living room. Pressboard dresser and nightstand, a twin bed covered with a worn spread of beaded cotton, a thin pillow with its zippered edge leaking out of a yellowed pillowcase. A sense of trespass came over me, as if McGriff and I just stumbled into a Pharaoh's tomb.

"She got slapped around some, then took a strong blow like yours only more near the side of the head. The actual cause of death was strangulation. We found her on her back with a little bitty skirt pushed up to her waist and her panties down around one ankle and a big rip in her blouse. Now if the killer ripped that blouse during a struggle, we'd find marks on the skin underneath. Cuts, scrapes, bruises. But she was clean. Tests aren't in yet, but I don't think there was any sexual assault involved."

"How do you know?" I said.

"Just a feeling I get."

McGriff rose and stepped past me into the other bedroom. It was completely empty, the green carpet still showing the imprints of recent furnishings.

"Here's where we found you," he said, opening a small closet.

The carpet was new, thick and springy, which explained my impression of laying alongside a fairway. I patted my hand between two brown splotches joined together like a snowman.

"Mine?" I said.

"A lot more ended up on your shirt. We sent it for lab tests to see if there is any other than yours mixed in. Tell you the truth, I doubt it."

I stared at the snowman. If Ellis told me the blood in my mouth almost suffocated me, why did so much soak into the carpet?

"The place wasn't ransacked, but there isn't much to toss," said McGriff. "Her purse was under the bed, with not much in it. Are you missing anything?"

I showed him my watch. Not the world's most expensive timepiece, but worth a few vials of crack from a forced sale. I counted out the money in my wallet. Four-hundred odd dollars cash, plus a bank credit card.

"About what I usually carry," I said.

"Okay, let's get out of here," said McGriff.

Outside, I stared across the courtyard while he locked the door and restuck the yellow tape. The sprinklers had shut down. The bikini lady dragged a lounge chair onto the grass and aimed it at the sun. Music still blared from the open window.

"Anything come back to you?" McGriff drew up beside me.

"Nothing," I said.

"You got in your car after playing your round at Bay Hill. You drove two hours north to a seedy old apartment complex. Why?"

"I don't remember, dammit," I said.

He measured me again, as he had while driving the car. His eyes seemed to enlarge until they filled the lenses of his glasses with his deep brown pupils. I had the feeling that behind those eyes he replayed my answers slowly, comparing my tone of voice, facial expressions, and body language with a paradigm of a truthful answer.

"You married, Lenahan?"

"No."

"Involved with someone?"

"Yeah."

"She with you on Tour?"

"Not yet. She's in Europe."

"Pardonez moi," he said.

"What are you driving at?"

McGriff patted his pockets. "Damn, sometimes I wish I smoked. Gum?"

I pulled a piece from the pack he offered and slipped it into my mouth. Peppermint, powdery cool on my tongue.

"You meet lots of babes out there, right?" he said.

"Could if I wanted to. I don't."

"Why not?"

"I had some trouble a while back," I said. "Wasn't exactly blacklisted, but close enough. I caught a streak of luck last summer, and here I am. I don't believe in blowing second chances."

"So you avoid the near occasion of sin."

"Something like that."

"But you agree the occasion is there," said McGriff. "The babes are there."

"Okay, let's suppose I met her at Bay Hill. That's two hours away. We couldn't meet up somewhere closer to Orlando?"

"Depends on why you met her, doesn't it?" he said. "And we're not just supposin'. You were in Gainesville. That's a fact."

Across the courtyard, the long-haired guy unlocked his bike and gave us a long look before pushing off through an archway.

McGriff peeled another stick of gum, spit the old wad into the foil, and chewed up the fresh one. He didn't offer me any this time.

"She rented this place about three weeks ago," he said. "Refused to sign a lease, but paid the manager one month's rent and two months' security up front in cash. Said she'd let him know about a second month when the time came, but the time hadn't come.

"The furniture's rented, too. Same deal from an outfit on the other side of town. She never installed a phone. She had no job that we know of. The letter carrier never delivered a scrap of first-class mail to her. Manager says she wasn't here much, but kept her lights on all the time. The people upstairs complained about an argument on a Monday two weeks ago. They called the manager, and by the time he got off his butt, all was quiet. Ms. Moran was alone, sweet and apologetic as pie."

"Did anyone see or hear anything yesterday?" I said.

McGriff smiled sourly. "Something happens in a retirement complex, and we get more witnesses than we need. We get eyewitness accounts, we get theories why so-and-so would have done this or that, we get volunteers sitting with us on stake outs. Something happens at a student complex like this, and no one sees anything, no one hears anything. What we have is someone who saw a black male, someone who saw a white male, and no one who could put the two of them together. A complex like this gets lots of traffic during the day. Students coming and going to class, friends visiting. Even if the residents were inclined to talk, they don't pay the traffic much attention."

"Someone found me," I said.

"Paperboy found the door ajar and heard you moaning inside," said McGriff. "He called us."

I drifted back to the door. The frame was warped, the paint was cracked. The stained glass light in the center was actually cheap plastic. The bolt couldn't stop a marginally competent picker. I'd passed through this door less than twenty-four hours ago, for reasons I couldn't remember, let alone fathom. My head ached, my knees shook with the constant effort of keeping myself balanced. My mind whirred, searching for a chink in the wall of memory. Something was going on, something more complicated than retrograde amnesia.

I sensed McGriff talking.

"What?" I said.

"One more stop," he said.

Our stop was the Alachua County Medical Examiner's Office, a whitewashed concrete bunker of a building in the center of town, not far from the tall pines and the gothic brick of the University of Florida campus. My knees quaked as we ambled down the corridor, and I wasn't sure where my shakiness left off and my apprehension began. An attendant led us to the drawers. My breath swirled in the chill, and I wondered, illogically, if ice crystals might form.

I'd seen the rawness of death more often than I cared to. It was much different from what we see in funeral parlors, and not just because of the satin and flowers. Death has a heaviness about it. A waxy fleshiness. A sense of gravity dragging the body into the earth. Loosening muscles. Pooling fluids. Sagging cavities.

I wasn't prepared for Cindy Moran. She was so long and slim the attendant pulled forever before the top of her shrouded form cleared the end of that claustrophobic drawer. Her ankles and knees pressed together almost daintily. Her hands folded across each other just above the navel. Her hair was black, cut in a stylish wedge, but mussed. Her face was serene, her skin pale and unmarked except for a tiny bluish-red splotch like cheap rouge on one cheek and two red splotches unfolding like bat's wings beneath her Adam's apple. She had a small mouth, with lips pursed in a slight, prideful smile. An elegant sweep of neck joined a delicate jawline. Cast her in bronze, and she'd be Nefertiti's death mask.

"So?" said McGriff.

"Nothing."

"You don't know her?"

"I don't remember knowing her," I said.

"Don't play word games with me, Lenahan. Do you know her?"

"No."

"Close her up," he told the attendant sharply, and stormed out.

I didn't try to keep up because I knew he'd wait for me outside. He leaned out of the midday sun, stuffing another stick of gum into his mouth. In a stupid way, I almost felt bad for him, as if he'd read *The Merck Manual* and decided a trip to the scene would crack my amnesia, and, when that didn't work, he'd try a trip to the body. But now neither worked, and his whole grand scheme was a bust. I almost forgot I was the guy trying to remember.

"You know, Lenahan," he said. "I had the luxury of checking you out last night. I talked to a Detective DiRienzo. Know what he told me?"

Chicky DiRienzo was the entire detective squad of the police force back in my hometown of Milton. He combined a gorilla's body with a reptile's brain and a world view that sounded like a child's garden of clichéd aphorisms. *The rich are all dishonest. Smart people lack common sense. Sitting too close to the TV ruins your eyes.* We'd butted heads on several occasions, mainly because his vaunted common sense led his investigations to my door. Via five or six wrong turns.

"I can imagine," I said.

"Lots of things. I wrote them all down for future reference. But I happen to like the things that stick in my mind. And what stuck was the last thing he said. He said, 'Murder isn't Lenahan's style. But if there's a train wreck, Lenahan isn't very far away.'"

"Are you going to arrest me?" I said.

McGriff laughed. "Right now you're a poor excuse for a material witness. So what I'm going to do is get you your car and hand you your keys. You get your memory back, you contact me. If I need you, I'll know where to find you."

CHAPTER
THREE

McGriff bailed my car out of a private pound in a seedy section of town and bid me adieu. I called Judge Inglisi collect from a nearby payphone. His clerk knew enough to accept the charges and to drag his esteemed honor off the bench.

I'd known the Judge since my teenage years, our friendship enduring incarnations as golfer/caddie, mentor/student, and partners in the practice of law. We ran a busy suburban New York law office until he caught a notion to run for county judge. He won—another nail in the coffin of the democratic process—and I decided against continuing the firm on my own.

"You're going to become a golf pro," he'd intoned repeatedly, as we boxed our books and files. "Only an idiot makes a job out of something he loves."

But never say the Judge isn't adaptable. Within minutes after I became a full-fledged touring pro, he appointed himself my business manager.

"Where the hell are you?" he barked into the phone. "I've already gotten two calls from tournament people at Bay Hill asking for you."

His tone of voice painted a vivid picture in my brain. He paced his chambers with the collar of his robe thrown open and the phone pinched in a fold of his jowls. Meanwhile, his clerk scrambled out of the way.

"What did you tell them?" I said.

"Never mind what I told them. I lied like a bastard, as I've often done to save your irresponsible ass. Now I go back to my first question."

"I'm in Gainesville."

"Refresh my Florida geography. Gainesville is nowhere near Orlando, right?"

"About two hours north."

"What the hell are you doing up there?" he said.

"I don't know."

There was a pause, pregnant with judicial ridicule, followed by a solid thud. Another image: the Judge plopping himself into his huge catcher's mitt of a chair. I could see him against his nineteenth floor window, reclined almost parallel to the floor. The world's heftiest astronaut awaiting liftoff.

"You don't know," he said slowly, squeezing every syllable for maximum sarcasm.

"I do, in a way. I just spent the night in a hospital with a concussion."

"In Gainesville?"

"Apparently I finished yesterday's round and drove up here. Do I know anyone named Cindy Moran?"

The Judge muttered something I interpreted as a negative.

"The police think I do. They found me in her apartment.

She was dead and I was unconscious from a blow to the head, probably with a blackjack. The police don't know what to make of me because I don't remember coming to Gainesville or who Cindy Moran is, or was."

"Did you get arrested?" he said.

"No. A detective just gave me back my car, told me he'd be in touch. They are holding my shirt for tests. It had some blood on it."

"And you don't remember anything?" said the Judge.

"I have retrograde and post-traumatic amnesia." I didn't cite *The Merck Manual.* The Judge isn't impressed by book knowledge, which he thinks is available to any idiot. In his mind, he's the world's leading exponent of a type of intuitive genius last seen in Leonardo da Vinci.

I explained the parameters of my memory and described the apartment and Cindy Moran's body. My amnesia shielded me from the Judge's considerable nit-picking powers, so he confined his comments to general pronouncements on my intelligence.

"Do you have any idea what you've done by missing that round?" he wound up.

"Uh—" My dim awareness was unrelated to my concussion. The Tour had rules against dropping out of a tournament. Since I never expected to find myself in that predicament, I never paid attention to the specifics.

"It's big trouble, okay?" said the Judge. "And your amnesia doesn't extend back six years, so I don't need to remind you what little provocation the Tour needs to fry your ass."

I gulped audibly.

"Stay the hell away from Bay Hill. I'll call the officials

there and give them a story. If I can't save your reputation, at least I'll save mine."

"What do I do?"

"Get over to Sawgrass. I'll contact Meg and tell her to pack your stuff and bring it along." This was the Judge I knew, the man who made an art out of barking orders via telephone from a thousand miles away. Meg was my caddie and not intimidated by bluster. Even the judicial variety. "Did the doctor give you anything for the concussion?"

After all these years, did I finally detect an ounce of sympathy in the man? I almost dropped the phone.

"A prescription," I said.

"Good. Wait till you're in your hotel to take it. Maybe it'll knock you out until I fly down."

I heard stories of people with post-concussion syndrome who hopped into cars, quickly forgot their destination, and drove in endless circles, completely unaware they were lost. Never happen to me, I thought. I knew north Florida from my years as apprentice golf pro and mini-tour competitor. The state road from Gainesville to the east coast curves past lakes lined with towering cypress, plunges through thick stands of live oak, and skirts wide savannahs dotted with palms and cattle. So I was surprised when I entered and re-entered the river town of Palatka from about four different directions before I got back on track.

I hit the coast at St. Augustine, turned left at Castillo de San Marcos, and headed north on A1A, the road that hugs the Atlantic from Miami to Fernandina Beach. Huge dunes, stitched together with sea oats and sea grape, obscured any view of the ocean. But salt smells gradually permeated the car's interior, and the sky beyond the dunes blurred with the distinctive haze of air over water. The dunes ended south of Ponte Vedra, and a more leaden type of haze—Jacksonville—filled my windshield until I turned off A1A.

My eventual destination—eventual, as in next Monday—was the Sawgrass Players Club, the site of the PGA Tour's richest and most prestigious event, the Tournament Players Championship. My immediate destination, however, was the Sawgrass Marriott, located right outside the club's gates.

I left my car with a valet and walked into an atrium the size of a cathedral. Passing quickly from the cool of the car, into the heat of the outside air, and again into the cool lobby, must have swelled my brain. By the time I reached the front desk, my quiescent headache was seriously a-pounding. The desk clerk was one of those young ladies with the eager look of someone who could belt out inspirational songs on cable TV.

"Are you ill, sir?" she said.

I worked the pill bottle out of my pocket. The thought of swallowing another pill dry turned my stomach, but the nearest water fountain was too long a trek for my rubbery legs.

"Yes, I am. Do you have any water?"

She fetched me a paper cup in about ten seconds flat. Ah, the sympathy of total strangers. Grease on the wheels of civilization.

I swallowed the pill, gave her my name, and explained I arrived three days before my reservation. For once, I didn't mind the wait, as she struggled to inform the hotel's computer system that humans occasionally change their plans. Even if those plans are etched in electrons. By the time I received my room card, I felt steady enough to walk.

I bought a *Gainesville Sun* from the newspaper rack and caught the elevator with my designated bellhop. The gentle ascent practically hammered me through the floor. I couldn't manipulate the card into the door lock and paid for my clumsiness by overtipping the bellhop. After he left, I drew the curtains tight, switched on the reading lamp, and sprawled out on the bed with the newspaper.

WOMAN MURDERED AT CAMELOT, read the headline. A subhead added: Pro Golfer Survives "Surgical" Attack. A color picture showed police and EMS crews wheeling a body bag out of the apartment. Detective McGriff stood stage right, a notebook in hand as he spoke to someone out of frame. The story mentioned few details—nothing I didn't know from my visit to the apartment with McGriff—and certainly nothing to jog any memory about Cindy Moran. No age, no occupation, no tag line station in life. Just a young woman with a name. The "surgical" in the subhead paraphrased a police spokesman, who actually said the "perpetrator was like a surgeon the way nothing in the apartment was disturbed, except for the two people in it." As for me:

> Police refused to speculate whether the survivor, Kieran Lenahan, was present at the apartment during the attack on Ms. Moran, or whether he arrived afterward. Lenahan, a professional golfer, was apparently visiting Ms. Moran after playing the opening round at the Bay Hill Classic at the Bay Hill Club in Orlando earlier in the day. He was found in a different room from Ms. Moran, unconscious from a head injury, and was taken to Shands Teaching

Hospital, where doctors were optimistic about his chances.

So much for the *Gainesville Sun* police beat. I turned to sports, more out of habit than any deep, abiding interest in the complete list of Bay Hill scores. Tommy Garth Hunter was among a group of four tied for the lead with 67. My 74 sank more than halfway down the page, fortunately without any cross-reference to the big story on page one.

I swept the paper off the bed, shut the reading lamp, and rolled over onto my back. Daylight leaked over the top of the curtains, turning the stippled ceiling into the surface of the moon. My eyes wandered as I examined the few facts I knew for sure. *I was found with a dead woman. I am a professional golfer. The perpetrator was like a surgeon. I could have died.*

I couldn't get my mind around it, maybe because my mind wouldn't let me. How much of life really catches our attention? My first time behind the wheel of a car threw the entire world into high relief. I remembered the exact color of the sky that Saturday afternoon, the size of the buds on the trees, the makes and models of every car parked along Poningo Point Road. I remembered a gaggle of young kids playing Frisbee in a yard and easing off the gas in case the disc sailed into the street and I needed to hit the brake. I remembered a couple on ten-speed bikes flashing through an intersection two hundred yards ahead. I'd driven that road through Milton a million times since and couldn't call one other instance to mind. But sometimes life catches too much of our attention and the only way to deal with it is to build a wall.

Daytime naps disoriented me, and, after yesterday, even a Zen snooze could land me in the booby hatch. But I was just too damn tired. I drifted off to sleep and awoke to the sound of the door opening. I listened with post-concussion detachment to voices speaking in whispers and heavy objects thumping to the floor. I didn't stay detached for long. Someone shook my shoulder.

"Where's your money?"

Was it robbery now? I came up flailing.

"Kieran, it's—"

A hand grabbed my wrist and wrenched it around my back.

"—me. Meg."

"Eh? Meg?" I let myself go limp. I didn't need ligament damage on top of a concussion. "What's this about money?"

"For the bellhop," said Meg. "Jaysus, Kieran, bad enough I had to drive all the way here. I'll be wrassling you for tip money now, too?"

Out in the foyer, the same bellhop who showed me to the room waved sheepishly from behind a small mountain range of luggage. Trapped by my previous flight of philanthropy, I reached into my wallet for another overly generous tip. If I really wanted to spend money wisely, I would have paid the bellhop to stay. But he had a job, and eventually I needed to face Meg by my lonesome. As soon as he left, Meg dragged a suitcase to a dresser and began to unpack.

"Well," she said, noticing I'd settled back onto the bed. "My job description does not include personal valet."

"You're pissed."

"Angry," she said, tossing shirts and socks helter-skelter into drawers. "I'm up here three days early, missing out on Orlando and on the free buffets. This is costing me."

"I'll pay."

"Oh, you'll be paying," said Meg. "But right now you'll be helping me unpack."

I stood over the pile, idly tugging at the handles. Everything felt as heavy as a set of barbells. Finally, I dragged out my briefcase and wedged it between the bed and the nightstand. I'd used this briefcase throughout my entire legal career. It accompanied me onto the Tour, not out of any sense of nostalgia; rather, it was a convenient place to store my important papers.

"You call that unpacking?" said Meg.

Meg Black was one of the few female caddies on the Tour. She'd won several women's amateur golf titles in Ireland and emigrated to the States with the idea of caddying on the men's tour while deciding whether to turn pro herself. I assumed the logic for this plan existed somewhere, though not in my particular dimension. A mutual friend in the Irish consulate hooked us up in late December, just before I was scheduled to fly west and pick up the Tour in California.

I hired Meg over the objection of the Judge and with the blessings of Georgia Newland, my current significant squeeze who, by coincidence, was about to depart as a costume designer for the European engagement of a Broadway musical. We met for a get-acquainted dinner—Kieran and his two ladies. At first blush, forty-ish, haughty, classically beautiful Georgina and twenty-something, spunky, demijock Meg seemed polar opposites. I worked like hell to hold the conversation together, alternating between the witty employer and the warm lover. I never realized the two women were communicating on some other level until sign off.

Meg: "You have nothing to worry about, Georgina."

Georgina: "I knew that before we finished our appetizers."

More recently, Meg dressed down a sportswriter in Palm Springs who hinted at physical intimacy between us.

Physical intimacy had crossed my mind, but at Indy speed. Meg was a petite blonde who filled out the overalls and bibs caddies wore on Tour and still managed to look dynamite in cutoff jeans and tee shirts. Her sole drawback was her mouth, and not because of her blistering Dublin ire. She had Irish teeth, meaning short on fluoride and orthodontia and stained from the cigarettes she smoked before quitting when she came to the States. Smoking is a little known fact about the Irish. People associate the Irish with drinking, and that certainly is true, with the pub being the social focus of every little village from Mayo to Waterford. But the Irish also smoke like fiends. An American stranger might offer you a cigarette once a decade. In Ireland, you can't talk to an Irishman for ten minutes before he's shaking a pack in your face.

"First you don't show at the practice tee," Meg said. "And I'm after asking every golfer in creation if they'd seen hide or hair of you. Ten minutes before tee time, I lug the bag to the tee and hope to find you standing there with a huge big grin on your face. All I find are a bunch of officials who surround me like Roman soldiers. I'm not about to tell them what I think I know about your whereabouts. So I deny you thrice, like St. Peter. Your tee time passes, and you're officially disqualified from the tournament. They take me to the will-call tent and tell me the sponsors are raging. I wash my hands of you like Pontius Pilate. I tell them to call the Judge."

I wanted to guide this monologue back to what Meg thought she knew about my whereabouts. But she was too caught up in Easter season imagery. There is an old story about Bobby Jones delaying the start of a playoff for the 1929

U.S. Open so his opponent, Al Espinosa, could attend Sunday Mass. Then Jones whipped him by 23 strokes. Jones would have loved Meg, who attended Mass regularly, regardless of my Sunday tee time. One week, in Tucson, I carried my bag for the first hole because the sermon ran extra long.

"I don't know what the Judge told them," she continued. "But he calls me an hour later and says I should pack up all your belongings and meet you here."

By now every stitch of my wardrobe either hung in closets or was tucked away in drawers. Meg ran a look of disgust up and down the length of me, focusing for the first time.

"Where did you get that shirt?"

"The hospital," I said.

"You had an accident?"

"Sort of."

"What does that mean?"

"I didn't have an accident in the strictest sense of the word," I said.

"Grand," she said. "I knew something would happen when you said you were going to Gainesville."

"When did I say that?"

"Yesterday on the seventeenth tee," she said. "Kieran, this is no time to be slagging me."

Slagging was Dublinese for teasing, only without the jocular connotation.

"Why?"

"You didn't say, but I wager she was behind it," said Meg.

"Who?"

"Tall, thin, black hair." Her face registered that special distaste women reserve for each other. "Walks like she has a stick up her arse and smiles like she just sucked a lemon."

Near enough the body I saw in the morgue to give me a shudder.

"Do you know her name?" I said.

"You never introduced me," said Meg.

She folded her arms and cocked her head to stare hard with her right eye. Time had come to move this discussion to a more serious plane. I scraped the *Sun* from the carpet and folded it back to the front page. Meg curled up on a chair and read the headline story with a smirk on her face.

"I don't remember any of it," I said after she tossed the paper aside.

"You don't. Are you slagging me again, Kieran?"

"I'm not. I have amnesia." No throwing in the medical terms with Meg.

"How convenient," she said.

"It's true," I said. The desk clerk would have believed me. "I have a vague memory of arguing with you on the seventeenth tee. And then I woke up in the hospital."

I explained that most of what happened since we arrived in Florida had been wiped from my memory. Meg tsk-tsked. Her doubts went beyond devil's advocacy; she didn't believe a goddam word I said.

"Are you playing this week?" Meg said, jumping to her feet. "Because if you're not, I'll drive on to New Orleans and have some fun instead of hanging around this elephants' graveyard."

"I'm playing."

"Grand." She brushed past me and snagged the strap of my golf bag, which still lay on the floor in the foyer. Fully loaded, the bag tops eighty pounds. But little Meg swung it

onto her shoulder as easily as an empty knapsack. "If I lugged
this up here, you're going to practice. Meet you on the range."

"But, Meg, my head's pounding," I said.

"Take two aspirin," she said. "I'll be waiting."

One hour and another dose of Ellis's pills later, I strolled out
into the white of a Florida afternoon. Across a wide lagoon,
a corner of the Players Club angled into deceptive proximity.
The practice range, however, was a good hike away even for
someone in his preconcussion prime. So I retrieved my car
from the valet and drove.

Inside the gates, the Players Club already showed early
evidence of next week's activity. Signs marked special parking areas for contestants, the media, and spectators. A television tower rose above a stand of pines. The clubhouse is a
sprawling building constructed in an architectural style I'd
call "mostly roof." I checked in at the club manager's office,
then quickly descended to the locker room, where three valets
scattered to find me a fully appointed locker.

I'd been on tour almost three months and still felt uncom-
fortable with the courtesy cars, the tons of complimentary
merchandise, the hordes of gofers willing to do my bidding
because I could work a golf ball across the sky. A psychologist
I met at a pro-am suggested I needed to get in touch with
my inner child, an entity far more able to handle moral dilem-
mas and philosophical questions than my outer adult. Even
if I didn't believe the inner child concept to be a New Age
justification for immature behavior, it wouldn't erase my sense
of alienation. My inner child remained a caddie, humping bags
for ten bucks a round and wolfing peanut butter sandwiches in
a corner of the caddie yard.

Two dozen golfers spread across the wide crescent of the practice tee. Some blasted drives toward the distant mix of pine and palm trees. Others drilled iron shots at flagsticks cut into several dummy greens scattered on the range. A dozen of the golfers were touring pros, including one who pulled out of Bay Hill at the last minute because of a hand injury. People might laugh at the idea of golfers being injured. After all, we don't have linebackers chasing us in between shots. But constantly pounding the turf takes a toll on a golfer's hands and spine. Plus, the delicate and complex motion of the golf swing falls well out of kilter if one muscle or ligament is out of whack.

Three of the pros gathered with Meg, who reeked of a coconut sunscreen she slathered on, except during monsoons. I wanted to think my colleagues inquired after my health, but with Meg still in cutoffs and tee shirt, I knew better. They mumbled hello and scattered to their respective tee boxes, leaving me to feel distinctly plague-ridden. Oh well, I still had Meg. But a few minutes in the sun didn't brighten her disposition.

"Warm up with this," she said, poking the grip of a club into my hands. "It's your pitching wedge, in case you don't remember."

I took a few easy practice cuts, bracing myself for head pain that luckily never materialized. Satisfied I could swing without losing my balance, grip, or mental stability, I scooped a ball from the pile Meg had staked me and aimed at the nearest green. I chunked the first shot. It flew like an early NASA rocket: up, down, barely a few yards forward.

Meg exhaled sharply. I kept my head down and addressed another ball, concentrating on nipping the blade of the wedge right where the ball's curvature climbed out of the bristly turf. This shot flew straight at the green, bounced once, then spun back to a foot from the stick.

Not a sound from Meg. I stayed cool, didn't even lift my eyes, just lined up another ball. This one followed the exact same flight path. Bounced, grabbed, rolled back, kissed off the other ball.

"Guess my muscle memory doesn't have amnesia," I said, letting another fly. The result wasn't the same, but damn close.

"Oh yes, you surely recovered from that," said Meg.

I hit five more decent shots before the comment registered.

"I've been playing badly?" I said.

"Kieran, stop slagging me."

"Dammit, Meg, I don't remember. Okay?"

She folded her arms, tucked her chin, and kicked three balls rapid fire at me. I stick-saved each one, then lofted them at the green.

"We've been in Florida three weeks," she said wearily, "and so far you've finished dead last, you missed a cut, and you were disqualified. You're playing the worst since you got into this."

"Into what?" I said.

"My life. Just practice, Kieran, okay?" She kicked another ball, which got past me, caromed off a wooden tee marker, and bounded onto the range.

Not knowing what nerve I just touched, I did exactly that. I practiced, working my way methodically toward the longer irons. I couldn't ask what had been wrong with my game without risking a rain of golf balls aimed at my ankles. But these shots felt awfully crisp and awfully smooth. Maybe I'd been overswinging and the blow to my head forced a return to tempo. If so, did I unwittingly unlock the secret of the game: better golf through head trauma?

Halfway through my dozen allotted five-iron shots, I noticed a young kid standing beside Meg.

"Sorry, no autographs right now, son," I said, full of myself.

"I don't want your autograph, and I'm not your son."

I straightened up, noticing now that the kid wore a white dress shirt and green tie, and realizing he was a teenaged Tour employee. Nice combination, clean-cut looks and disrespect for his elders.

"What is it?"

"You're wanted at headquarters," he said. "Right now."

CHAPTER FOUR

I brought different sets of expectations to my two careers.
Law never thrilled me. I didn't yearn to argue arcane legal
principles before the Supreme Court. I didn't sit in my office
and stare at the front door, waiting for my first leg-off case
to roll in with a seven-figure contingency fee. I didn't lie
awake nights conjuring ways to help rich clients hold onto
their pelf. Judge Inglisi and I practiced meat-and-potatoes
law for the good people of Milton: closing house deals, drawing wills, keeping the town's incorrigibles out of Sing Sing,
incorporating small business that rocketed into success or
petered out into oblivion. We attended christenings, wed-
dings, and funerals. We joined civic organizations and donated
time and money to charitable causes. Basically, we lived our
clients' lives. (At least I did. Who can say for the Judge, who
lives life like no one else.) When the firm split up, Merchant
Street gnashed its collective teeth, and the Milton Weekly
Chronicle ran an edition bordered with black. Only the police
rejoiced, and even there, the joy wasn't unanimous.

Golf, like law, is a mansion with many rooms. But only one room would satisfy me. I wanted—oh, all right—I needed to play on the PGA Tour. For me, the Tour was the Supreme Court, the seven-figure contingency fee, the epitome of golf.

Carving out a spot on the Tour is no easy matter. In the old days, each tournament ran a Monday qualifying round for five, ten, sometimes twenty tournament berths. Marginal players, known as rabbits, chased the Tour from site to site and played in these qualifiers. If you won a berth and managed to survive the 36 hole cut, you were automatically invited to play in next week's event. A good player could theoretically play his way onto the Tour and never look back.

Things changed when the Tour went corporate. To play regularly on the Tour, you need a playing card, something as rare and as valuable as a New York City taxi medallion. The Tour grants playing cards, also known as exemptions, to approximately 140 players each year, based on a variety of automatic exemption categories. Some of the categories are straightforward. For example, winning a tournament earns a two-year exemption. Some of the categories are complicated, and I won't bore you with examples. The idea behind the "all-exempt" Tour is to guarantee spectators, advertisers, and the corporate tournament sponsors the strongest possible fields week in and week out.

But the Tour also makes room for new blood. The 140-odd yearly automatic exemptions fall well short of the standard tournament field of 156. To make up the gap, the Tour runs an annual event called Q School. In these multi-round grinds, hundreds of players (including college grads, former Tour players, and club pros) compete for the holy grail of a year's exemption. With so much at stake, Q School is a joyless affair. Golf without a soundtrack, and with tension as thick as midafternoon in the Everglades.

I spent a year as an assistant at a club outside West Palm Beach, doing scut work, smiling at the members, and practicing whenever a free moment rolled my way. At year's end, I tried Q School. I didn't expect to qualify; this was an experience for building a career, a rite of passage, dues, whatever you wanted to call it. I missed qualifying for the big Tour, but finished high enough to earn a spot on the mini-tour, a kind of minor league of golf.

I kissed the country club good-bye and steeled myself for a year of traveling by car, sleeping in rest stops and stroking putts on linoleum floors while my clothes tumbled in coin dryers. The money was small and the perks nonexistent, but the competition was keen and the camaraderie enjoyable. I played with Thomas Garth Hunter, Chris Jennings, Sam Young, Ned Nelson—guys who later made it big on the Tour. It was a year of pleasant memories, and, looking back, I could still feel the burgeoning sense of optimism, the confidence that I rode a slow roll toward a successful second Q School. Then came Sarasota.

We spent long hours wherever we played, mainly because any clubhouse beat the motels for ambience. Guys would gather in the locker room hours before their tee times, eating breakfast, watching TV, reading the Bible. The morning before the Sarasota tournament, I walked into the clubhouse locker room to find the TV blank, the coffee and buns untouched, and everyone jammed between two rows of lockers. No one spoke, no one read the Bible. The tension felt like Q School, only different.

Tommy Garth Hunter spotted me first.

"The police are investigating us for gambling," he said.

This was absurd. There wasn't enough money floating around the mini-tour to interest even a small-time racketeer. The absurdity must have registered on my face because a general shuffling rose as everyone handed me their subpoenas.

"Twenty of us got them," said Hunter. "It's no joke."

No, it wasn't. Testimony was to start that afternoon and run through the end of the tournament. I knew the law enforcement mind-set from too many experiences. Once some publicity-hungry state attorney sank his teeth into these guys, he wouldn't let go. I set up a storefront legal clinic right in the locker room. I grilled the guys from all possible angles, spoon-fed them canned answers, generally prepped them on how best to gum up the works. Four days later, the state attorney dropped the investigation.

I never realized my activities attracted a silent audience until Q School. The PGA Tour officials "lost" my entry fee, and after I scraped up a second stake, rewarded me with graveyard starting times. Out on the course, marshals stalked me every hole to make sure I didn't disturb a single blade of grass. And if I needed a ruling, well, the verdict didn't break my way. I didn't even place high enough to keep my mini-tour card.

I returned home to Milton and took a job as head pro at Milton Country Club. Six years later, a crazy series of events landed me a sponsor's invitation to the B.C. Open in upstate New York. The tournament is named after the comic strip caveman because his creator lived nearby, and the tournament promoters thought B.C. a wittier local hook than a pair of Endicott-Johnson shoes. The late September date, chancy weather, and out-of-the-way venue combine to keep the big names away. But the golf course is beautiful, the people are especially nice, and pros savvy enough to play there once, make a point of returning again and again.

I rode an insane hot streak and plowed through a field Judge Inglisi called "ten acres of nobodies." I didn't care. The win earned me a two-year exemption on the Tour. But poetic justice can exact a heavy price, especially when most people don't share your ideas of poetry or sense of justice. I felt a definite, though indefinable, sense of resentment from the other players. It wasn't my being on the Tour that bothered people. No one knew me well enough to hate me, as I quipped to Meg during one of our rare light moments. Rather, it was my route onto the Tour that raised hackles. Guys who'd suffered in the crucible of Q School thought I'd achieved heaven by detouring around purgatory. Guys who'd won big-time tournaments treated my B.C. victory as cartoon golf, like something Judge Inglisi played on his six-foot video screen. And the Tour brass couldn't stomach my triumphant return to their kingdom.

Right now, the teenaged boy chauffeured me in an electric golf cart toward the heart of the kingdom, because the Sawgrass Players Club not only hosted the Tournament Players Championship but also housed the corporate headquarters of the PGA Tour, Inc. Like most large corporations, the Tour's official corporate name bore only a vestigial relation to its original purpose. American Can makes more than tin cans; Nabisco makes more than biscuits; and the PGA Tour, Inc., doesn't just stage weekly golf tournaments. The Tour is basically a nonprofit corporation, and is justifiably praised for the millions of dollars its tournaments raise for charities. But during its thirty-year existence, it expanded into profit-making ventures such as marketing, golf course design, and resort development. This dual purpose spawned PGA Tour Investments, Inc., to erect a barrier between the nonprofit and profit-generating activities. Tour headquarters and the offices of PGA Tour Investments stand side by side on TPC Boulevard. I hoped my invitation to headquarters was charitable.

My chauffeur stopped the cart barely long enough for my feet to hit the pavement before he zoomed away. Inside, I identified myself to a suitably bubbly receptionist. Her bubbles froze into a cool smile, and she directed me to a conference room where I was expected. People zipped past me in the corridors. The men all wore shirts and ties, the women neat skirts and blouses. I could have been in any Fortune 500 corporation, not the center of professional golf-dom.

I found the conference room and yanked on the heavy door. Inside, a conversation ground to a dead halt. Nothing like instant silence to make you self-conscious.

My spikeless golf shoes squeaked on the carpet while the four of them arranged themselves at the conference table. Henry Chandler played one season on the Tour in the early 1960s and distinguished himself to no one except a fellow pro who later became the first commissioner of the PGA Tour. Years later, Chandler received an invite from his good buddy to leave his savings and loan mortgage desk and sign on with the Tour's executive offices. Chandler never looked back. Tan, short, built like a bulldog, he had outlasted his buddy and two successors and rose to become tournament director. Peter Haswell was Chandler's assistant. Sandy-haired and rubbery-faced, he leaned back with the languid air of someone just called away from afternoon cocktails. Sally Lang was the vice-president of sponsor relations. Her neat hair and spiffy suit covered a heart of pure grind. Both she and Haswell had been champion golfers at Southern colleges and both preferred the minutiae of corporate management to professional competition. Atwood "Woody" Harrington was vice-president of player relations. Affable and athletic, with the blond locks of a romance-novel cover hunk and the U-shaped face of a college jock, he was my only friend in the PGA Tour, Inc. who ranked higher than janitor.

I settled onto a lone chair set about ten feet from the foot of the conference table and tried to decide what to do with my arms. Folded across my chest, perched on the arms of the chair, gathered in a mass of fingers and knuckles on my lap, nothing worked. With the exception of Woody, the razor-precision of these Tour staffers always made me feel unkempt. A Visigoth on the Palatine.

"The Commissioner is in Europe," said Henry Chandler, "meeting with the directors of the European and Asian golf tours. But he is aware of what happened and is very concerned."

A nice touch to invoke the Commissioner. He certainly must have appreciated being dragged away from whacking up billions of dollars in worldwide golf revenue to take a phone call about a Tour rookie missing his tee time. I almost cracked my knuckles before sailing into contrition mode.

"I'm sorry," I said. "I realize how many people I've inconvenienced. The sponsor, my playing partners—"

"The Commissioner doesn't care about the second round at Bay Hill," said Chandler. "Do you think he can't smooth things over with the sponsor's CEO? Do you think you're such a big draw that fans will stampede the exits if you don't play?"

"The Commissioner's concern," said Sally Lang, "is the Gainesville incident."

The Gainesville incident. I could practically hear the trumpet fanfare blaring offstage. Did the Tour think whatever happened to me could be mentioned only in euphemistic terms?

"We've all read the newspapers," said Chandler. "We've tried to talk to the police, but the detective in charge of the investigation won't take our calls."

"We want to hear your side, Mr. Lenahan," Peter Haswell said through his grin.

The formality irked me. Even at its highest level, golf was a friendly game totally free of the in-your-face antics so prevalent in the major team sports. Golfers went by their first names; the stars earned nicknames, preferably ones geared for trademark protection.

I ran my eyes along the line. Woody Harrington leaned back in his chair, as if ducking out of anyone's line of sight. He made a patting motion with his hand, signaling me to keep calm. But Henry Chandler stared at me like a bad lie in a sand trap, Peter Haswell grinned without mirth, and Sally Lang pursed her pale lips as if daring me to speak the truth. Maybe I was in more trouble than I thought.

"Didn't you all speak to the Judge?" I said.

This threw them into an exchange of confused mutterings, until Woody piped, "Judge Inglisi, Kieran's business manager."

"Oh him," said Sally Lang. "Yes, he called me."

Of all the people for the Judge to phone. I imagined their conversation in her sour smile. Full of "dearies" and "honey-buns," the Judge treating it less than seriously because he had a "little girl" on the other end. How he'd survived this far into the '90s without a sexual harassment suit was beyond me.

"He said Mr. Lenahan's been under lots of stress lately," Sally Lang continued. "I suggested that he avail himself of the many players' services the Tour provides, including referrals to qualified mental health therapists. Isn't that true, Woody?"

Woody started to bail me out, but Chandler cut him short.

"Whether you want therapy for your stress is your own business," he said. "Point is, we don't care what this Judge Inglisi character has to say right now. We'll speak to him later. Right now, we need to know what happened in Gainesville yesterday. From you."

I honestly wanted to remember, so I rolled my mental tape back to the seventeenth tee at Bay Hill. Maybe the pressure would snap me out of my amnesia.

"Well, uh, I played my round at Bay Hill." Nothing broke. My voice sputtered.

"And?" said Henry Chandler.

"Oh yeah. I shot seventy-four."

"Is this necessary?" said Woody. "Can't you see Kieran's woozy?"

"He answered that question fine," said Peter Haswell.

"He hasn't said a damn thing we don't already know," said Chandler.

"That's because Woody piped up," said Sally Lang.

"Actually I feel fine," I said. "Tired and sore, that's all. Where was I? Oh yeah, I shot my seventy-four, then drove up to Gainesville to visit Cindy Moran."

"And exactly what was your relationship to Cindy Moran?" said Chandler.

"We're friends."

"Friends?" said Chandler.

"That's right, friends," I said.

Chandler leaned back in his chair, a weary, now-I've-heard-everything slouch.

"Was she an old friend or a new friend?" said Haswell.

"Aw come on, Pete, just ask if she was a golf groupie," said Woody.

"I think Peter's phraseology is just fine," said Chandler. "Mr. Lenahan, was she an old friend or a new friend?"

"Depends on your point of view," I said. "I'm new on the Tour, so all my friends are new."

"And were you—" Sally Lang searched the ceiling for more clever phraseology.

"Friends," I said. "Nothing more. Just friends."

"Mr. Lenahan." Chandler pressed forward. "You expect us to believe that you drove one hundred twenty miles in between the first two rounds of a PGA tournament to visit a friend. For what reason?"

"To see her new apartment," I said.

Chandler shoved his chair back in disgust.

"Mr. Lenahan," said Sally Lang. "We are all familiar with your history. Most of us would prefer that you not play on the Tour at all. But you earned your playing exemption, and we are duty-bound to honor it. However, that doesn't mean we need to tolerate your every indiscretion. Now in the context of your other activities, the Gainesville incident—"

"What other activities?" I said.

"Your caddie," said Haswell. "She's a—"

"She's a damn good caddie. Nothing is going on between us, if that's what you mean."

"I can vouch for that," said Woody.

I didn't know how Woody could vouch for anything about me and Meg. But what was the point of having a friend in high places, if he couldn't throw a roadblock in front of the occasional inquisition.

"I'm sorry," I said. "I should have been up front from the start. The reason I sound so vague is because I don't remember what happened in Gainesville."

"You're telling us you have amnesia?" said Chandler.

"A bad case," I said. "Most everything back to Doral has been wiped clean."

"How convenient," said Sally Lang.

Henry Chandler glared, Peter Haswell's rubbery face went to pieces, Sally Lang pinched her temples. Even Woody bit back an odd grin.

"If you've read the newspapers, you know as much as I do," I said. "Check with the hospital if you don't believe me."

The four of them spoke sharply among themselves while I probed my skull for any sign of a headache. So what if Cindy Moran had been more than just a friend? There were enough bachelors on Tour to keep the golf groupies in business, and the Board certainly didn't react to every tryst. Was something going on here? Or was it just personal? The little old troublemaker, me.

The huddle broke. Henry Chandler cleared his throat.

"I don't need to remind you that the Players Championship is our biggest event of the year," he said. "Starting Monday, the focus of the entire golf world will be right here. I, that is, we expect you will do nothing to reflect badly on the Tour or this tournament. Nothing. We will speak to the hospital about your amnesia. We will speak to your manager. We will conduct whatever investigation necessary to present our findings to the Commissioner. He and the Tour Policy Board will have the final say."

"On what?" I said.

"Suspension," said Chandler.

CHAPTER
FIVE

Woody Harrington caught up with me outside.

"Sorry, Kieran," he said. "I wish I could have done more to help."

"Don't worry. I don't expect you to stick your neck out for me." I maneuvered us into the lollipop shade of a palm tree. "Is Chandler serious about suspension?"

Woody had a slight touch of walleye. It didn't affect his distance vision, but up close he needed to bob his head to keep you in focus.

"You know the routine," he said. "We staffers just work here. The Policy Board asks us to look into something, we look into it. We report back to the Board, the Board meets with the Commissioner, and then the Commissioner does whatever the hell he pleases."

"But suspension for this?" I said.

"I thought you don't remember what happened."

"I don't."

"Then how do you know it isn't worth a suspension?" said

Woody. He twisted a square knuckle into my ribs. "Only kidding, Kieran. There is no way I'll recommend a suspension. I don't care what you did."

"Thanks," I said. "Any idea why the Board is so interested?"

"Chandler took the call from one of the Board members, and we got word you were on the practice range, so we called you in." Woody stared off toward the television tower. "It's probably because of the Players. Everything gets a bit nuts here this time of year. But who knows? The Board has its own agenda, and that can have precious little to do with running golf tournaments."

"Like what?" I said.

"Hey, Kieran, I just work here."

Woody Harrington had a longer golf pedigree than most of the Tour hierarchy. The current Commissioner never played professional golf. Player seats comprised a minority bloc on the Tour Policy Board, which was dominated by directors appointed from private industry. The vast majority of the staffers came out of college with degrees in business administration. Not Woody. He captained the Oklahoma State golf team three years running, almost won the NCAA championship twice, and played his first Tour event the week after graduation. This was in the mid-70s, before exemptions and Q School, when a golfer of Woody's talent earned a spot on the Tour by a kind of divine right.

Woody won five tournaments in three years. A gregarious sort, he delighted the crowds by celebrating his victories with somersaults into the nearest sand trap. His fifth victory celebration turned out to be his last because his somersault pancaked into a flop, compressing a disc in his lower back.

The next five years saw three operations and four attempts at comebacks. Nothing worked. He quit golf completely and tried different career alternatives: television commentator, newspaper columnist, club designer. Nothing satisfied him, until Henry Chandler offered him a job with the Tour.

I first met Woody during my second attempt at Q School. He worked as part of the crew that marked the course before each tournament round, spray painting the ground-under-repair and drop areas, staking the boundaries of water hazards, pressing little yellow markers into the greens where the pins would be cut for the next day's play. During the tournament itself, he observed a senior official twist a rule against me. He argued in my favor, lost, and after the tournament, personally apologized for the unfair treatment. I never forgot.

Woody rose rapidly through the Tour hierarchy during the ensuing six years to become vice-president of player relations. He earned a reputation as being a "player's man," someone who understood the players' lives and who performed the tiny acts of mercy that made life on the road bearable. When I won at B.C., he sent the first congratulatory telegram. (Judge Inglisi had telegrammed earlier, but not with congratulations.) When I arrived in California to start my first year on tour, he personally delivered an orientation package. As I said, one of those tiny acts of mercy to make life on the road bearable. The bond we'd forged during that Q School six years ago had strengthened during the last two months. We both worked for the PGA Tour, but we were both outsiders in our own way.

"Your amnesia is on the level, I hope," said Woody.

"I wouldn't lie about that," I said.

"I'm glad. Not because you have amnesia, but because

now that you've said it, Henry Chandler will follow through with the hospital."

"He won't be disappointed."

"You really can't remember things as far back as Doral?"

"No, and whenever I try to work up a memory, I get a splitting headache as a reward."

"And this woman they found you with?" said Woody.

"I don't know a thing about her. Or, to be accurate, I don't remember knowing a thing about her."

"Did the doctors say when your memory would return?" said Woody.

"The hospital was too interested in pushing me out the door before the meter ran out on my insurance."

"You're on your own?"

"Medically speaking. I have a prescription for my headaches. Nothing else." I recalled Woody's odd grin when I mentioned the amnesia. "Would it help if I remembered?"

"Depends on what you remembered," he said. "Let's say the lady was a groupie, and you were there for the obvious, and it happened to be the wrong place at the wrong time. The Board might not like it, but I doubt you'd get much more than a fine. Now if it turned out to be something else."

"Like what?"

"Hard to say, Kieran. Let's see what you remember and when you remember it."

A group of Tour employees came chattering down the path. Woody greeted them with a stuck-on smile calculated to usher them along.

"Do you remember the Jason Oliver interview?" he said when they passed out of earshot.

That I remembered.

Jason Oliver was golf's ultimate gadfly, its malevolent clown-prince. Perfectly ambidextrous, he sometimes mixed left-handed and right-handed clubs in his bag. And that was just for starters. Oliver was an old-style left-wing radical among arch-conservatives, an eclectic bundle of New Age mysticism among serious Christians. While most pros plastered themselves like walking billboards, he refused all product endorsements, preferring "clean shirts, monochrome visors, and a simple black golf bag to the patchwork logos of corporate shills." He traveled from tournament to tournament in a converted school bus powered by natural gas. An electric model, he often stated, was on the drawing board.

His galleries were just as loopy, turned out in sandals and garlands, wild hair and long beards. Many carried cardboard placards in the hope of flashing a cause for the TV cameras: "Save the Whales," "Save the Canada Geese," "Free [the outlaw *du jour*]." Some didn't know a thing about golf, just followed for the spectacle. A few wandered into the nearest woods to get high.

Just before Doral, back before the mists of amnesia socked in my brain, a golf cable channel broadcast an interview in which Oliver accused several pros of using both legal and illegal drugs to enhance performances during tournaments. He refused to name names, but hinted darkly that "they know who they are, and the Tour does, too."

"Oliver dropped out of sight after the interview," said Woody. "As you might imagine, lots of people want to talk to him, including the Commissioner."

"Why doesn't he just suspend him?" I said.

Woody didn't catch my tone. "Not that easy with Oliver. Everything he touches becomes a *cause célèbre*."

"But he can suspend me," I said, adding a dash more acid.

"Hey, Kieran, I'm on your side, remember?" said Woody. "Oliver's agent tells me Oliver and his wife will be here Tuesday, maybe Wednesday. And from what I hear, lots of the guys are gunning for him. Now Oliver doesn't stay at any hotel, he doesn't mingle in the bars. The only time any of the guys see him is during the rounds. I've been trying to hook him up with some levelheaded soul to minimize the chances of an embarrassing scene during the tournament. But no one will volunteer. So-and-so might not personally object to playing with Oliver, but one or more of his good buddies will. The Players is my baby. I can't have any incidents spoil it because Chandler and the rest of them want to see me fall on my ass."

"Why?" I said.

"Some corporate infighting," said Woody. "Nothing you need to hear about."

"You want to pair me with Oliver," I said.

"That's what I planned. And then your problem came up. Now I'm thinking maybe we can help each other."

"How?"

"The Board is more concerned about Oliver than whatever the hell happened to you in Gainesville," said Woody. "If I can impress it upon them that pairing Oliver with you is the best chance of assuring a tranquil Players Championship, your suspension gets delayed at least a week. And maybe it blows over."

"Let's try it," I said wearily.

"I'll do my best to make it happen." Woody pumped my hand. "And when Gainesville comes back to you, make sure you tell me. Deal?"

Meg had vacated the practice range, but I found her skipping stones on the glass-smooth lagoon beside the putting green. She took the news of this latest impending disaster with uncharacteristic silence—one might say numbness—and barely smiled at the irony that my sudden compatibility with Jason Oliver, of all people, could deliver me from damnation.

"I always wanted to join the circus," was all she said before tossing a few balls to the turf and sticking something in my hand.

"What's this?" I said.

"Your putter."

My what? It was six inches of brass pipe filled with lead and stuck on the end of a shaft.

"Kieran, you bought this from a lad at Honda two weeks ago. He said he found it in his da's attic. You liked the feel. You paid fifty quid for it."

Liked the feel? It felt like a goddam wood maul. But no debating the facts with Meg. She'd been at Honda body, mind, and soul. Until my amnesia lifted, I'd been there in body only.

I stroked a few putts badly. Meg's putting skills were superb—something mine definitely were not—and most of our arguments occurred over the reads and speeds of putts. She adjusted my stance, separated my hands, tucked this elbow in, pulled this elbow out until I looked like a figure on an ancient Greek urn. The putts rolled no better.

As dusk fell, mist from the lagoon slickened the putting surface with evening dew. I sent Meg packing with everything but my putter and three golf balls. I didn't need practice so much as the mindless activity of rapping putts at the end of a mind-blowing day. During one of my turns around the empty green, a figure stepped out of the mist.

"Evenin', Kieran."

I squinted into the ribbing of fuzzy shadows a stand of palms laid across the fringe. The figure, shambling arthritically, slowly resolved into Daniel Neale.

During the '60s and '70s, Danny Neale practiced law in Gainesville. As a sidelight, he represented University of Florida football players in negotiating their rookie NFL contracts. He did this *gratis*, out of love for the game and the Gators, who considered him their No. 1 fan. The players called him Uncle Dan'l, and the name stuck. When NFL scouts came to town, they knew the road to signing a rookie ran straight through Uncle Dan'l's law office.

Then the rules changed. The contracts mushroomed, agents usurped the negotiating process, Gator seniors decided that their expectations and Uncle Dan'l's didn't quite jibe. Uncle Dan'l made a stab at working for one of the large management combines. He made more money than he ever dreamed possible, but he wasn't happy. "The kids changed," he said in an interview published by a golf monthly. "People think you're talking in racial code words when you say that. But I'm not, and it's true. The kids changed. When I started, most of the kids coming out of UF were damn flattered the NFL wanted them. They knew they were good players, but they were flattered just the same. Nowadays, they want signing bonuses and huge salaries and cars and mansions for their mothers, and then they hold out for half of training camp when the plain fact is they ain't done nothing yet. I told them so, and they just looked at me like I came from another planet. Maybe I do."

He quit the agency, cast about aimlessly for a while, then decided to cultivate new fields by catching guys on the golf mini-tour. He had a good eye for talent and for the guts necessary to bring that talent into full bloom. His current stable included Tommy Garth Hunter, Ned Nelson, and several other guys I knew from my mini-tour days. "I'd like to add your name to the list," he'd often said, his whiskey voice full of allusion to the circumstances that would always keep us at odds.

We traded the usual pleasantries for only the briefest moment before he cut to the point. Uncle Dan'l might move as slow as a meandering blackwater river, but he never wasted time.

"Got yourself in a fine bit of trouble," he said. He had the palest blue eyes I'd ever seen, like he flushed his pupils with chlorine bleach. Thick love handles bulged over the waistband of his golf slacks. He held his arms out from his body, fingers spread as if trying to air-dry his hands.

"I've been there before."

"Throwing you off the Tour is different from keeping you off in the first place," he said. "Degrees different."

"Thanks for the analysis," I said.

"Now don't get your back up, Kieran. I'm not here to gloat over your misfortune. I'm here to offer my services."

"How?"

"Mediating your problem with the thrones and dominations. Or whatever those pencil pushers like to think of themselves."

"Thank you, no," I said.

"Don't need the help?" said Uncle Dan'l. "Can go it alone. I've heard this tune before."

"I have representation," I said. "Judge Inglisi."

"Your business manager." Uncle Dan'l grinned. "Having some slick New York judge rather than a fuzzy old backwoods Florida lawyer is nice for being in a court of law. But you're not in a court of law, Kieran. You're in a monarchy, and the people with the ear of the king aren't necessarily the closest by."

"I'll take my chances," I said.

"I know you will," said Uncle Dan'l. "You always were the real gambler of the lot."

I went back to the hotel, ordered a room service dinner, and sulked about Uncle Dan'l. I'd read him wrong once and couldn't afford another mistake.

Uncle Dan'l and I went back to the Sarasota gambling scandal. He was in the locker room that morning, standing off to the side with his straw hat pushed back on his freckled scalp and his watery blue eyes drinking in the panic. He didn't say much, just drew me off into another rank of lockers after the guys stuffed their subpoenas into my hand.

"I remember that no-good bum from law school," he said of the state attorney who headed the probe. It was all the encouragement I needed.

I never asked if the charges could be true; the idea seemed too far-fetched. I rallied the guys with all my lawyerly zeal, while Uncle Dan'l stayed in the background. "Looks prettier to have you defend the boys," he said. But he advised me from the locker room and the practice tee, dropping nuggets of advice that, in retrospect, seemed too uncannily prescient to be wisdom or coincidence.

A few years later, in the depths of my Milton exile, Tommy

Garth Hunter visited during the Tour's northeast swing. Hunter had been my closest friend on the mini-tour. His Canadian background gave him a wry outlook on the excesses of American society, and he took great delight in pointing out how many "American" personalities had actually been born in Canada.

We were well into afterdinner cognacs when he let something slip.

"That gambling ring," he said, "was no myth."

The ring worked like a murky blend of fantasy football and an old-fashioned Calcutta, where spectators bet on teams of golfers like racehorses. Using a computer, an organized crime operation assembled the upper tier of mini-tour players into four-man teams. These were virtual teams because the players were ignorant of their participation. At least at the start. Gamblers would place their bets, the players would play their regular tournament rounds, and, at the end of the week, the computer tabulated the results. Some teams advanced, some were eliminated. All the while, the stakes escalated. In the later stages, so much money rode on the weekly matches that a player might arrive for the final round of a tournament and find a wiseguy toting his bag. The wiseguy would dictate the player's target score for the day was 75. That is, 75, or else the player might not make it to the next tournament. But the player was lucky. Instead of grinding for a share of the official purse, he could relax, plunk a shot or two into a water hazard, and pocket ten grand tax-free.

Hunter tried to convince me that he hadn't taken a dime in bribes, that his reputation as a player surpassed any amount of money slipped to him under the table. I didn't believe him, and, anyway, believing him was beside the point. That conversation did more than just redefine a friendship as just another couple of guys in the same line of work. My entire world shifted. I hadn't been the crusader protecting innocent friends from the jaws of the System. I'd been a naive rube with a convenient talent for obfuscation.

I wheeled the food cart into the corridor and sat in the dark, pondering the different routes Hunter and I had taken. His trajectory since Sarasota had been ever upward. He sailed through the same Q School that sent me packing back to Milton. His huge frame, thick dark curls, four top-ten finishes, and Uncle Dan'l's management earned him name-recognition few Tour rookies ever enjoyed. Early in his second year, he won a tournament in the desert. Uncle Dan'l issued a press release saying Hunter grew up in a small town on Hudson Bay that closed up for two weeks every spring while polar bear herds migrated through. A golf columnist, picking up the subtle cue, christened Hunter the "Polar Bear." The nickname stuck, not only because of Hunter's ursine physique, but also because of the conscious allusion to Jack Nicklaus, the Golden Bear.

Though a major championship still eluded him, the Polar Bear kept manufacturing victories in lesser events. Last season had been his most successful: three victories, fifth-leading money winner on the Tour, and a well-publicized endorsement contract paying $30 million over the next ten years. Just for swinging a certain set of golf clubs, hitting a particular brand of golf ball, and wearing a white golf shoe designed to resemble a polar bear's claw.

Good ole Uncle Dan'l, I thought, comparing my earning power to Tommy Garth Hunter's. He never does anything for nothing.

I crawled under the sheets, my skull suddenly feeling as light and resilient as two inches of lead. The first dream cycle plopped me back into that same mansion. I weaved through the party, this time catching glimpses of the woman who'd eluded me the last time. A curve of shoulder, a sweep of thigh. *Walks like she has a stick up her arse,* a voice spoke within my dream-mind.

I climbed a short flight of stairs and floated down a long corridor. The sounds of the party receded. Doors slammed shut on each side as I passed. Finally, the corridor angled into an open room. She stood against the window, her back toward me. My putter lay on the floor beside her, its head separated from its shaft.

Something whirred behind my ear. I turned. It spun close and very fast. But in the logic of the dream I could see the unmistakable dimples of a golf ball pressing against the fabric of the black Banlon sock.

I jumped up with a start. My heart thumped in my chest, my head pounded. I staggered into the bathroom and gulped a pill.

The rest of the night passed with only the vaguest sense of sleep.

CHAPTER
SIX

Sometimes the little things affect you. I'd like to say I'm psychic, that the dream of the woman in the mansion drove me back to Gainesville. I'd like to say I'm sensible, and that Woody Harrington's solid advice persuaded me to pursue my lost memory. I'd like to say I'm careful, and that Uncle Dan'l's offer meant I should take nothing for granted. In truth, it was that stupid putter. How could a confirmed cheapskate not remember paying fifty bucks for a worthless piece of old plumbing?

I showered, dressed, and carefully worked a room service breakfast around the stitches in my tongue. My head felt better, though not one hundred percent. If I moved too fast, a warm pressure spread from behind my ear and heat waves shimmered before my eyes. Life on the verge of a migraine.

After breakfast, I rang up Meg at her motel. No answer. I phoned the practice tee. Meg hadn't arrived yet. I left word I was taking the day off.

Rumors of yesterday's tipping rampage must have spread

through the hotel staff because the parking valet buffed the seat with a chamois before allowing me into my car. He visibly deflated in the rearview mirror as he unfolded the single I'd pressed into his hand.

I drove well south of St. Augustine before turning west. Part of the idea was to avoid a rerun of yesterday's Palatka fiasco. The rest was to retrace at least part of my path from Orlando to Gainesville. Maybe it would jog a memory.

The day was beautiful. Northern Florida enjoys a definite, if short-lived, spring. Some signs are obvious, like azaleas and magnolias in bloom. Others are extraneous, like the sudden influx of students from Northern colleges. I focused on the sky, which seemed poised in a momentary clarity between the wispy cirrus of winter and the humid haze of summer.

I noticed the car east of Ocala, shiny and black, with the sun winking off its windshield. There were thousands of them on the road, with nondescript bodies differentiated only by a piece of molding or some plastic doodad. I sped up the I-75 entrance ramp, and the car followed.

I-75 evoked no special memory of Thursday. It looked like any other Interstate: two ribbons of pavement divided by a swath of green, all dipping, curving, and looping into the distance. No Cindy Moran lurked along the roadside. No electromagnetic traces of earlier thoughts hovered in the air.

South of Gainesville, the highway crossed a perfectly flat plain called Payne's Prairie. One hundred years ago, the prairie was a lake, with steamboats and packet rafts plying the water between Gainesville and points south. According to local legend, a rift opened up in the lake bed, and the water drained away like a bathtub into subterranean aquifers. Very much like my memory.

I swung into Shands Hospital. The black car tucked into a parking space several rows away. I thought about waving, but kept my eyes averted as I hurried out of the sun and into the ER. Several lies and five minutes of wrong turns later, I found Dr. Ellis in his office.

"What can I do for you, Mr. Lenahan?" he said.

"I want to know why I can't remember things going back almost three weeks."

"You had a concussion. Amnesia is a normal sequela."

"I know what's normal. I want to know about me." I laid out everything Meg had told me, including the putter.

"Maybe your caddie is testing you," said Ellis. "You said she is skeptical about your amnesia."

"She wouldn't lie, dammit!" I slapped the desk.

"Easy, Mr. Lenahan." Ellis flicked his intercom and ordered someone to fetch my X-rays. I retreated to a chair. He buffed his glasses, held them to his lamp, and buffed them again. The X-rays arrived before he needed to repeat that charade a third time. He jammed the plates into the shadowbox and, after a moment, started to hum thoughtfully.

"Your amnesia reaches back three weeks?" he said.

"That's when we arrived in Miami for Doral," I said. "I remember finishing last, but nothing of the tournament itself. Honda is a blank. So is Bay Hill, except for the snatch on seventeen that led me to think a golf ball clocked me."

Ellis shut off the shadowbox and folded his hands on the desk.

"Do you know computers?" he said.

"Not very well."

"Same here. I've learned how to use them. I can access records, perform diagnoses, track a patient's progress. I know what keys to hit to perform the tasks I need to perform. But I don't have a clue about what's happening inside the machine. Our understanding of memory is largely the same. We know about the limbic system. We know that different sensory aspects of a particular memory reside in different parts of the brain, and that another part reassembles them into an integrated memory. But how it happens, well, we're all like me at the computer. About all I can say is, one day your memory will come back."

"Yesterday it was little balls in tubes, today it's computers," I said. "I can't live on analogies, Doc. I need to know why I was in that apartment, who Cindy Moran was, and how I knew her."

Ellis reached for his glasses again. I grabbed his wrist.

"Are you going to help me, Doc? Or do I read about what happened to me in the newspapers?"

Ellis slid his wrist out of my grasp, all the while staring at me as if I might snap if he moved too fast.

"Back in the early seventies," he said, "a big alligator capsized a man fishing in his canoe and mangled him pretty badly. The doctors here sewed him up, about a thousand stitches. Inside, he had tendon and ligament damage. Physical therapy lasted a solid year. After that—" Ellis tapped his temple.

"He didn't remember the attack?" I said.

"He remembered it too well," said Ellis. "He stayed on for psychiatric counseling. It wasn't just alligators that scared him, either. If he saw a tree frog, he freaked out.

"One of the ward attendants got friendly with him. They talked about fishing and hunting. The attendant signed him out one day, and they headed to a lake on the University

campus with some pretty big gators. First, they watched from
the car. The patient shook and sweated, but didn't freak out.
The next day, they got out of the car. The day after that,
they took a few steps toward the water. The day after that,
a few more steps. Soon enough, they got to the banks, and
the patient stared in the eye of a seven-footer floating a few
yards off. Next thing that happened, the patient slipped into
the water and slowly waded toward the gator. The attendant
wanted to scream, but he knew better. The gator and the
patient stared at each other, and then the patient started
swimming and the gator started swimming alongside. After
awhile, three more gators joined it, and they all swam like
great friends.

"He never missed a day after that, except for one when a
hurricane hit. People dubbed him 'Gatorman,' and came from
miles around to see him swim with those gators. He'd hug
them, ride them. They even let him cuddle their young. He
never got a scratch from any one of them. Then one day, no
Gatorman. People thought the gators got him. The police
sent skin divers, boats with grapples. But they never found
any trace of him."

"Is there a point to this, Doc?" I said.

"Yes," said Ellis. "If you can't just wait for your memory
to return, you'll need to swim with the gators."

"I've been to the apartment with McGriff, if that's what
you mean," I said. "I've seen her body. Nothing's clicked."

Ellis took a deep breath. "Go back by yourself. Steep
yourself in Thursday afternoon. I'm sorry, that's all I can
suggest."

The parking space McGriff showed me yesterday was open, but I didn't swing in just yet. If I wanted to swim with Thursday's alligators, I needed to recreate the scene as accurately as possible. I followed signs to the manager's office and parked nearby. The black car kept its distance, slamming on the brakes and reversing out of sight as I stepped outside. I tried not to laugh.

The woman seated behind the desk identified herself as the manager's wife. She was plump but pretty, with blond hair so wispy she could have been halfway to bald. I took the honest approach, and told her who I was, what I wanted, and why. Funny, the desk clerk at the hotel offers me more sympathy in twenty-five seconds than Judge Inglisi has in twenty-five years. I blab my amnesia to this woman like she's my shrink. Life imitates talk show.

"Don't remember anything?" she said. "Funny, none of us knew enough about her to forget."

"I heard she'd been here less than a month," I said.

"Three weeks yesterday. We're under strict orders from the owners not to rent without written leases. The big turnover times are September and March. That's when the bulk of the new students come in at the University. We have a ten percent vacancy rate. That's high. So Drew, my husband, took it on himself to rent some of these units month to month. You can bet the owners aren't happy one of our month to monthers got herself killed."

"She wasn't here much, right?" I said.

"Hardly at all," she said. "She had some kind of tiff one

night that the upstairs neighbors complained about. By the time Drew got there, it was over."

"Did she drive a car?"

"She didn't reserve a parking space. But that doesn't prove anything because we have such a big lot with so many visitors' spots."

She opened a shallow cabinet, and lifted a set of numbered keys off a hook.

"One more question," I said as she handed me the keys. "Did you ever see me around here?"

"I think I would have remembered," she said.

I drove my car back to that parking space and followed the path into the courtyard. Shafts of sunlight poking through the live oak lit rainbow patterns in the spray of the sprinklers. A lounge chair lay open on the grass, getting drenched. A huge titanium lock hooked the frame of a mountain bike to a lamp post. Music played in an apartment, and curtains fluttered out of an open window. Familiar, yes, but only from my visit with McGriff.

I turned a corner, walking slower, and then edging forward like a man in a strange, darkened room. But the darkness wasn't out here in the physical world; it was inside my own mind. I reached the door without bumping into any furniture.

The crime scene tape was gone, with small, crumpled bits stuck in the juniper like Christmas ornaments. I knocked and waited, but not for someone to answer. Nothing. I slid back the deadbolt and unlatched the door. I cupped my ear to the tiny crack as if listening for the past. Nothing. I knocked hard enough for the door to open a few inches. Still nothing.

I stepped inside. Someone had drawn the curtains, and the entire apartment was dim. I switched on the ceiling light in the kitchenette. The furniture was gone, probably reclaimed by the rental company after the crime scene unit finished lifting fingerprints. The apartment looked even shabbier than yesterday, with faint smudges of grease where the couch once lined the wall. I thought about telling Henry Chandler I drove to Gainesville to see Cindy Moran's apartment. What a joke.

I inched down the small hallway toward the bathroom where water once again dripped in the toilet. I stood between the two bedrooms. Cindy Moran's taped outline was gone from the carpet. My bloodstain had lightened; the nap of the carpet was raised as if Drew the manager had tried to scrub it out with bleach. I stood completely still, trying to visualize the scene as it may have looked, trying to replay the sounds I might have heard before the back of my head exploded. I saw nothing but an empty stretch of carpet, and heard nothing but the dripping water. Suddenly angry, I pushed into the bathroom and jiggled the flush handle. The dripping immediately ceased, as if the entire plumbing system cowered beneath my rage. I slumped against the wall, dug my fists deep into my eye sockets. I couldn't remember a thing about Thursday. I just could not remember a thing.

A hand touched my shoulder. Meg. She tugged my arm and I followed, docile in my desolation. We sat on the living room floor with our backs against the wall. Her coconut sunscreen smelled like home.

"Sorry, Kieran," she said.

Nothing like hearing the Irish say an Irish name. They get every subtle inflection just right. No one said my name quite like Meg. Not even Georgina in the throes of wild abandon.

"About what?" I said.

"Following you."

I said nothing, pretending not to have noticed.

"And for doubting you. You don't actually remember."

"Not a thing," I said.

We sat for what seemed to be several minutes in complete silence. The drip in the bathroom started up again, but I didn't move. Meg tentatively worked her arm around my shoulder, then quickly pulled it back.

"You met during the Tuesday practice round at Doral," she said. "We were on the third hole. You hit your approach to the green. I pulled the putter from your bag and tamped down your divot. You were about twenty yards ahead. She must have ducked under the ropes because a marshal was trying to pull her away. You told him she was your friend."

"I did?" I said.

"That was a lie. You never saw her before."

"Did she follow me?"

"For the rest of the round," said Meg. "Afterwards, you had a drink in one of the corporate hospitality tents. She missed Wednesday, but she followed you all four rounds Thursday through Sunday."

"And I never introduced her to you," I said.

"No."

"Sorry," I said. "Did I see her any time off the course?"

"You mean did you date her?" said Meg. "I wouldn't know whether you did at Doral. But she showed up at Honda after the Wednesday practice round. She watched you on the range, and then you spoke. You went out to dinner with her that night. That was when you bought that putter. I thought you did it to impress her. Give the poor kid fifty quid for his da's shillelagh."

"Did any of my playing partners at Doral or Honda talk to her?"

"Not that I saw. She actually seemed reticent about other people. She certainly gave me a wide berth."

"Who did I play with in those rounds?" I said.

"None of the regulars. Local pros who filled out some empty spots in the field. No one we'll find at the Players."

"Did she show up at Bay Hill?" I said.

"No," said Meg. "But her absence affected you. I could see that plainly. You were in a very distracted state."

"Like our argument on the seventeenth tee?" I said.

"I thought you had amnesia."

"I remember that," I said. "It's what made me think a golf ball hit me."

"It wasn't only about the line of the putt but the putter as well," said Meg. "I wanted you to stop using it. You flatly refused. I told you a putter salesman wanted to show you a new line of stock after the round. You said you were going to Gainesville."

"Did I say why?"

"No," said Meg. "But it was plain to me your woman was involved."

And it was plain Meg was miffed about more than me using a wood maul for a putter.

We locked up the apartment and returned to the manager's office. Outside, a mountain bike leaned against an azalea bush. Inside, the manager's wife spoke on the phone while the long-haired guy from yesterday loomed over her desk as if waiting for her to finish. He had deep-set eyes and a cleft in his chin. He looked at Meg, then at me. I nodded, and so did he, a tacit sign he recognized me from my visit with McGriff.

The manager's wife sounded angry, and I gathered a crew she'd hired to plaster and paint some vacant units hadn't shown up. Inbred manners prevented me from dropping the keys onto the desk and scooting out the door. I believed in properly thanking a person who did me a favor, and a proper thanks occurred when the favor was complete. Otherwise, the transaction lacked closure. Sometimes I ended up listening to one half of pointless conversations. Sometimes those conversations aren't so pointless.

"You want no part of it?" she said. "Drew hired you. You signed a contract."

My face must have rearranged itself.

"What's the trouble?" said Meg.

But I was already out the door, walking double-time toward Cindy Moran's apartment. I stopped where the courtyard path intersected the path from the parking lot. My car sat at the other end of the archway. *"You want no part of it."* I took a deep breath and started walking.

Only I wasn't walking; I was floating. And it wasn't a fresh Saturday morning, but a hot Thursday afternoon. Camelot kaleidoscoped around me. Loamy smells, humming air conditioners, pots thick with spider plants hanging from wooden balustrades. I reached the door. In the present, I fumbled for the key, and turned back the deadbolt. In the past, a past that rushed out at me like sunlight blazing through a rift in a cloudbank, the door was slightly ajar. I knocked, and it opened with a stuttering creak of its hinges. I stepped inside, and walked as far as the tiny hallway. *"You want no part of it. Too late. It's already done."* I recalled a faint sound, like the whir of a distant helicopter. But before I could remember whether I'd seen Cindy laid out as McGriff described, or standing as the woman stood in the dream, the memory burned up like a jammed strip of celluloid.

"Dammit, dammit, dammit." I pounded the bathroom doorjamb. "Dammit, Meg, I almost had it."

"Kieran," she said, "we have company."

CHAPTER SEVEN

He was Gainesville P.D., and one of a growing breed. Tall, strapping, dazzling with metal, and creaking with leather in a way once reserved strictly for motorcycle cops.

"Are you Kieran Lenahan?" he said.

I nodded, and nodded back at myself twice in his reflective lenses. He turned his head to a tiny radio clipped to his epaulet.

"Subject located," he said.

Static erupted and then fell away, leaving a human voice in its wake.

"Bring him up."

"He's accompanied by a female Caucasian," said the cop. "Approximately five-two, blond hair, early to mid-twenties."

Meg snorted, irked at being reduced to a physical description on a radio run.

"Bring her, too," came the response.

They rogered this and that, and then broke off.

"Let's lock these premises and return the keys to the office," said the cop.

"And then?" I said.

"That was Detective McGriff. He wants to talk."

The Shetland-sized German shepherd in the back seat of the patrol car explained the leather.

"I'm a K-9 officer," said the cop. "I was the nearest unit when we were apprised of your presence."

Oh. I caught Meg's eye and shrugged. Jargon killed me.

He opened the front passenger door. "We'll all need to squeeze in front. Regulations."

Meg took the middle. I slammed the doorlock with my elbow and turned sideways so the dog wouldn't slobber on the back of my neck. We passed nothing that looked like a police station. A stretch of auto dealerships gave way to small houses made of pastel-painted cinderblock, and then to scrub pine.

"I thought you said McGriff wanted to see me," I said.

"He does," said the cop.

A Piper Comanche skimmed low, fixing on a line of tall orange light stanchions that led to an airport. The cop signalled for a left turn. Up ahead, a rough-hewn wooden sign poked out of the solid wall of pine. Ironwood Golf Course.

Judging from the parking lot, Ironwood catered to back-woods Florida. Finned Cadillacs, pick-ups with gun racks, huge Chevies thick with a dozen coats of paint. We left the K-9 cruiser, walked through the clubhouse, and out onto a patio overlooking the putting green. McGriff sat at a table, his arms spread across the backs of two empty chairs. A thin canvas golf bag lay at his feet. He stared at a TV angling down from above the outdoor bar. Sweat glistened on his arms and darkly streaked his red golf shirt. He leaned forward for his pilsner glass and noticed us.

"Afternoon, Lenahan," he said. "You must be feeling better to come all the way back to Gainesville."

"A little," I said.

"Good to hear. Head injuries are nasty things." He rose halfway out of his chair to shake Meg's hand. "Meg Black, I take it."

"I am," said Meg, flushing.

"Don't be flattered," I said. "The detective spends hours on homework."

McGriff let that pass with a wink. He told the K-9 cop to swing back in an hour, and kicked two chairs as an invitation to sit.

"Beer, iced tea?" he said.

I declined; Meg opted for iced tea. McGriff waved for the bartender.

"Before we engage too much in mysterious machinations," he said, "I had a feeling you would return, so I arranged with Camelot's management to allow you free access to the apartment. They also were to call me when you arrived."

"Before you congratulate yourself," I said, "I came back only to see Dr. Ellis about my amnesia. He told me a parable about someone named Gatorman who was attacked by alligators and then swam with them to overcome his phobia. That's why I went back to the apartment."

McGriff mugged a smile in Meg's direction. I wondered if he knew enough about us to realize he could turn her into an amused audience by spinning me on a skewer. But he retreated, and focused on the telecast of Bay Hill's third round.

"Ned Nelson's making a move," he said.

The TV showed Nelson's compact frame hunched over a putter. The graphic showed him three under par for the day and two under for the tournament, but not yet on the first page of the leader board.

"He's still a bit far back," I said.

"Really?" said McGriff. The bartender brought Meg's drink, and McGriff signed for it. "Do I detect sour grapes?"

"Why?" I said.

"Well, you're here and he's there playing for millions," said McGriff.

"This isn't the first time I'm missing out on a payday." I looked at Meg, who nodded as if to say "Amen to that." Then I remembered I was dealing with a cop, and decided to explain myself. "What I meant was that twenty guys separate him from the lead. That's more important than the five stroke deficit."

"But you know Ned, right?" said McGriff.

"I know him."

"And you know Chris Jennings and Sam Young and Thomas Garth Hunter."

"I know lots of guys from the old mini-tour who are now on the big Tour."

"And of those, Tommy Garth Hunter's made it the biggest so far, right?" said McGriff.

"Fair enough," I said. "What's your angle?"

"No angle. Just homework, like you told the lady." McGriff nodded courteously in Meg's direction. "You helped those guys out of some trouble some years back."

No angle, my ass. "Look, Detective, I helped those guys

out of a jam. And given the same set of circumstances, I'd help them out again."

"Now don't get all lathered up," said McGriff. "Meg, does he get this excited on the golf course? Lenahan, you want to move back into the shade. You're looking a little red in the face."

"No, I'm fine," I said.

McGriff spun his chair and lifted his feet onto a wrought-iron railing that separated the patio from the putting green. We all three faced the same general direction, away from the TV and out over the golf course. I could tell the course had been carved out of pine forest, contoured by bulldozers, and seeded with the kind of bent grass that grew best in Florida's sandy soil. It wasn't lush. The roughs had already baked to brown, and the fairways would follow suit without adequate watering.

In the distance, a foursome trudged along the brow of a hill. One of them stopped, dropped the bag from his shoulder, and pulled a club out of the bag. Staring off beyond the hill, he switched the club as if gathering his concentration or waiting for the group ahead to clear. Finally he settled into a squat almost as deep as a baseball catcher's. Even at this distance, I could see he held his hands abnormally low, with the club almost certainly toed up instead of laying its sole flat on the turf. He swung. The turf erupted. The ball flew arrow straight before dissolving into the blue.

"That's Dewey Peek," said McGriff. "Ever hear of him?"

"No."

"If he still had the game he had thirty-five years ago, we'd be watching him on the little screen now," said McGriff.

Dewey Peek's foursome descended out of sight.

"You didn't bring me here to talk golf," I said.

"You're right." McGriff drained the last of his beer. "There have been some developments on my end. I want to know if there have been any on yours."

I don't like talking to cops. They tend to hear either too much or too little of what you say, depending on their agenda. But a couple of things weighed in favor of immediate candor. First, I respected McGriff. He wasn't another Chicky DiRienzo, the kind of detective who handled an investigation the way a child handled a bumper car. As I'd glibly told Meg, McGriff actually did his homework. Second, despite my epiphany in the apartment, I was still in the dark. If Meg could place me with Cindy Moran at Doral and Honda, dozens of other people could do the same. So I related exactly what Meg told me. McGriff listened, made some notes on the back of a scorecard, tossed a few confirmatory questions Meg's way.

"Did your swim with the alligators help your memory?" he said.

"I remember walking from my car to the apartment door," I said. "It's still sketchy, but I remember. I think the door was unlatched, and my knock pushed it open."

"You remember that, too?" said McGriff.

"Sketchily."

"Was she alive when you got there?"

I closed my eyes and tried to will myself back, to inject myself into that exact place at that exact time. Nothing.

"I can't remember," I said, "but what sparked my memory was overhearing the apartment manager's wife speaking on the phone. She said 'You want no part of it.' That's what Cindy Moran told me."

"Want no part of what?"

"I don't know."

"Well, what do you think it means?"

"I don't know," I said.

" 'You want no part of it,' " McGriff said thoughtfully. "Do you remember her inflection when she said it?"

He demonstrated several different interpretations, repeating the words as a harsh warning, a surprised reaction, and a sarcastic observation. This last sounded as if I had been every bit a part of something. But what? McGriff let the words linger, then swung his gaze over to Meg.

"Don't ask me what it means," she said. "I never spoke to the woman."

"All right. Okay. At least that's something," said McGriff.

I had the distinct impression it was neither all right nor okay, it was more than something, and he didn't believe me.

"Here is what we know," he said. "Her name wasn't Cindy Moran. We have no ID on her yet, but the real Cindy Moran is still very much alive out on the panhandle near Fort Walton Beach. Your lady assumed Ms. Moran's identity."

"How?" I said, realizing that the revelation had moved me to the edge of my chair. Meg leaned forward as well.

"Simple, really," said McGriff. "The real Ms. Moran and her husband applied to refinance their home mortgage. The application is being processed in a Gainesville branch of their bank. You ever talk to your credit card customer service line?"

"I try not to," I said.

"It's a hassle, right?" he said. "All those questions to verify if you're you. Well, a mortgage application has all that information in one convenient place. Social security number, job history, phone number, d/o/b.

"We think that someone lifted the info off the Moran application and sold it to your Cindy Moran. She called the credit card companies and used the information to have duplicate cards sent to her at a Gainesville address. This isn't a long-term scam. But long enough to hit up the real Ms. Moran for ten grand in cash advances."

"You should be able to trace her with this," I said.

"We're trying," said McGriff. "The address where the duplicate cards were mailed is bogus. But we're watching the mail in case it was a routine drop. We're also running down everyone with any possible access to that mortgage application. Naturally, that's turning out to be everyone from the branch manager to the janitor."

McGriff waved for another beer and poured it slowly down the side of his glass.

"Do you plan on retrieving more of your memory?" he said.

"Maybe."

"Then let me set you straight about that parable Dr. Ellis told you," he said. "Gatorman was no survivor of an alligator attack. He was a Vietnam vet with post-traumatic stress syndrome. He swam with the gators on campus, like Ellis said, but he didn't just disappear. He ended up in Europe, dressed in a tuxedo and playing a human mannequin in little town squares. After that, he went insane."

Officer K-9 dropped us back at Camelot. Heat billowed up from the macadam. My headache poked at the edges of my temple. Maybe it had been there all along, and I just hadn't noticed.

"I'll follow you back to Sawgrass," said Meg.

"I might hang around awhile," I said.

"Why? Your amnesia's breaking. The cops will find out about the woman. Let them do their job."

"But I'm close to something. I can feel it."

Meg choked off a harangue, slammed herself into her car, but didn't start the engine. I leaned against my own car. The sunbaked fender sent a chill up my spine. Okay, so what if I hang around in Gainesville? What would I do? Haunt Camelot? Drive around aimlessly? Wait for McGriff to dispatch the nearest unit to grab me for more enlightenment? Swimming with real alligators seemed an easier task. At least better defined.

"Hey, pal."

The long-haired guy straddled his mountain bike in the archway. He kicked forward, and rolled into the sun.

"I can help you," he said.

"How do you know I need any?"

"Because Suzanne inside told me you don't remember anything, and because the cops are putting the squeeze on you."

"What kind of help?" I said.

"Info about the lady."

"You knew her?"

"Never spoke to her in my life," he said, "but that might be an advantage."

A car door slammed. In a moment, Meg stood beside me.

"What is this about?" she said.

"He says he has information about Cindy Moran," I said.

"Good stuff," he said. "Photographs."

"Let's see them," I said.

"Whoa, man, the viewing isn't free."

Meg yanked my arm.

"Kieran, this is a trick," she said.

"Wait a second." I squirmed out of her grasp. "How much?"

The guy's eyes locked on something over my shoulder. I turned in time to see a police car speed past on the road outside.

"Let's go to my place," he said. "We can negotiate there."

Meg followed reluctantly. We crossed the courtyard, waited for him to lock his bike to a post, and climbed a set of open stairs to a second floor unit opposite Cindy Moran's.

"My name is Larry Stuart," he said, "but people call me Stu."

He opened a door into a disaster of post-hurricane proportions. Books, newspapers, and balled up clothing littered every inch of floorspace.

"Stay on the newspapers," he said. "You won't hurt anything that way."

"Like what?" I said.

"Negatives, contact strips," said Stu. "It's not neat, but I know where everything is."

Meg and I crossed a river of trash on a bridge of old *Gainesville Suns*. In the kitchenette, dozens of plastic cups stood on the counter, filled to various depths with slimy coffee and floating cigarette butts. A dingy towel hung on the corner of the bathroom door. One bedroom was sealed off with black felt lining the doorjamb and threshold. A chemical smell leaked out, which was preferable to the possible alternatives.

"My darkroom," said Stu.

The other bedroom was filled with cameras, tripods, lights, and screens. The walls were papered with prints. I recognized the sunbather, among the subjects, and didn't imagine she would have consented to some of the candids. The only discernible piece of furniture in the bedroom—in fact, anywhere in the apartment—was a bed raised four feet above the floor by a crude plywood platform.

Stu lifted the mattress and pulled out a manila envelope.

"Has anyone else seen these?" I said.

"No."

"Not even the cops?"

"I don't like cops." He pried open the clasp and peeked inside the envelope. The photos were eight by tens. Six riffled beneath his thumb, each separated by a thin piece of cardboard.

"Uh uh," he said when I reached out my hand. "First you pay."

"How do I know they'll tell me anything I don't already know?" I said.

"They will."

I looked over at Meg. With her arms clasped across her belly and her nostrils pinched tightly against the assorted odors, she suffered from a bad case of the creeps.

"How much?" I said.

Stu gathered his hair in one hand, calculating.

"Two hundred," he said.

"Kieran, let's leave this instant," said Meg.

I raised a hand to stop her. "How about one hundred now and a hundred after I see them, if they help me?"

"Kieran, are you mad?" said Meg.

Maybe. But the window gave Stu a straight shot at Cindy Moran's front door. If he put even half of this optical wizardry to good use, the pictures could be worthwhile.

Stu tugged at his wad of hair. "How do we decide if they help?"

"We talk about it." I opened my wallet and winced with psychic pain as I counted out five twenties. Meg groaned. I could almost hear her thinking, First the putter, now these pictures.

Stu took the twenties, counted them twice, and stuffed them into the pocket of his jeans. Then he handed over the envelope.

I spread the photos side by side on the mattress. They were a grainy black and white, obviously shot at night. Each showed the entrance to Cindy Moran's apartment. The front door was open, and light from within splashed on the junipers and laid a bright trapezoid across the path and onto the grass. In three of the photos, a wiry man faced the doorway. He pointed inside, and even the poor resolution couldn't mask the sinews exposed in his neck. He was shouting. Two showed the profile of a woman edging out the door. Cindy Moran, with her chin thrust forward, taking the other half of the argument. The last showed the man full face, walking away from the door with his hips cocked in a determined swagger. He had thin features, scraggly hair, and a goatee. Grease stained his tee-shirt, and a large oblong belt buckle caught a glimmer of light from the closing door.

"These don't tell me anything." I slipped the photos one by one into the envelope. "They're barely worth a hundred and definitely not worth another."

"What if I find you this guy?" said Stu.

CHAPTER
EIGHT

Medically speaking, it was a clog in the arteries leading from the heart of Gainesville. Six highways converged at a node of shopping centers, gas stations, and fast food joints. All the usual suspects were there, the corporate tandems we've come to expect since the days of Macys and Gimbels. Can't have a Publix without a Winn-Dixie, a Mobil without a Gulf, a McDonalds without a Burger King.

Meg drove while I rode shotgun and Stu directed from the back seat. We parked at the edge of a Gulf station. Stu jumped out and walked up to a teenager pumping gas into a station wagon. They spoke briefly, and then Stu jogged back.

"The guy we're looking for is named Eddie Fort," he said. "He's supposed to be working right now, but he hasn't shown up."

"Does he know where Fort lives?" I said.

"I asked. He doesn't. But he says Fort's usually late, and the boss is this close to firing him." Stu pinched a millimeter of air between thumb and forefinger.

We camped across the street in the window booth of a sandwich shop. There passed three of the longest hours in recent memory. A pill and a seltzer gave me heartburn, which worsened with two bites of a BLT. Meg played with her food, probably dreaming of New Orleans. Stu tried to make lighthearted conversation, which was about as welcome as a fruit fly. He was into me for a hundred, and maybe a hundred more. I didn't need to entertain him, to boot.

Finally, Eddie Fort emerged grandly from a rust-eaten Camaro. His boss, hefty in bib overalls, greeted him with a half-Nelson and an ass-boot in the general direction of the pumps. Eddie bounced well. The boss drove out, a customer drove in, and Eddie set to work.

Stu and I crossed the highway on foot while Meg idled in the car. I met Eddie Fort coming out of the station office with change for his customer.

"Eddie Fort," I said.

"Yeah." He didn't break stride, so I grabbed his arm. "What the hell—"

"I want to talk to you about Cindy Moran," I said.

"Who the hell's that?" He squirmed. His arm was skinny, but the muscles felt like wire cables. I needed all my strength to keep hold.

"This is who." I showed him one of the pictures, and he froze.

"You a cop?" he said.

"Bank security. I'm tracing a stolen credit card."

"Hey, I don't know nothing about nothing," he said, trying to break free. "I ain't talking."

I whipped his arm around his back, pushed his clenched fist to a section of spine he could reach only with a backscratcher.

"You're talking to me right now, Eddie," I said.

"I got a station to run," he gasped.

"Give the money to my friend there," I said. "He'll work the pumps while we talk. I doubt the Gulf Oil Corporation will notice any decline in performance."

Eddie handed the money to Stu. I kept my hold on Eddie's arm as I walked him behind a wall of oil drums piled near the rest rooms.

"Enough, okay?" he said. "Shit."

I let go. He leaned against a drum, rubbing his sore wrist with his good hand. The goatee was gone, the skin of his chin raw and red from a recent shave.

"You know what happened to her, right?" I said.

He grunted.

"The cops talk to you?"

"No."

"You want to keep it that way, right? You talk to me, it goes nowhere."

"How do I know?"

"You don't," I said. "But right now, you have nothing to bargain with."

Eddie considered his position. At least, I think he did. He had the dullest blue eyes I'd ever seen, and they gave no hint of any brain activity backstage.

"I met her about a month ago at the Alibi Lounge, right around the corner there," he said. "I just got off work. She was sitting at the bar, and I squeezed in next to her to order. She didn't look like the Alibi type. Too clean. And I was sweated up from the job. But she started talking. She went by the name Carla Cole. We had a few drinks, and, next thing

I know, she's inviting me back to this rooming house in the student ghetto across the street from the University."

Eddie leaned around the drum, saw Stu pumping a Mercedes, and settled back.

"We stayed thick like that for five or six days," he said. "We'd meet at the Alibi, drink, go back to her place, and make out. I never nailed her. She always had some excuse. But I knew it was gonna happen soon. Man, I was stoked. Here I got thrown out of Bucholz High in tenth grade, and I got this really nice looking college chick hot for me. I thought maybe I should even take some courses somewhere and get smart so we could talk about more things.

"One night we meet, and she's acting strange, like something's bothering her. We leave the Alibi right away, but instead of going back to her place, we drive down 75 to Ocala and park on this small bluff overlooking a stud ranch. It's dark now, and the ranch house is lit up like a Christmas tree. All kinds of fancy cars are pulling up and fancy people getting out.

"Carla starts sobbing about how that's her daddy's ranch, and how he doesn't give her nothing because she accused him of molesting her. She goes to the University on scholarship. But the tuition is due and something's holding up the scholarship money, and, if she can't lay her hands on some cash real soon, she'll be thrown out.

"Hell, I don't have that kind of money. But I know this guy who comes in the station, name of Waldo Wilson or Wilson Waldo or something. He runs a company that cleans office buildings after hours, and he has another business on the side. I put the two of them in touch, and two days later she has a credit card.

"The next night, she doesn't show up at the Alibi. I drive to her house, and her roommates tell me she's moved out. I think they mean thrown out of college. But they say no. She never was in college.

"I didn't know whether to feel depressed or stupid." Eddie picked a scab of dried oil from the drum and flung it away in disgust. "I mean, did she just want the credit card?"

"Maybe she liked you," I said.

"Maybe." He laughed ruefully. "I went to the Alibi, but she never showed. A few days later, one of the roommates came in here and told me she saw Carla living in Camelot. I drove over there after work and, sure enough, found her. She had some bullshit all ready for me about how she hated to leave me like that, but there were things about her I couldn't understand. I said, 'Yeah, like you're so smart and I'm so stupid.' She just smiled this real superior smile like I just explained everything. Really ticked me. So I started yelling, and then this guy comes out of one of the back rooms. He looked mean. Real mean. Like he had this thick streaky hair, and dark eyebrows shaped like horns, you know? He had a hand in his pocket, like he held a gun. I couldn't see what she'd be doing with a guy like that. So I just said, 'Fuck you both,' and left. That's the last I saw of her."

Daylight was near gone by the time Stu walked off into Camelot with my second hundred bucks. I was too tired for a drive to Ocala, so I floated the idea of spending the night in Gainesville. For once, Meg didn't challenge me to a joust.

We convoyed to a mess of motels and shopping malls situated for easy-off, easy-on access from I-75 on the western edge of Gainesville. Settling on a high-rise Days Inn, I ordered two adjoining rooms. Meg immediately countermanded me.

"One room with two double beds," she said, and then whispered to me, "You're already two hundred dollars over budget."

Meg Black, my very own accountant.

I paid cash to prevent my real accountant, the Honorable Big Jim, from questioning why I returned to Gainesville when I should have been convalescing at Sawgrass. Up in the room, Meg announced she wasn't logistically prepared for a night away from the current roost.

"I thought I was already over budget," I said, assembling another fifty bucks from my wallet for sundries.

Overcome once again by post-concussion fatigue, I stretched out on the bed and stared at the dark panelled walls. Drapes hung thick and heavy on the windows. Unmatched screws protected paint-by-number coastal scenes from thievery. The stalk of a table lamp sprouted from the dorsal fin of a dolphin. Tacky tacky tacky. Yet comforting at the same time. I generated a small psychic space, which I ascribed less to psychological lacerations than to the simple fact of growing up in a cramped, working-class neighborhood. I preferred tight, tree-lined fairways to wide desert expanses. I preferred my garage apartment to four bedroom town houses. This room, despite the decor, felt cozier than the Marriott.

Meg returned with take-out Chinese food. The picture window faced west, and we ate at a small table with the curtains pulled back, the lights dimmed, and the last streaks of sunset firing up the sky.

"It's easy on your eyes," Meg said of the candle power.

After dinner, I descended the balcony stairway and set a

course to circumnavigate the motel grounds. I'd dismissed Ellis' marbles and tubes as another useless analogy. But a few of the marbles had rolled out in Camelot that afternoon. Maybe a walk would dislodge a few more. Instead, my thoughts trailed back to my unlikely kinship with Eddie Fort. You go through life with a mental conception of yourself. A face in the mirror, a shadow on the grass, a mix of experiences, ethics, scruples, and morality. Then wham, you get hit on the head. The mirror distorts, the shadow fades with the sun, the mix curdles. You find you were involved with the same woman as some skinny-assed high school dropout pump jockey. You the lawyer, the professional golfer, the man who prides himself on being principled. And the kicker is, the kid knows exactly why he fell in with her; you don't have a clue.

I bought a soda from a vending machine and trudged up to the balcony. The curtains were drawn against the picture window. I dragged a chair to the railing and sat with my feet propped high. Glare from the security lights washed out the stars. Mist boiled off the surface of the swimming pool. Traffic hissed on I-75.

For as long as I remembered, sitting alone and staring into the night gave me a sense of expectancy. At home, at the top of the stairs leading to my garage apartment, I knew what to expect. A client, my girlfriend, the Judge, a neighborhood acquaintance, any number of people might materialize out of the dark of the driveway and shake the stairs with their first footfall. Here in Gainesville, tomorrow in Ocala, I didn't know what to expect.

I went inside. The only light came from a music video on the TV. Meg lay asleep in her bed, with a row of airline issue Irish Mist bottles empty on the nightstand beside her. The covers reached only to her waist, exposing a frilly nightgown embossed with the smiling green gator mascot of the University of Florida.

What did she have in mind, I wondered, and clicked off the TV.

I didn't ask and Meg didn't tell, her idea of morning conversation being only slightly more civilized than a donnybrook. I dawdled over a diner breakfast, while she attended Sunday Mass at a church with rocketship architecture. We drove to Ocala in one car. Five minutes off the I-75 exit, we were in thoroughbred country. Big fields, white fences, training ovals with clay as red as Mars, driveways lined with live oaks running straight at columned mansions. Eddie Fort's directions took us to one such driveway leading up to one such mansion. The sign leaning against a varnished prairie schooner read "Downer Dirty Ranch—Nix Downer."

We parked in a huge circle of gravel in front of the house. In the distance, I saw the bluff where Eddie Fort parked that night. No way could he have seen fancy people getting out of fancy cars from so far away. But I knew all about visions seen through the prism of hopeless romance. I remembered lots of things that never happened from my days as a foolish young buck. Now I just wanted to remember Thursday.

A black man in livery answered the door. I told him I wanted to speak to Mr. Downer about his daughter Carla. He closed the door without saying a word.

"What does that mean?" said Meg, whose understanding of the Deep South ended with *Gone With the Wind*.

"We wait," I said.

The door opened presently, and the man led us around

the veranda to a rear porch thick with potted plants and white wicker. Two more liveried servants leaned over a table. They stepped away to reveal a huge man dressed in faded denim.

"I have no daughter Carla," he said. "I have no daughter at all."

His voice was gruff with years of tobacco and bourbon. But beneath the gruffness, I sensed the suspicion that anyone who arrived at his doorstep unbidden carried some secret plan to lop off a part of his spread. I took a step toward him. He lay his arms on the table. They were big arms, as ruddy and sunbaked as his face. He palmed something metallic in his right hand. I took a second step and a third, betting he wasn't the derringer type.

"Late twenties," I said. "Five-eight to five-ten, dark hair, face like an Egyptian queen. Called herself Cindy Moran, Carla Cole, who knows what else."

"Called?" said Downer.

"Whoever she is, she's dead."

His eyes never left me, his mouth never moved. But at the word *dead*, his entire body twitched as if someone beneath the table jabbed him with a needle.

"Sit down, Mr.—"

I introduced myself and Meg and, since it mattered to a man like Downer, identified us as golf pro and caddie. Downer never heard of either of us, evidence that he spent his time constructively.

Behind the porch, a man in jockey silks mounted a chestnut two-year-old. A gun fired. Meg jumped, and, at the same instant, Downer clicked a stopwatch with the thumb of his right hand. He alternately stared at Meg and me while the horse raced around the oval. At almost the precise moment, he turned to clock the finish.

"Not bad," he muttered. He pocketed the stopwatch and turned his full attention on me. "How did she die?"

I gave him the *Gainesville Sun* account of the murder. He had thick features, with deep creases across his forehead and around his mouth. His sunburn accentuated the white hair of his sideburns and temples. I judged him to be in his early sixties, with a hardness cultivated by not allowing other people to do his work. His servants set his table, but he pitched his own hay.

"What's your connection?" he said.

"I was attacked by whoever murdered her," I said. "But I don't remember anything about it. Don't even remember knowing her."

I told him about Eddie Fort. When I reached the part about child molestation, Downer reacted for the first time. He laughed.

"I met her at the Preakness four years ago," he said. "She sat in the adjoining box with a breeder from Tennessee. Her name was Diane Danora, and she was the most beautiful woman I'd ever seen. I invited her down for a weekend. By Saturday night, we were engaged. My lawyer insisted we sign a prenuptial agreement. Diane bridled at that, but I promised her I'd tear it up after one year.

"A month passed, two. I was happy. But then I started seeing things I didn't like about her. She was a wonderful person, always bouncy and perky, loved the horses. But if you crossed her, watch out for her temper. My lawyer noticed, too. We talked, and I finally gave in and hired a private detective to look into her background.

"The detective was new, but very thorough. Racked up a lot of hours and a lot of air miles tracking down her past. Really got into her head, is how he put it. But it was worth every dollar I paid him, and I paid him a lot.

"She'd done time in Ohio for insurance fraud, then she bilked some elderly people around Pittsburgh out of their pension money. She got probation for that, but only because Pennsylvania never found out about Ohio. And that wasn't the half of it. She'd pulled some scams, big ones, that she never got caught for. Stuff with computers and credit cards I didn't understand even when it was laid out in front of me. But I understood one thing: she was no goddam good.

"We had it out. She didn't admit to any of this, but she didn't deny it, either. She packed the same suitcase with the same clothes she brought for that first weekend and walked out. Only time she returned was to sign the divorce papers. The prenup gave her a quarter of a million bucks. My lawyer told me to offer a hundred grand and she wouldn't kick. He was right."

"When was that?" I said.

"Two, three years ago. I never saw her again, but I always had the sense she was never that far away."

The crew at the oval shouted about whether Downer wanted another time trial. He walked to the porch rail and yelled a horse's name. Meg and I joined him.

"If I had to guess," he said, "she was planning something big."

"How do you know?" I said.

"That detective found a pattern in those big scams she pulled off," said Downer. "Just before one, she'd go through a bunch of false identities in quick succession."

"Building up shells to throw off pursuers," I said.

"More like a mutating virus, if you ask me," he said.

"Who was the detective?" I said.

"Don't matter," he said. "I called him a few months ago when I suspected someone monkeying around with my horses. He'd closed up, finished, gone. Lost his license, I heard."

A gun sounded. Another horse and another jockey exploded out of the starting gate. Downer checked his stopwatch.

"I doubt someone killed her at random," he said, his eyes following the red dust erupting from the track. "She had a tongue like a serpent, and she could create a powerful anger in a man. I know."

I heard a pop, followed by a tinkle, as tiny glass shards dropped to the wood floor. Downer had crushed the crystal of his stopwatch.

CHAPTER
NINE

Since the Players' buffet lines wouldn't open until tomorrow, I felt a moral obligation to offer Meg dinner when we arrived back at Sawgrass. I intended my offer as a cash stipend; she interpreted it as a shared experience. Feeling too tired to argue, I followed her lead. While she buzzed to her motel room to freshen up, I returned to my hotel suite to rinse Gainesville from my pores.

Hot water drummed my shoulders, back, and neck, loosening muscles but no marbles. I stepped out of the shower and wiped the mist from the mirror. I'd lost count of the gray hairs years ago, though I continued to console myself by calling them premature. My skin was crusty from three months in the sun. Tiny veins, like snippets of red lint, squiggled subdermally on my cheeks and nose. A furrow I once thought would smooth out when I quit the practice of law cut even deeper across my brow.

I probed the back of my head, sparking ladyfinger explosions of pain. Meanwhile, Cindy Moran floated all around me, a ghost in the fog that spiralled into the ceiling exhaust fan. Thinking about her only made her less accessible, like a dream that vanished at first light. What the hell did I see in her? What was her interest in me?

A knock returned me to normal space/time coordinates. I cinched my bathrobe and answered the door.

"Kieran, I'm famished," Meg said, breezing in, "and you barely decent."

She wore a pleated skirt, ribbed cotton blouse, and gladiator sandals. Hardly haute couture, but stunning on Meg.

I ducked back into private quarters and paused several times in my dressing to spy through the door crack. Was this the same Meg who carried my bag six days a week? The concussion must have rearranged my perceptions.

For dinner, we drove to Sawgrass Village at the intersection of TPC Boulevard and A1A. The name Sawgrass Village connotes a peaceful coexistence between the quaint and the modern, overlaid with a veneer of professional athleticism. The Tour's analog to an Olympic Village. In fact, it's a J-shaped promenade of stores and restaurants abutting a retention lake decorated with fountain and gazebo.

Meg chose a steak joint with the predictable golf cachet. A good number of pros would hang out here during the tournament week, and I quickly spotted several early arrivals in the crowd. The hostess sat us in line with a six-foot TV screening fuzzy images of Bay Hill's final round. Meg slid her chair close to mine.

"For the view," she explained, and fell instantly enthralled by the dogfight between Ned Nelson and Sam Young.

We ordered drinks and appetizers. Meg peered at the

screen; I spaced out. Halfway through the nachos, Tommy Garth Hunter sailed in.

"Hiya, Kieran. Hiya, Meg."

I was surprised to see Hunter so early on Sunday. Even though Bay Hill was an easy three-hour drive, most of the finishers wouldn't arrive until Monday. Hunter must have read my mind.

"Dropped like a rock the last two rounds," he said, "so I decided, why not head up here, eh?"

He whipped an empty chair from an adjoining table and settled down. This was pure Hunter, inviting himself to dinner on the assumption Meg and I would just enjoy the hell out of the Polar Bear seated in our midst.

"How's your head?" he said.

"Fine," I answered, and he knew from my tone the subject was closed.

Wide gulfs separated me from the other players on the Tour. With the twenty-something rookies, it was the gulf of age. With the vets, it was life experience. Hunter was the lone exception. Even though our friendship fell off its special plane when he admitted his role in the gambling ring, we kept a bridge open. Actually, it was Hunter who verbalized the basis for our friendship.

"Do you know the biggest difference between Canada and the United States?" he'd asked me early in that mini-tour season. "The American West was settled by a series of land grabs. The Canadian West was settled by the Royal Canadian Mounted Police. It gives us a sense of order that you Americans don't have. But you're the one exception I've met since I've been here. You're a systematic kind of guy."

This may have been an astute observation, but it sounded

funny coming from someone as personally disorganized as Tommy Garth Hunter. His rickety Volvo was forever packed from floorboards to ceiling with junk, and he blundered from tournament to tournament only with divine intervention.

"Out of this chaos comes a simplicity of purpose," he once told me. Then he smiled his disarming smile. "That should be the motto on the Hunter coat of arms."

I sat quietly while Meg and Hunter concentrated on the telecast, and Hunter analyzed every nuance Ned Nelson and Sam Young faced over the last few holes.

"Can't be too far left on that fairway," said Hunter. "Left looks like the best landing area from the tee, but right's the spot. That's the genius of the architect."

I couldn't remember where I'd landed on that hole, but gathered from Meg's accusing glare it must have been well left. I forced a sheepish grin. In fact, I felt a twinge of jealousy. Was I jealous about how Hunter had siphoned off Meg's attention? Or was I jealous about how smoothly Hunter operated, twisting a banal discussion about course management into a lively barroom rap? Hunter always had been the edgy type. On the mini-tour, he'd been notorious for working his jaws during a round. If his partner squelched the nervous chatter, he'd resort to chewing Lifesavers, cough drops, scoring pencils, chopsticks, even twigs plucked from trees. But the Hunter I reacquainted myself with when I reached the Tour was a man completely at ease with his surroundings. A $30 million endorsement contract works wonders with the human nervous system.

As they rattled on, I withdrew into a laundry list of doubts and discomforts. I loved golf and the exotic Tour locales. But did I love them more than I hated the hotel rooms, the restaurant meals, the chow lines, the fast exits and forced marches to the next tournament? And then there was the sense of disconnection. In Milton, I felt rooted to the community. I had my apartment, my pro shop at Milton Country Club, my pupils, my customers, my local pub, Georgina. The Tour was a virtual community, like something on the Internet. A thousand or so people who came together for five or six days, evaporated on Sunday, and coalesced someplace eerily similar on the following Tuesday. Maybe the Judge had been right. Only an idiot makes a job out of something he loves.

"Now this putt breaks more than Ned expects," said Hunter. I recognized the seventeenth green, felt Meg's eyes sweep me as the camera closed in on Ned Nelson's feet and his putter poised behind his golf ball.

I wondered whether Gainesville had been a sign that I was out of my element. Maybe my love of golf was too pure to be debased by life on the Tour. Maybe I shouldn't wait to be suspended. Maybe I should voluntarily withdraw. This brainstorm held a certain appeal, judging by the sense of relief that coursed through me as the unthinkable slowly became the possible. The Judge could broker a deal where I quietly slip off the Tour and return just as quietly at season's end to defend my title at the B.C. Open. No messy press releases, no embarrassing petitions for reinstatement. The Tour gets me out of its collective hair for the heart of the tournament schedule. I get a chance to reassess my career without closing a door behind me. Everyone wins. The Judge could pull this off as easily as settling a pedestrian knockdown lawsuit.

Ned Nelson sank a twenty-footer to snatch the Bay Hill

title from Sam Young. The restaurant crowd cheered, and
Meg excused herself for the loo.

"Nice bum," said Hunter. He hooked another empty chair
and propped up his feet. A couple of buddies settling in for
some male bonding. At least his sneakers weren't trimmed
with the bear claw motif.

"She's my caddie, Tom, that's where it begins and ends."

"Looks like she's on the prowl tonight, just the same." He
raised his eyebrows. "Would you mind?"

"Yes, I would. Thank you."

He nodded, always an ambiguous gesture with Hunter. A
few other pros stopped by the table. They greeted me curtly,
then jawed with Hunter about good buddy Ned's victory. I
didn't care. By this time tomorrow, they wouldn't have Kieran
Lenahan to kick around anymore.

"I didn't rush up here to get a head start on the Players,"
Hunter said when the pros drifted off. "I came up here
because of you."

"I said I'm fine, Tom."

"Gainesville is a rough town," he said. "I know. I apprenticed at Gainesville Country Club, remember?"

"I don't want to talk about what happened. Even if I
wanted to, I shouldn't. You understand. And Gainesville *is* a
rough town. Nobody knows that better than me." Uncon-
sciously, I lifted my hand to my head.

"Did Uncle Dan'l contact you?" he said.

"Friday night."

"Can he help you?"

"I asked him not to," I said.

"He's done well by me," said Hunter.

"That's true. But Uncle Dan'l and I differ on some subjects, like professional ethics." My words even sounded sour to me, so I forced a smile and backtracked. "The Judge flies down tomorrow. He'll handle my situation with the Tour."

Hunter grinned, possibly at the idea of me relying on the Judge when I could have Uncle Dan'l buzzing in the ears of Henry Chandler, Peter Haswell, and Sally Lang.

"And thanks for the concern, Tom. I took a bad shot, but if I don't play this week, it won't be because of this." I tapped my temple.

Meg appeared, shouldering and ducking her way through the crowd.

"I hope you know what you're doing," Hunter whispered before breaking out into smiles at Meg's return.

He took his leave, wishing Meg the best and me poignant good luck. As he ambled away, I thought of a swaying footbridge crashing into a deep canyon.

Sometimes matters slip out of your control. Not in the sense of careening downhill in a car without brakes, but with the gentle giddiness of an amusement park ride. We drove back to the Marriott for Meg to collect her car, and for me to turn in early. But without so much as a word, we strolled past the swimming pools and down to the edge of the lagoon. A coolish breeze rustled palm fronds as the hush of a Sunday evening descended. The hotel's pontoon boat bobbed gently in its mooring.

"Aren't you the pensive one," said Meg.

"It's nothing. I'm just tired," I said, coming within a millisecond of confessing my plan to leave the Tour before Meg locked her arm around mine.

"Poor dear," she said.

We walked along the lagoon, swaying with every step, talking about everything and nothing in particular. My senses, so long packed in bubble plastic, slowly sharpened. A shore bird cried in the distance. Oceans and craters freckled the moon. A whiff of fertilizer wafted across the water from the Players Club.

Quiet again, we headed toward the hotel entrance. Our hands brushed, then held fast as we crossed the atrium. Meg leaned casually against the doorjamb as I fumbled with the room card. Inside, she sat me down on the couch, swept two locks of hair behind my ears, and, after precise hesitation, planted her lips on mine.

I broke off, after my own precise hesitation.

"What about Georgina?" I said.

"She still has nothing to worry about," said Meg, staccato as she strafed my neck.

"Why?" I said, bending her backwards.

"Because she's in Europe," she said after her breath returned.

That settled the faithfulness issue. Meg plucked the blouse from the waistband of her skirt. I eased it over her head. She unhooked her bra, and the theoretical became flesh.

Two hours later, Meg slipped out of bed and stood at the window. I couldn't believe the sight of her, clad only in the moonlight while one hand clutched the drape and the other twisted the hair falling on the nape of her neck. She reminded me of statues the ancient Romans copied in marble from even more ancient Greek bronze originals. Since marble is heavier than bronze, the Romans fashioned struts to keep various body parts from breaking off. Meg didn't have struts; she just defied gravity.

I rolled onto my side, rustling the sheets. She turned and wrapped the drape around her in mock prudery.

"Where did this come from?" I said. I didn't normally stop to debrief these developing situations, rational thought being an all-time mood-breaker. But Meg's turnabout had been sudden and extreme.

"You couldn't tell?" she said.

Tell from what? Hateful stares?

"I've felt an attraction from the start," she said. "But you didn't touch me until I saw you alone in that apartment yesterday. So alone. So bereft."

She untwined herself from the drape and came back to the edge of the bed.

"For three months you carried yourself as if you were invincible. Yesterday, I saw you aren't."

"Invincible? Didn't I finish last at Doral and miss the cut at Honda?" The west coast swing had been equally successful, but no need to remind Meg.

"I don't mean in golf. I mean in life. There's a difference." She raised a leg to straddle me. "Does Georgina do this for you?"

"Oooo," I said. "I don't remember."

Later still, I took my turn at the window while Meg slept. The moon had set. A drunk staggered around one of the pools, somehow not falling in. He stopped, fumbled with a piece of paper, and held it up to a spotlight angling down from a palm tree. A good night of sex usually fills me with bravado, if not genuine confidence. But I'd started in such a post-concussion funk that the double play with Meg barely brought me to normal levels of pessimism. I didn't shelve the idea of ducking out before the Commissioner suspended me. But I did resolve not to worry about things I couldn't control, and not to muff the things that I could. After the evening's sour start, this was a downright heady attitude.

I awoke with a good head, which I attributed less to Ellis' pills than to a psychic sense of the virtual community coming together at the Players Club. Forget about yesterday's doubt and depression; I loved the Tour. Not the corporate entity represented by Chandler and his cronies, but the Tour that existed in my head: golf balls whooshing off the practice tee and rippling across the thin grass of the putting greens; huge television vans disgorging miles of cable; equipment companies erecting hospitality tents as palatial as Versailles; the blimp hovering silently overhead. Nobody was going to run me out of here, at least not without a fight.

I roused Meg from bed. All business on a Monday morn, I resisted her invitation to shower together. I wanted to hit the sunshine sometime before noon. While she mixed the water, I fiddled with the extra club I kept in the hotel room for emergency practice sessions. I took several swings, freezing myself at various points along the arc to inspect the positions of my knees, shoulders, arms, and wrists.

The phone interrupted my search for perfection.

"Where the hell have you been?" said Judge Inglisi.

"When?"

"Since you called me last Friday."

"Gainesville."

"Didn't I tell you to get over to Sawgrass?"

"I did."

"I know you did," said the Judge. "You checked into the goddam Marriott. Don't you pick up your messages?"

"Messages?"

"At the goddam reception desk. I'm on a first-name basis with three shifts of bell captains for the twenty calls I made since Saturday morning."

"Sorry," I said. "I wanted to force myself to remember what happened."

"And did you?"

"I've pieced some of it together. It's complicated."

"Kieran, someone clocks you with a blackjack and you either remember or you don't. What's so complicated?"

The shower cut off, leaving Meg singing in high fidelity. I cupped my hand around the phone.

"I'd rather not talk about this now," I said.

"What did you say?" said the Judge.

"I'd rather not talk about this now."

"Well, we'd better talk soon, because I have a four o'clock meeting this afternoon with somebody named Henry Chandler and a few other yo-yos. I think your buddy Hannigan is one of them."

"Harrington," I said. "Woody."

"Yeah, him," the Judge said dismissively. "And this complicated story of yours better be good because I'm going into this thing to save your ass, not to get my jock-strap handed to me. Especially after the worst goddam flying experience of my life."

The Judge held a private pilot's license and had a penchant for aerial high jinks. I'd sooner take a turn in an industrial-sized washing machine than strap myself into the right-hand seat of the Cessna he owned with nine other suicidal maniacs. Commercial airline flights bored the Judge. Too smooth, too much altitude, too many people violating his personal airspace. I wondered what happened.

"Randall Fisk is what happened," he said.

"You flew down here with Fisk?" I said. Randall Fisk covered golf for a countywide newspaper chain back home. He'd probably wangled an all-expenses-paid trip down here with a promise to report on my exploits, which I hoped he'd restrict to golf matters. Never could tell with Fisk, who suffered equally from delusions of muckraking and overly extended metaphors.

"I had no choice," said the Judge. "He booked his flight with his home computer, right down to the seat assignment."

"Randall tends to wax eloquent," I said, assuming the Judge had his ears melted.

"I wouldn't have minded if just words came out of his mouth," said the Judge. "But he blew lunch twice. Not once, twice. And in between, he scarfed down something the airline passed off as ravioli. Then we shared a cab, and, don't you know, he's booked the same hotel as me. There should be a law on this goddam personal computer stuff."

"At least he shouldn't puke on solid ground," I said.

"I didn't wait around to find out," said the Judge. "I cancelled that reservation and booked into a different place."

"Where?"

"Look out your window."

I parted the shades. A man, whose brown pants and pink shirt assumed the approximate shape of a giant strawberry ice cream cone stood beside one of the swimming pools. One hand pressed a cellular phone to his ear. The other lifted a pair of binoculars to his eyes. A blinding flash of sunlight burned off the lenses. Meg chose that precise moment to skip across the room behind me, minus even a towel.

"Who's that?" said the Judge.

"Who's who?"

"That pair of jugs," he said. "Kieran, is that who I think—?"

"Kieran," said Meg, "do you have anything I can throw on? Oh, sorry. I didn't realize you were engaged."

"It is," said the Judge. "Georgina's gone to Europe two months now and you're balling Molly."

"Meg," I said.

"Meg, Molly, what's the difference? How long has this been going on?"

"Hours," I said. "I've had a rough few days."

"Not as rough as the next few months might be," said the Judge. "I'll meet you on the practice range in an hour. That's if you can come out to play today."

He rang off as Meg returned, wearing one of my shirts like a mini-skirt and toweling her curly locks.

"Who was that?" she said.

"No one."

Meg walked past me and leaned over the balcony rail, stretching her leg muscles taut.

"Doesn't that man down there look like the Judge?"

"Sort of," I said.

I headed for the Players Club while Meg returned to her motel to change into less conspicuous caddie togs. Much of what I imagined in the hotel in fact occurred in the material world. The blimp hovered quietly overhead, pitching slightly as thermals wafted upward from the landscape. Network road-ies scurried hither and yon, wiring the course for the weekend telecast.

The practice range, so relaxed on Friday afternoon, crackled with activity now that the Tour had come to town. The golfers carved out tiny plots to work on their games. Pearly white golf balls sparkled in the sun. Moist brown divots scored the flat green turf. Yellow nylon ropes held back the galleries that thickened here and there, treated to the sight of the golfers rooted to one spot with their shotmaking skills on repeated display.

Inside the ropes, characters as identifiable as caricatures darted from tee box to tee box, sometimes interrupting, other times waiting for the fleeting breaks in a golfer's practice routine. Media types trolled for quotes and interviews. Agents and managers pitched business opportunities. Golf gurus fid-dled with their clients' swing mechanics, while sports psychol-ogists pumped up confidence levels. Then came the carnival barkers of the Tour, the equipment reps and tournament reps.

Equipment reps worked for sporting goods companies. They carted wagons laden with the latest club designs, know-ing that an advertisement featuring the right club in the right golfer's hands translated into millions of dollars in sales. Tournament reps worked for the promotional committees of other Tour events. They tried to populate their tournaments with the best possible field with selling points often unrelated to golf. They might offer first-class childcare, super accommo-dations, fun activities for the wife and kids, courtesy cars, anything to extract a promise from a pro to play in that particu-lar tournament on that particular week.

For years, golfers complained that their "business office" had devolved into a commercial bazaar, where the marginal players practiced in solitude while the successful players fended off myriad pests. The Tour diplomatically ducked the issue, until a temperamental equipment rep named Leo Tomalini slugged a journeyman pro who refused to test a super-hi-tech pitching wedge. The incident precipitated a series of experiments, from corralling the reps, gurus, and sportswriters in a bullpen, to allowing only five extraneous people on the tee in thirty-minute shifts.

The controversy filled the golfing press for several months, with hundreds and thousands of column inches devoted to the respective positions of the golfers, gurus, reps, and the media. Even I, from my Milton outpost, fired off a letter to the editor of a major golf monthly, opining that "the hallmark of civilization is the luxury to argue about stupid things." The letter never was published.

Predictably, the golfers lost out. The Tour restored open access to the practice range, with the decree that "everyone involved use common sense and good judgment in balancing all competing interests."

On this bright morning, no smoke lingered over the old battlefield. Club shafts sparkled in the sunlight. Balls climbed skyward, dissolved into the deep blue, and reappeared on earth. Spectators lined the gallery ropes, one thick knot gathered behind Tommy Garth Hunter and another behind Ned Nelson, who held court with a gaggle of golf scribes. I retreated into the shade of a corporate hospitality tent to wait for Meg, and found myself elbow to elbow with Kenny Palumbo.

No one quite understood Kenny's role on Tour, which he

followed from tournament to tournament the way bummers dogged Sherman's army during its march to the sea. But everyone accepted his presence, as if he performed some sort of public service or represented the Tour's penance for sins yet to be revealed. He ran errands, haunted buffet lines, gossiped with reporters, and generally prostrated himself at the disposal of the pros and Tour personnel. All the while, he slipped M&M candies out of his pants pockets and replaced them with golf balls nicked from baskets on the practice tee. He'd sell these balls and other scraps of pilfered equipment to spectators from the trunk of his old Buick Riviera.

Kenny kept his hair shaved almost to bald and wore an oversized Tam O' Shanter that, combined with his puffy jowls and bloodless lips, gave the impression of the dwarf Dopey, aged into midlife by computer enhancement.

I'd spoken with Kenny at just about every tournament this year. He struck me as a soul mate to characters back home whose quirks earned them reputations as eccentrics. These people bounced through life in a protective bubble, indulging in behavior that would land someone like me in the slammer. Kenny could babble endlessly in a corporate hospitality tent without anyone raising an eyebrow.

I picked him up in his usual conversational midstream, my presence allowing busboys to scatter and the bartender to escape to the far end of the counter.

"I have this thing on my hand," he said. He peeled a Band-Aid from the back of his hand, exposing a penny-sized welt as red and as moist as a crushed cherry. "People keep telling me I should see a doctor, but I'm never in one place long enough."

I muttered something inconsequential. He droned on about his hand and the sun and how the welt was nothing to worry about, just something he picked at when he was bored, not some kind of melanoma as people imagined. The topic petered out. Kenny leaned over the bar to scoop ice into a paper cup.

"Are you sorry you didn't listen to me now?" he said.

"Listen to you about what?"

"Come on, Kieran. It was all over Bay Hill by Friday night. That dead lady."

"You knew her?"

"Knew her? I hooked you up with her."

My neck snapped so fast my headache returned for one dizzying moment. I hustled Kenny out of the tent and down a cart path that curved behind a rank of portable toilets.

"You hooked her up with me?" I said.

"Hey, Kieran, don't get all hopped up." Kenny wrenched his arm out of my grasp and tucked his shirt back into his waistband. " 'Course I hooked you up with her. We talked about this at Honda. Don't you remember?"

"No."

"Geez, you're flakier than I thought."

"I had an accident, Kenny."

"Yeah, right. You got bopped on the head, and everything you want to forget fades away."

"Run it by me again," I said. "We met at Doral, right?"

"Kieran, I told you all this at Honda."

"I told you I don't remember, goddammit."

"Geez, Kieran, calm down," said Kenny. "It was the Tuesday practice round. I was leaning into the trunk of my car when this beautiful lady came up behind me. She knew my name and said she heard I was the man to know about meeting people on the Tour. Well, I didn't fess up right away. I got into some trouble with that in Georgia last year. So I made some noise for awhile, until I satisfied myself she wasn't undercover. I asked what was she interested in. 'New blood,' she said. So I started naming the new guys who just came on in January. Some guys I helped out before, and some guys I didn't. When I reached your name, she stopped me like she wanted to hear more.

"I told her you quit law to become a golf pro and would have made the Tour a few years ago, except for some trouble I didn't understand. So you went home and worked as a club pro, got yourself invited to the B.C. Open, and won the thing, and here you are. I told her to be careful with you because you had that girl caddie who looked after you pretty close. Then she asked me if you had an agent or a business manager, and I told her I heard your business manager was a judge up in New York. I didn't know his name, but she could find out from the Tour."

"Why did she want to know that?"

"She didn't say, but it made me think, maybe she wasn't after what I thought she was after. Anyway, I went to the marshal's tent and found out who you'd paired up with for the day's practice round. She took it from there."

"Did you see her talking to anyone else?" I said.

"I spotted her a few times at Doral and then at Honda. The only guy I ever saw her talking to was you. Hey, Kieran, I don't take money for this, if that's what you're saying. Most other things, yes, but not this."

"But we talked about her at Honda?" I said.

"Boy, you must really not remember anything," said

Kenny. "You and I struck up a conversation, just like up in the tent. I asked how things were, and you started right in about this lady and how she wanted your help with a business deal."

"What kind of deal?"

"You didn't say," said Kenny. "I'm not sure if you knew. All I know is what I told you, which is when ladies and business mix, there's nothing but trouble."

That memory rolled back. *You want no part of it.* A derisive laugh followed, but I wasn't sure if that was part of the memory or something I engrafted now.

"I took your advice, right?" I said.

"Does anyone?" said Kenny.

A yell interrupted us, and we jumped sideways as an electric cart flew past. It skidded to a stop, then reversed up the path. The driver was Woody Harrington.

"Kieran, I've been searching all over for you." Woody stopped the cart between Kenny and me. "Oh, morning, Kenny."

Kenny mumbled something, nodded at me, and walked away. Woody lifted his straw hat and wiped his brow with his forearm.

"What did Palumbo want with you?" said Woody.

"He offered to buy some of my used golf balls cheap. Too cheap." I watched Kenny disappear into the crowd near the practice tee. "What does he do here anyway?"

"Nothing much," said Woody. "If he weren't so popular with the players, I'd run him the hell out of here. May have to anyway. We've had complaints about him selling bogus souvenirs."

"Aw, Woody, he seems like a nice enough guy."

"Kenny Palumbo's only nice if he has his hand in your pocket," said Woody. "Anyway, where the hell have you been? I called your room all weekend."

"Away," I said.

"With all that's going on, you just disappear?" said Woody.

"I went to Gainesville to try to get my memory back."

"Did it help?"

"Not much."

"Damn," he said. "We have a meeting with your business manager this afternoon."

"I know. He told me."

"There's been a lot of talk among us about your story." Woody's head bobbed to keep me in focus. "I don't need to tell you no one believes it. The hospital didn't help matters."

He handed me a form with the fuzzy print of a cheap fax machine.

"What's this?" I said.

"A release for your medical records. No one at Shands Hospital will even talk to us without it."

"Goddam that Ellis," I said.

Woody twisted open a fancy ballpoint pen, and I scratched the signature line.

"I hope this proves you have amnesia," said Woody.

"It will," I said.

"I have to warn you, Kieran, there's a drumbeat building for your suspension."

"For this? The worst case is I was found in a compromising position with a dead woman, which I wasn't. That's a suspendable offense?" I almost launched into describing Kenny Palumbo's activities as the Tour's own Pandarus. But I didn't quite trust Kenny's candor, and Woody probably knew about it anyway.

"It's too complicated," he said. "Too much goes on that you players don't know about."

"Like what?"

"Take my word for it," he said. "That's why you should give me some type of story. The Board reacts better when they aren't punching in the dark."

"I can't," I said.

"You know I'm on your side," said Woody. "You know I need you here to help me with this Jason Oliver problem."

"I know."

"Then goddammit, Kieran, can't you give me something I can use?"

"Sorry, Woody, I wish I could."

"You're making it damn hard, Kieran." He kicked off the foot brake, and the cart rolled away.

CHAPTER
TEN

I expected at least a few minutes of practice time before the Judge made his fashionably late appearance. But Meg hadn't yet arrived on the tee, and since she customarily stored my bag in the ladies' locker room, I was clubless as well as clueless. I ducked back into that same hospitality tent, which buzzed with a livelier air now that Kenny Palumbo had taken his eccentric roadshow elsewhere. None of the assembled golf aficionados betrayed any recognition of the certified golf professional sipping ice water in their midst. In fact, a middle-aged thug wearing the registered trademark of the corporate host tried to eject me before noticing the contestant's badge pinned to my belt loop. Made me wonder why the Tour would consider suspending a high-profile player like me.

The Judge finally blipped onto my radar screen. He waddled through the crowd, stopping occasionally to scan the tee and showing no sign of surprise or recognition when he spotted my idleness.

"You don't look so bad," he said, elbowing his way through the crowded tent.

I knew better than to expect sympathy from the Judge. Since I was obviously alive and apparently well, he felt no moral obligation to delve into my medical condition.

He lifted the straw hat from his head and mopped sweat from the reddened tracks the band printed across his thick brow. Gray hairs, worn long to accommodate the northern winter, bristled in sweaty spikes. He took the cup from my hand, pressed it to his temples, then doused himself. Ice cubes bounced off his shoulders and clattered to the wooden floor. A woman, hit by the spray, squealed in surprise. Her escort, a gangly gent, scowled in defense of the lady's honor. A busboy leaped in, toweling furiously. The Judge, noticing none of this, handed the empty cup back to me. Then, with considerable flourish, pulled a stack of letters from his waistband and slapped them against my chest.

"I'm not your mailboy," he announced.

No, the Judge was not my mailboy, though I didn't want to focus any more attention on us by dignifying him with an answer. Writing to a touring pro is a lot like shooting skeet. You might know his general direction, but not how far to lead him. So the PGA Tour accepts mail at its headquarters and forwards it to the players at the different tournament sites. I received about a dozen pieces of forwarded mail each week. Some of it was junk. A few were from fans, mostly middle-aged wannabes intrigued by someone who reached the Tour at a relatively advanced age and after a career in law. Anything important or business-related, I packed into a manila envelope and mailed to the Judge.

The six letters in my hands had been mailed to me, care

of Judge Inglisi at his home address. The handwritten letter is the grandest form of communication. It is to faxes and voice mail what the Orient Express is to a Boeing 747. Slow, but stately. You need to care enough to cradle the pen in your hand, refine your thoughts, drag the pen across the paper. Arduous, but personal, right down to licking the flap. I read the letters as much out of respect as a desire to delay the inevitable conversation about Gainesville.

The first was from Pete O'Meara, for three years my shop assistant at Milton Country Club, reporting how my successor was "frigging up the works." The second, from an elderly tailor and former client named the Dutchman, contained an exquisitely sewn Lenahan coat of arms "suitable for stitching onto a golf sweater." The third was from Una MacEwan, a neighborhood lady whose son I helped to bury on consecrated ground; the enclosed picture of her tiny grandson, "looks just like Jackie, doesn't he?" The fourth was from William St. Clare, Jr., a Milton lawyer who almost sold me out when the Westchester County D.A. charged me with arson/murder after my pro shop burned down. He'd inherited some Inglisi & Lenahan clients and needed advice on how to handle one hardhead in particular. The fifth came from Adrienne Miles, who'd touched a spark in me even as I suspected she'd murdered her husband. She'd relocated south of Cleveland and reminded me her "door was open" if I qualified for the World Series of Golf, played in Akron at summer's end.

I tossed St. Clare's into the trash and folded the other four into my pocket. The last letter bore no return address. It had been mailed certified return-receipt-requested, and I could only imagine the Judge's fit of pique when he drove to the post office to sign for a letter addressed to me.

I tore open the envelope, scratching my finger on the point of a staple.

"Damn," I said. A drop of blood filled the tiny hole and instantly clotted.

"Should I call an ambulance?" said the Judge.

My sour retort stopped halfway up my windpipe as I skimmed four sheets of heavy bond legal paper. I reread carefully, making sure each separately numbered paragraph registered before going on to the next. When I finished, I carefully refolded the sheets into the envelope.

"We need to go to Gainesville," I said.

"Again?" said the Judge. "You haven't even told me why you went there the first two times."

"I'll tell you on the way."

The Judge drove because he always drove, whether it was his Cessna, his Ferrari, or the car I rented for my four-week swing through Florida. A steering wheel was a macho symbol to the Judge, who thrived on the idea of powerful machinery reined in under his control, even though his own mechanical prowess ended with the clothesline pulley. The Judge fumed because he always fumed when he encountered something he could not understand. Judges are accustomed to presiding, to exerting control, to having their opinions carry momentous weight, even when those opinions border on the ridiculous. They aren't geared for the confusion and ambiguity mere mortals encounter everyday. Most of the time he confined his tirades to the idiot lawyers unfortunate enough to find themselves trapped in his courtroom. Without the perspective of a longtime association, these lawyers could not know the Judge's blusterings from the bench were comparatively minor barometric disturbances. They never experienced the force-five storm that brewed whenever he detected my "congenital predilection for sticking my nose into other people's problems." And that was *before* I told him about my weekend exploits.

I began with my visit to Dr. Ellis. The Judge listened calmly enough, probably because he discerned a medical reason for traipsing around northern Florida when I should have been following his direct order to repair my sorry skull in my hotel. He pretended to retch when I related Ellis' alligator parable and made kissy sounds when Meg showed up at the crime scene. But he thundered, "Now we are getting somewhere," when I mentioned my epiphany, quickly followed by, "That's it?" when I explained exactly what my epiphany had been.

He reacted badly to McGriff ("A homicide detective who's a friggin' golf nut?"), but listened intently when the story turned to Larry Stuart's photography hobby. Who can figure the Judge? I thought I was beginning to capture his interest when the Eddie Fort encounter elicited only a weak warning that I could probably be charged with criminal impersonation.

"All right, all right, the lady was a con artist," he said, when I finished with the Nix Downer visit. "What's your point?"

My point waited, while he punched us into overdrive, screamed past a line of cars, and tucked back into our lane as an oncoming semi blared its horn. Then I handed him the affidavit.

The Judge assumes his judicial persona at odd times and in odd places, and not always when he's on the bench. When this occurs outside the courtroom, he confuses the rules of evidence with the rules of life. Try discussing global warming with him. You can trot out computer models, NASA satellite data, reams of scientific evidence, and he'll just say, "They don't prove it to me." *Ergo*, no global warming. Same thing with the afterlife. Line up a group of interfaith theologians and people who have seen a white light during open-heart surgery, and he'll answer, "The mind plays tricks with wishful thinking." On the other hand, the Judge claims he saw a UFO dipping into the Hudson River near West Point one evening as he flew his Cessna back to Westchester County Airport. No further proof needed; flying saucers are real. I predict the Judge will move to Arizona and live out his days in an Airstream trailer, waiting to be beamed aboard.

The Judge read the affidavit with all his judicial scrutiny, somehow managing to keep the car between the white lines.

"Okay," he said, tossing the affidavit to the gusts of a/c blowing around the interior. "Let's assume she sent you the affidavit. Tommy Garth Hunter taking beta blockers is a big deal?"

"Very big."

"Big enough to kill for?"

"Yes."

"Prove it," said the Judge.

I started with beta blockers, which most adult Americans know are a class of drugs prescribed to control high blood pressure. In times of stress, the body automatically initiates an ancient mechanism biologists call the fight-or-flight response. Adrenalin surges, the heart kicks up, nerve endings prickle, the windpipe constricts, digestion ceases, and blood pressure shoots to the sky. On the cellular level, the process starts when epinephrine fits into the body's beta receptors like keys into so many locks. Beta blockers control blood pressure by filling the keyholes first, short-circuiting the fight-or-flight response.

"So what?" said the Judge, who believes the AMA guidelines about fat, cholesterol, and exercise apply to everyone in the world but him, and therefore considers beta blockers about as relevant to his existence as the planet Neptune.

The fight-or-flight response girds the body for battle, not for a golf swing. Golf club grips slip in sweaty palms, tight muscles truncate shoulder turns, concentration dissipates into the sheer effort to breathe. Tranquilizers might help, so might a shot of booze. But each would impair a golfer's judgment. Enter beta blockers. Their glorious side-effect is the suppression of outward signs of nervousness. Your insides may roil, but your palms will remain dry and your golf muscles won't shake. This is a tournament golfer's dream, maintaining an inner edge while eliminating the physiological effects of nervousness most damaging to a golf swing, and giving the appearance of holding onto your head while your competitors are losing theirs.

"So what?" said the Judge. "They aren't illegal, and they aren't recreational."

"But using them could be very expensive for someone like Hunter," I said.

"Why? Would the Tour make him disgorge his winnings?"

"Worse," I said. "He could lose his endorsement contract."

Golf endorsement contracts go back to 1898, when two-time British Open champion Harry Vardon signed with the Spalding Company to play a gutta-percha golf ball. By the 1930s, all major equipment companies started signing pros to advisory staffs, who promoted their sponsor's products by genteel example. In return, the pros received all the equipment they needed, with golf clubs tailored to their specific style of play. In 1939, Ben Hogan and Byron Nelson, two of golf's biggest stars, pocketed $1,500 each.

The world has changed radically since 1939; endorsement contracts even more so. Hi-tech golf equipment companies raise capital by public stock offerings and pump millions into advertising, all to grab a piece of a market with an insatiable appetite running the gamut from $2 golf balls to $500 titanium drivers. The cornerstone of these ad campaigns is still the professional endorsement, the familiar face who smiles and says, "I play with this club, and now you can, too."

Tommy Garth Hunter's endorsement contract with Trident Golf Company was the current gold standard among Tour professionals. He endorsed golf clubs, golf bags, shirts, hats, shoes, and umbrellas. He licensed the use of the Polar Bear's distinctive bear claw logo. In return, he received $3 million per year for ten years.

"Unless Trident cancels the contract," I said, after sketching out the terms of Hunter's deal.

"What's a reason for cancellation?" said the Judge. "If those ugly-assed bear claw shoes don't sell?"

"Behavioral objectives," I said. "A company won't invest in a personality if that personality turns out to be a jerk. Now Uncle Dan'l probably drove a hard bargain negotiating that contract, but I don't think he could have escaped without a behavioral objective clause."

"So if the Tour suspends Hunter for using beta blockers," said the Judge, "the endorsement contract can be cancelled."

"It doesn't need to go that far," I said. "If Trident independently found out about a serious problem like using beta blockers during tournaments, it doesn't need to wait for the Tour to act."

CHAPTER
ELEVEN

We pulled into a gas station just outside the Gainesville city limits and, from a phone book, learned that Dr. Sharon Paulling's office was located near the intersection of Main Street and University Avenue, the heart of Gainesville's grid pattern of thoroughfares. The Judge nosed the car into an angled parking space in a cobblestone square fronting an old columned courthouse. On foot, we passed several storefronts that hadn't succumbed to the cutesy makeovers popular in college towns. This was old Florida, humid, soporific, laden with Spanish moss that barely ruffled in the sluggish breeze. Just as long as I averted my eyes from the new construction rising above a line of distant palms like a child's building blocks gone wild.

We found Dr. Paulling's office tucked away on a quiet side street lined with royal palms. The office itself looked like a beached riverboat, with a double-level veranda wrapping around the side, and lots of wooden festoons and curlicues dripping from eaves and soffits.

The waiting room was empty except for a young woman draped over a chair in the reception bay. She was all arms and legs, with a long purple lock swooping down from an otherwise slicked-back head of black hair. When she swivelled, the lock swung enough to reveal a phone tucked between her shoulder and ear.

"Uh, gotta go," she said, and snapped to attention, which meant she hung up the phone and twirled the lock with her finger. She had a fashionably pale face and a gold ball stuck to the dimple of her nose.

I introduced myself and the Judge, paused in vain for the weight of his judicial office to thump her on the forehead, and asked to see Dr. Paulling.

"Do you have an appointment?"

"No," I said.

"The Doctor's very busy."

"We'll wait," I said.

"For about one whole minute," the Judge snarled.

The Judge and I settled onto chairs. I don't strike immediate fear into people's hearts. But the Judge can, and occasionally does, resemble a Southerner's idea of a Northern mafioso. Especially when he lifts a glossy magazine out of its rack, rolls it into a tight baton, and starts whacking it against the open palm of his hand.

You might think the Judge employed his regal petulance to help me investigate my lead. This ain't necessarily so. He was either hot or tired or hungry, and rapped the magazine as a way of counting out the sixty seconds he graciously allowed me to connect with Dr. Paulling. But whatever its genesis, the act worked. The young woman, without taking her wide eyes off Don Inglisi, creeped her hand along the top of her desk and flicked a button on an intercom. Fifteen beats later, the door to an inner office opened.

"Never can tell who'll show up when the circus is near town," said a tall, handsome woman wearing a white smock.

"Sharon?" I said, and scrambled to my feet.

"What's it been? Seven years?" she said, accepting my handshake.

"Almost exactly," I said.

"Is this a business or a social call?" she said. She lay a hand on my shoulder, her fingers expertly probing the tone of my trapezius muscle.

"Social," I said, resisting the urge to say *pure coincidence*.

I introduced the Judge, who unfurled the magazine before shaking Sharon's hand. Backing away, he stitched his brow in angry befuddlement. *Tell you later*, I mouthed as Sharon leaned over the reception desk to look at her appointment calendar.

"I really need to get out of here. If you give me a moment, we'll have lunch," she said, and stepped back into her office.

"Where the hell do you know her from?" said the Judge.

"The mini-tour," I said. "Her last name was Gray back then."

Sometimes life runs in funny stretches, like a rain squall you never escape even though the sun lights the pavement just over the next hill. I hit a stretch in college where every woman I met was named Barbara. I hit another one, years later, where every woman I dated was separated with two kids. These last few days plugged me back into the mini-tour. Tommy Garth Hunter, Uncle Dan'l, and now Sharon Gray. Coincidence? Omen? Who could tell?

Two rounds into a tournament at Tallahassee, Hunter and I were dead even and ten shots ahead of the field. Sunday dawned perfectly clear and wonderfully warm. A golf day from a dream: just me and a friendly competitor battling for a tournament without any interlopers. I'd have noticed Sharon even without the day's trimmings. Tall and willowy, blond hair, alert green eyes, strong features likely to remain handsome into her dotage.

Hunter introduced us as we walked down the first fairway.

"Sharon's a Gainesville Country Club member," said Hunter, who went by "Gar" in his pre-Polar Bear days. He'd apprenticed at GCC prior to hitting the mini-tour.

"I drove here when I heard Gar was in the lead," said Sharon.

I knew there was a long story to this one.

Gar and I traded shot for shot, birdie for birdie. Several times during the round, I caught Sharon watching me. Not idly, not as a spectator. I found myself watching her, too, with a sense of improbable possibility. But for Gar Hunter, she would be mine, and but for Gar Hunter, I never would have laid eyes on her.

I blinked in sudden death that day, but, looking back, the outcome didn't matter. Sharon was intimately bound up in that day. I couldn't recall Tallahassee without remembering her, and I couldn't think of her without recalling Tallahassee.

I related this to the Judge, minus the sentimental details, before Sharon popped back out of her office. She looked terrific in her simplicity, the squint in her eyes and the hint of gray sweeping over her ears adding character rather than age. We headed on foot to a place called Lillian's, which she described as a quaint slice of old Gainesville. The Judge trailed a few paces behind, with Sharon graciously, though unsuccessfully, trying to include him in our conversation. Her small talk about the indigenous flora struck me as a touch forced. I wondered if she guessed the reason for my visit.

Lillian's was a converted music store on the cobblestone square. Antique instruments dangled on wires behind plate-glass windows. Inside, the decor was turn-of-the-century, with a tin ceiling and lots of dark, heavy drapery. A waiter wearing sleeve garters and a waxed mustache seated us beneath the only mote in this clear-eyed vision of old Gainesville: an oil mural of the Coppertone lady, supine on a cathouse chaise.

A waitress dealt us gold-braided menus, then recited the specials of the day. I barely listened, knowing what I planned to spring on Sharon and figuring it would ruin her appetite. I know it ruined mine.

"The brook trout is excellent," said Sharon after the waitress departed. "Now tell me, how does it feel to be on Tour at last?"

"The Tour," I said, "isn't what I expected."

Reaching into my pocket, I sensed every muscular movement, felt the roughness of the bond on my fingertips, saw myself as if peering down from the tin ceiling, asked myself if I really wanted to do this, while all the time knowing I must. I laid the affidavit on her plate.

She held the papers at arm's length before taking out a pair of tiny reading glasses. Dammit, even they became her. She didn't scan the pages for more than a brief moment; she knew what was there.

"My God," she muttered as she folded up her glasses. "Where did you get this?"

"The mail. Addressed to me, care of the Judge."

"Why you?"

"I'm not sure yet," I said. "Sharon, is this true?"

She steepled her hands in front of her face and took a long breath.

"You remember the Tallahassee tournament," she said.

"It's what makes this so tough," I said.

The corners of her mouth turned up in a fleeting smile.

"You know Gar and I were involved. It started with the very first lesson he gave me at Gainesville Country Club. He wrapped his hands around mine to show how a golf grip should feel, and I knew." She stared into her palms as if they held a tiny mirror.

"I realized we didn't have any future. He was much younger, you know, and that definitely was part of the attraction. My young Canadian stud. The relationship eventually grew stale and, by the Tallahassee tournament, it was practically over.

"The night before the last round, he called me with good news and bad news. The good news was he was in the lead, the bad news was being tied with you. He spoke highly of you. He called you the big brother he never had, although I have my own competing theory. He was petrified about the next day, because he knew he had to beat you to win that tournament. He didn't think he could."

"Pretty funny," I said, "since I can't touch his game now."

"It was true," she said. "He wanted me there, he needed me there. So I got up early and drove to Tallahassee because he wanted someone in the crowd completely on his side. But I couldn't be. Not by then. The pills were my idea. I always felt guilty about it, like I helped cheat you out of a tournament."

"But you continued to supply Gar with beta blockers," I said.

"He used them at Q School," said Sharon. "He used them during his first three or four years on Tour. I can't say how much. I'd send him sample packets of a dozen or so at a time. And I warned him about the nonbeneficial side effects, like bronchospasms, insomnia, and fatigue. It was nice, I guess, the little cards he'd send to signal me he needed a fresh supply. We were finished, but I felt something of us continued."

"How did the affidavit come about?" I said.

"It goes back to early January," she said. "A man called to say Gar had applied for life insurance and listed me as his personal physician. He wanted to ask me questions over the phone. I refused. First, I told him Gar wasn't my patient. Second, even if Gar were, I wouldn't answer questions over the phone. I didn't give the phone call a second thought until a few weeks later, when a woman arrived at the office. She reminded me about the phone call and said she brought forms for me to fill out. She was very curt, and I took an instant dislike to her."

"Did she give you her name?" I said.

"No."

I described Cindy Moran.

"Sounds like her," said Sharon. "She was very forceful. Almost scary. My receptionist had left for the day, and my last appointment was over. So, to placate her, I agreed to fill out the form. The form turned out to be the affidavit.

"I read it through, completely dumbfounded. I asked her how she knew such things, and she said that was none of my business. She had connections. I was just to sign the thing."

"And you did," I said.

"Well, Kieran, you see—" She paused, and gulped almost audibly. "Could we speak alone?"

"Yeah, sure," said the Judge. He threw in the napkin he had spread on his lap, and waddled toward the door.

Sharon watched him go. The background music kicked into something jazzy. The noise level rose as the maitre d' seated a large group to our left. Sharon took a long draught from a tall glass of lemon water. Her lipstick left a faintly perfect bow on the rim.

"I knew it would come back to me eventually," she said. "Time passes, and you think it heals wounds. But it never changes the facts of the past. Do you believe in ghosts?"

"I've seen things I can't rationally explain," I said.

"Do you think someone who never existed could have a ghost?"

"Sharon, I—"

"The night of my wedding, I woke up in the hotel room and saw a little girl sitting on the foot of the bed with her back toward me. I'm terrible at estimating a child's age, but I knew she was five, almost to the day. She slowly turned around, and said, 'You must tell him,' in her little girl voice. She was smiling, and not a happy or pleasant smile, either. I must have said something, because she repeated the same words and, the next thing I knew, I was screaming and flailing and kicking the sheets, and John wrapped me in a bearhug trying to calm me down. Some start to a marriage."

"Did you tell him?" I said.

"Not about the ghost, and not about what the ghost said. I made up a story about mixing too many drinks at the reception. The first of many stories, I'm not proud to say." She took one of my hands in hers. "I love my husband, Kieran. He's a good man who's done a lot of good for Alachua County. He's planning a run for Congress this year. If anyone even knew about what Gar and I did—what I did, actually, because Gar never knew—it would ruin John in this district. So I signed the affidavit. True or not, I would have signed it. But it was true."

Her hands slipped off mine. The waitress loomed briefly, but receded when she couldn't get our attention.

"I had to make a choice, Kieran, between John and Gar. I had something with Gar I never could have with John, but I chose John. I hoped it would go away. But when I heard about the murder at Camelot, I knew it was connected. And when I saw your name in the paper, the picture was complete. This could hurt Gar badly, right?"

"Very," I said.

"He told me about his childhood," she said, "and how his father would beat him. Terrible beatings with a strap. He'd never commit to anyone and never have children, because he feared becoming his father. His Polar Bear nickname is such an irony. That little town on Hudson's Bay was the last place his whole family lived together. What I mean, Kieran, is that Gar isn't a violent person."

I stood to leave, and she grabbed my arm.

"I tried to visit you at Shands," she said, "but you already were released. I thought you should know."

The Judge and I found McGriff's Ford blocking our car in its parking space. I introduced McGriff to Big Jim as "the detective I told you about last Friday" and Big Jim to McGriff as "a county judge and my business manager."

"Spending an awful lot of time in Gainesville lately, eh, Lenahan?" said McGriff.

"Visiting an old friend," I said.

At that moment, Sharon Paulling exited Lillian's. She stopped dead at the sight of me, then turned sharply and double-timed up the sidewalk.

"I see," said McGriff, with the hint of a laugh. "Didn't know you had so many friends here."

"I take them where I find them."

"I have some news," said McGriff. "Not a lot, but some. Tests on your shirt showed only your blood."

"What you expected," I said.

"We always hope," he said. "What about you? Any pieces of memory fall into place?"

"Nothing," I said.

McGriff cocked his head just enough to take in the Judge. "What about you? Do you know anything about the lady Lenahan came to visit last Thursday?"

A highly reactive chemistry brewed in the Judge. He expected the mantle of his office to transcend the boundaries of his jurisdiction, with all the attendant ass kissing. And he hated to be addressed as *you*.

"I'm his business manager, not his guardian angel," he said.

"Get anywhere with that credit card lead?" I asked McGriff.

"Not very far," he said. "We picked up someone named Waldo Wilson who runs an office cleaning company. He had access to the stolen mortgage application. We traced back from him to a kid named Eddie Fort. He knows both Wilson and the victim. But that hasn't panned out into anything substantial. He did say a bank investigator questioned him about this over the weekend. Funny thing, the bank tells us it hasn't opened an investigation yet."

"Meaning what?" I said.

McGriff stroked his fuzzy chin. He knew I played bank investigator, and he knew I knew it.

"Oh, maybe someone else got burned and decided to take it personally," he said. "You still have my card. Call me when you remember something." He yanked on the gearshift. The engine pitched higher as it settled into gear. "And don't check out of the Sawgrass Marriott without informing me."

"Why didn't you tell McGriff about the affidavit?" said the Judge. He was driving us back to Sawgrass at record pace, every minute saved being an extra minute devoted to lunch before his big meeting with the Tour staffers.

"The same reason you won't mention a word of anything I told you or anything you heard today to the Tour," I said.

"Better clue me in," said the Judge.

"You agree that Cindy Moran and this other guy planned to run a scam?" I waited for his grudging assent, which sounded like a burp. "And she knew enough about Tommy Garth Hunter to contact two people from his past, Sharon and me."

"So?"

"So I can't blindly help McGriff until I know how I fit in,"
I said. "Same thing with the Tour. Stick with the presumption
that I went to Gainesville to have sex with Cindy Moran. It's
what they believe anyway."

"Not much I can do with that story," said the Judge. "I
paint her as a scam artist, and you as a rube, and I might save
your ass."

"I want my whole ass intact. Saving my Tour career doesn't
save me from McGriff, if he decides to pursue the wrong
theory."

"You're hamstringing the hell out of me, Kieran," he said.

We rode several miles in silence. The Judge mentally polished his presentation to the Tour officials while I grappled
with the thought of the Polar Bear gone feral.

"What do you plan on doing?" he finally said. "Arresting
Hunter yourself?"

"No. I'm going to find out if my good buddy had the
opportunity to kill Cindy Moran."

"He played at Bay Hill, didn't he?" said the Judge.

"So did I, and I got to Bay Hill in time to get clocked."

"How far are you going to take this?"

"Tommy Garth's opportunity," I said. "That's all."

"Then you turn everything over to McGriff," he said.

"Everything."

"Even if your memory hasn't returned and you still don't
know how you fit in."

"Yes, Judge," I said, struggling to keep my voice from
falling into sing-song.

"And if I quash your suspension—God knows how I'll do

that without spilling this scam—you promise to devote the rest of the week to the Players," he said.

"Promise," I said.

We shook on it, but as soon as our hands broke, I started mentally angling for loopholes. Sometimes it's fun to be an ex-lawyer.

CHAPTER TWELVE

I settled into a big chair in the Marriott's atrium as the Judge waddled off in search of grub. Outside the atrium window and across the lagoon, a small gallery trailed an anonymous twosome playing a practice round at the Players Club. I pored over the affidavit, cupping my hands to shield it from roving eyes. I'd given up hope of remembrance returning in a flash of fire and a puff of colored smoke. But the details were beginning to flow together, gathering speed and strength, as I picked my way upstream to the source.

Cindy Moran had included two old friends of Tommy Garth Hunter in her scam. But she easily could have picked Ned Nelson, Chris Jennings, Sam Young, or a dozen other pros. Each knew Hunter as long as I, and each was more attuned to Hunter recent activities, both on and off the Tour. But I'd learned enough about Cindy Moran to know she was careful. She'd cultivated me from Doral to Honda to Bay Hill. My friendship with Hunter was a prerequisite. My rookie status and my past troubles with the Tour were convenient touches.

But Cindy Moran chose me because I was a lawyer and therefore ethically bound to keep secrets.

Then the theory slid off-line. Cindy Moran and her accomplice had Hunter dead on the stick. He had used beta blockers
during tournament play in violation of Tour policy that almost
certainly would cost him his endorsement contract. Why
involve me?

She could have been trying to blackmail someone else,
maybe offering the affidavit to the highest bidder. This tied
in with her mailing the affidavit to the Judge. The affidavit
is safely out of her possession while she negotiates her price;
it lands with an attorney who she may have retained. Inventors
once used a similar technique, mailing plans and sketches
to themselves as a way of dating the genesis of their great
inventions. Any patent attorney can tell you the value of this
proof is negligible. And Cindy Moran's inexpensive form of
escrow hadn't worked, either. She'd been murdered.

I had only one candidate for a second target, and this was
the real reason I wanted the Judge mum on the scam.

The standard PGA Tour event is sponsored by a huge
corporation, if not an outright conglomerate. Advertisers pitch
products to the upper echelons of the demographic scale.
Huge galleries of fans line the fairways and jam the corporate
hospitality tents. A large share of the gate receipts is donated
to high-profile charities. The corporate sponsor gloms a full
week of priceless exposure, capped by the CEO presenting
the first prize check to the winner Sunday at dusk.

This edifice stands on a solid foundation—the honesty and
integrity of the men who compete on the PGA Tour. As a
group, the players adhere to a code of conduct quaintly out
of step with today's abrasive culture. No in-your-face antics;

no gloating; no taunts. As a group, the players are perhaps the most eloquent in professional sports, and the most accommodating to press and fans alike. Players actually penalize themselves for infractions only they know occurred. Any suspicion of cheating, any hint of players using drugs to enhance performance, any slight possibility that the tournaments are anything less than pure competition, and the entire edifice crumbles.

The PGA Tour is definitely a deep pocket, but it has too many layers of authority to make it an easy target for extortion. Who would Cindy and her accomplice have approached? The Commissioner? The Tour Policy Board? The sourpuss triad of Chandler, Haswell, and Lang? Any of a number of other Tour staffers with the fear of a scandal and the authority to dip into the till?

Even if Cindy Moran had been negotiating with the Tour, the currents of clues and assumptions still traced back to Tommy Garth Hunter. The scam threatened him personally, and he had the ability to strike quickly without running his options past a committee.

I locked the affidavit in the hotel safe deposit box, then drove to the Stadium Course. The practice range was just as crowded as this morning. Meg sat on the butt end of my golf bag, a towel draping her shoulders, her corn-colored hair spewing from beneath her golf cap, and a layer of sunscreen volatilizing into an atmosphere around her. I crouched to kiss her hello, but she made it very plain from her body language that her lips were off-limits. This wasn't simple workplace discretion.

"Where have you been all morning and into the afternoon?" she said.

"With the Judge," I said.

"A likely story."

"Something came up. An appointment. It was sudden." In some circles, invoking the Judge forgave a multitude of sins. This wasn't one of them.

"You couldn't have left word," she said. "I waited and waited, all types of men chatting me up, and me on the lookout for you in vain. Then I became worried, thinking that you're after falling back to sleep or suffering a relapse or worse. I went to your suite. The cleaning lady was there, and when I didn't find you asleep or unconscious, I became angry."

"Sorry," I said. "It won't happen again."

I touched her shoulder, but she spun out from under me and all but dusted off her shirt.

"What did you and his honor discuss?"

"Business."

Meg cocked her head, allowing me a chance to recant. She and the Judge had spent barely fifteen minutes in each other's company last December, but it was enough for them to form a mutual disadmiration society. I didn't know Meg's exact problem with the Judge and, since the Judge didn't usually travel with us, I saw no reason to discuss it. The Judge was an acquired taste I assumed Meg never would acquire. Like tripe. The Judge had been more cogent with his dislike.

"How the hell do you know if she knows anything?" he'd said after I broke the news about hiring Meg. "How the hell do you know if you can listen to her advice? What are you, an equal opportunity employer?"

But beneath all the sputtering, I detected his usual antipathy for the women in my life. The sole exception was Deirdre

O'Meara, my neighborhood sweetheart and redheaded object of desire in a ten-year soap opera that featured two near-death experiences (one for each of us). "Never should have let her get away," the Judge still said whenever her name came up, which mercifully was less often now that I was on the road. I'd been with Georgina Newland almost two years now, and he was just starting to refer to her by name instead of "that Amazon."

One of the Tour's bigger stars walked past, followed by his retinue of caddie, guru, psychologist, agent, wife, child, and half a dozen tournament reps. I claimed the vacated patch of turf. Meg performed the usual housekeeping while I loosened my back muscles with a club locked between my elbows and spine.

"The Judge brought down some mail for me," I said. "In it was an affidavit that implies Cindy Moran was blackmailing someone on Tour. I don't know how far she took it, but she obviously meant me to be a part of it."

"Who was she blackmailing?" said Meg.

A caddie interrupted to talk to Meg. I fanned the ground with my pitching wedge until their conversation ended.

"Tommy Garth Hunter finished ahead of us at Bay Hill, right?" I said.

"By three groups," said Meg. "He killed the lady?"

"Hold it, Meg, I didn't say that."

"But he's the name in the affidavit," she said. "What did he do?"

"I want to keep the details to myself," I said. "For your own protection."

"You sound like a credit card company," said Meg. "Who's

protecting the Judge? If he knows, you can share the information with me as well."

Meg folded her arms across her chest and tucked her chin tight. I lobbed a few wedge shots while she imitated an immovable object.

"I may have heard something about whatever's in the affidavit," she finally said.

"I doubt it."

"Why? We caddies talk about you golfers constantly. You fill our lives."

"Cut the sarcasm," I said, then thought better. "Okay, prove it. Tell me something I don't know about Hunter."

"He's married," said Meg.

"What?" I said. "I've known him seven, eight years. He never told me."

"He's been married ten," Meg said firmly.

"The Tour media guide doesn't list him as married."

"It wouldn't. They have an arrangement to allow her to stay in Canada as a landed alien, but they lead separate lives."

"Who told you?"

"His caddie," she said.

I knocked some balls out of the pile and shot them aloft like a metronome on the blink. The tee box was flat as a pool table, but my entire world had just shifted again into a sidehill lie. Like most people, I believe I understand what goes on around me. Not in the philosophical sense; our place in the universe and the meaning of life are open to serious debate. I'm talking about everyday affairs. I pride myself at peering beneath surface appearances to the truth below. Back in my lawyer days, I weighed not just the words, but the inflections and mannerisms of witnesses and adversaries. I drew dark inferences from innocent items like an unreturned phone call. If I didn't see the truth in full color, at least I knew its shadow.

My three months on the Tour had made me doubt my perceptions. As facts, Tommy Garth Hunter's marriage and the mini-tour gambling ring didn't shatter me. But the idea that I was skimming the surface of existence like a water spider raised a nagging question: what the hell was I doing out here?

I slid the wedge into the golf bag.

"All right," I said. "The affidavit accuses Hunter of using beta blockers during tournaments."

Meg let out a long whistle.

"Any idea where he is now?" I said.

"Ned Nelson, Chris Jennings, Sam Young, and himself organized a four-ball not half an hour ago."

"Nine holes or eighteen?"

"Eighteen, I believe," she said.

"I'm calling it quits for the day," I said. "If anyone asks, I'm still feeling a bit lightheaded. Meanwhile, you ask around for Hunter's whereabouts last Thursday afternoon. Be discreet. Someone's already been killed because of this."

The buffet tent was nearly empty, with afternoon just shading toward the late side. Huge overhead fans beat the air with rhythmic whumps. Sterno flames licked the bottoms of bubbling trays. Fruit and fish nestled in soft beds of shaved ice. I sampled each food group and positioned myself at one end of a long table, hard against the tent wall and with a natural aim at the entrance. People trickled in. Golfers and wives, caddies and guests. Kenny Palumbo heaped a tray, and exited quickly through a side flap. I checked my watch. The Judge's meeting with the Tour staffers was about to begin.

I spotted Jennings' caddie first, then Young's, Nelson's, and finally Hunter's. They formed up a tight circle near the beer cooler, grass-stained towels hanging over their shoulders and hair curling slickly beneath their golf caps. Only the sharpest observer could see the money changing hands. They finally fanned out along the buffet line. Meg came in, studiously avoiding my eye. She cut into line in front of Hunter's caddie and smiled impishly. I decided I'd rather not watch her work.

I needed to kill some time and chose the putting green as my weapon. With the afternoon waning, players came off the course at a good clip. Some went directly into the buffet tent. Others stopped at an area roped off for autograph seekers, and scribbled their signatures on scorecards, programs, or hats. A few dropped balls onto the green to work out their putting kinks.

I had at least a nodding acquaintance with all these guys. But I had the distinct feeling they deliberately avoided the area where I worked at missing my twelve footers. Ned Nelson and Tommy Garth Hunter made a quick circuit, with the obvious air of finishing off whatever bets started on the golf course. Ned, who should have been in an expansive mood twenty-four hours after his big victory, scrupulously avoided eye contact. Hunter flicked me only the slightest wave before he and Ned padded off toward the tent.

A few minutes later, Hunter's caddie emerged from the

tent, accompanied by Meg. I straightened up and cocked my head, as if asking her across the distance how she fared. She ignored me, until they turned out of sight.

I don't know how long I waited. Putting is an extremely boring endeavor, especially when your heart isn't in it. Suddenly, Meg stood beside me.

"Hit a putt," she said.

"I've been hitting putts for the last hour."

"Lag one there." She pointed at a practice pin in a distant, unoccupied section of the green.

I hit the ball, and we followed it out of anyone's earshot.

"Hunter's caddie says talk to Kenny Palumbo," she whispered.

I banged a long putt toward the other end of the green. When I looked back, Meg was gone.

I found Kenny Palumbo in the middle of the spectator parking lot. A bright blue tarp, held aloft by four slender poles, licked in the breeze. Beneath it, half a dozen people milled around the open trunk of the Riviera. Shade from the tarp just missed where Kenny sat in a seriously tilting beach chair.

"Golf balls, I got golf balls," he clucked. "Hardly used golf gloves, used once, owned by professionals. See this."

He tapped the arm of a woman standing closest and fished a golf ball from a plastic milk crate inside the trunk. Even from a distance, I could see the fanciful colors covering one hemisphere of the ball.

"Know what this is?" he said.

"An Easter egg?" the woman replied.

"Close," said Kenny, thick-skinned, or at least oblivious. "Touring pros use only a few different brands of balls, so they doodle their own distinctive markings for identification. These are collector's items now. Someday, they'll be folk art."

The woman muttered something to her husband, who tried to work a golf glove onto his hand. He tossed the glove back into the trunk, and the two strolled away. Kenny levelled his attention at a preteen leafing through a milk crate full of photographs.

"How much?" said the boy.

"Twenty bucks."

"For the lot?"

"The lot? Are you nuts?" Kenny leaped up and elbowed the boy aside. "These are all former Players champs. This guy won in 'eighty-seven, this guy in 'ninety-two, this guy in 'ninety-five."

"Why should I pay you if they'll autograph a picture for me for nothing?" the boy said as he walked off.

"Wiseguy!" shouted Kenny. He bent into the trunk to rearrange his stock as the rest of the customers drifted away.

"Eh, Kieran," he said, throwing a glance over his shoulder while he smoothed the price tags stuck to the bins. "These Monday crowds are tough. Not too many loose bucks in their wallets."

I lifted two balls from a bin marked "Professional—Used."

"Interesting how each of these balls was pictured in a magazine article." I dropped the balls and flipped a few pictures. "And these former champs, funny how they are the guys with the least distinctive signatures."

Kenny slammed the trunk. I barely got my hand out in time.

"Guys have been trying to run me off the Tour for years,"

he said. "Your pal Harrington is the latest in a long line. He says the players got the right to make money with their names and their autographs and their souvenirs. Hey, I got a right to make money, too. You tell him that."

We went back and forth until I convinced him I wasn't Woody Harrington's emissary or spy. Kenny opened his trunk for a passing knot of people. When they didn't stop, he closed it again.

"What are you here for?" he said.

"Information."

Kenny smiled as if I'd just asked to see the private stock. "How do you know I have any?"

I told him my caddie inquired of Tommy Garth Hunter's caddie, who suggested I contact Kenny.

"Tommy Garth Hunter, huh?" he said. "This'll cost you."

I could have strong-armed Kenny and saved money in the short run. But in the long run, I'd pay much more. From medieval court jesters to modern-day urban street whacks, fools operated under a type of divine protection. Kenny was just sly enough to paint me as a bully, rather than a victim of extortion. We haggled, eventually arriving at the theoretical possibility of a two-week paid vacation for Kenny, if his information checked out. He folded his chair, dismantled his tarp, and locked everything in the trunk. Then we climbed into the car. The windows were tinted dark enough that no one passing by could see inside. Remnants of his buffet dinner lay on the carpet.

"Fork it over," he said.

I counted out the bills. He leaned back against the seat and stuffed them into his pocket.

"I need to know what Tommy Garth Hunter did after Thursday's round at Bay Hill," I said.

"Interviews," said Kenny. "He was leading the tournament at the time."

"What about after the interviews?"

Kenny thumbed the bills in his pocket, probably wondering what it was worth going any further. People surrounded a nearby car, talking excitedly about what they'd seen today, until sinking inside and driving off.

"I was working the parking lot," said Kenny. "Hunter's caddie came looking for me. He's one of my suppliers. After we did our business, he said Hunter wanted me right away. I told him I couldn't close up right then because it was almost prime time. He said Hunter'd pay me.

"I met Hunter in a grove of trees near the edge of the lot. He said he needed a car for the afternoon, but didn't want one of the club courtesy cars."

"Did he explain why?" I said.

"He was going somewhere he didn't want to be noticed."

Many tournaments assemble a fleet of cars from nearby dealerships for the pros to use throughout the tournament week. Huge decals emblazoned on the doors advertise both the tournament and the dealerships. Kenny continued:

"He wanted a good car, not a piece of junk. I asked, what did I look like? A magician? But once again, I came through. I walked around the lot until I saw a bunch of kids getting into a decent looking car. I asked them how'd they like to drive around in a courtesy car all day. They said okay, but only if it was such and such a model and it had a full tank of gas.

"I got a courtesy car from the fleet and made the switch. The kids took the courtesy car, and Hunter took theirs."

"What time did Hunter return?" I said.

"He got back about seven or so. Those kids stayed out until midnight. Pissed me off because I signed out for the courtesy car and had to wait for them."

CHAPTER
THIRTEEN

I called the Judge's cellular from a phone bank near the buffet tent. The Judge usually needed at least three rings to fish the phone out of his cavernous pants pocket, and another three to raise the antenna and lower the mouthpiece. But I hung up after the second ring. Torches blazed around the tent as the sun dipped toward the flat horizon. Voices and laughter rumbled inside. The Tour is not a continuous party, at least not for the players. Early starting times and the need to be mentally and physically sharp cut into nighttime revelries. But with lots of the guys already up from Orlando, and with only practice rounds set for tomorrow, the tent would be hopping for hours.

I fled the festivities for the same reason I ducked the Judge. I didn't feel convivial.

You get past a certain age and finding a new friend becomes infinitely more difficult than finding a new lover. Life settles into an ever-deepening track, crossing, sometimes paralleling, but never quite dovetailing with another track. Sharing new experiences with other people—something that seemed to happen almost daily in youth—occurs rarely. And when it does, you remain guarded.

Tommy Garth Hunter was one of the few people in the kingdom of golf who emerged from the din of backslapping acquaintances and convenient contacts. I realized now that I never recovered from learning Hunter had participated in the mini-tour gambling ring. I had gazed deeply into a nickel-plated friendship and seen only my own reflection.

Now I wondered if I rushed Hunter to judgment, if I hoped he used beta blockers and killed Cindy Moran as further proof of my blunder in calling him friend.

Back at the Marriott, I found a message waiting for me at the desk: Call the Judge, ASAP. Amazingly, he answered on the first ring.

"Meeting's over. Get your ass here pronto," he said, and named a seafood joint in Sawgrass Village. From the sound of his voice, the meeting went well. At least in his estimation.

The Judge sat in a booth on the bar side of a stained glass room divider, not far from a huge tank of tropical fish. Two napkins dangling from his shirt collar flanked a plastic bib, all three sprayed Jackson Pollock-style with yellows and greens. The remnants of a lobster lay twisted on a platter.

"First thing I tried to do was psych out why suspending you is so important," the Judge said after I settled in. "I couldn't find any logical reason, which leads me to believe it's personal with you, and therefore completely understandable. That was some hostile group. Henry Chandler has all the charisma of a pit bull. That Haswell guy has a smile I wanted to drive a fist through. And that Lang lady. Let's just say I'd never hire her as my secretary."

"She's Vice-President for Sponsor Relations," I said.

"Whatever," said the Judge. He leaned backward and worked a cigar out of his pocket. The booth strained, but fortunately didn't burst into splinters. "I decided to say you visited Ms. Moran in Gainesville that afternoon for the obvious reason. That caused a ruckus among Chandler, Haswell, and Lang, who were very skeptical about your alleged amnesia. Well, with my grasp on medical lingo, I wasn't about to start shooting off my mouth. So I played it cool until your buddy Hannigan—"

"Harrington," I said.

"Yeah, him," the Judge said around his cigar as he fired up. "Until he piped up."

"What did he say?"

"He needs a lesson on whose side he's on. Started with a disclaimer about how he believed you, but still encouraged you to explain what you remembered. Sounded like a bunch of crap to me. You know, saying he believed in his good buddy's story, but leaving his conviction open to question. Luckily, a secretary came rushing in with a fax from that Gainesville hospital."

"Don't tell me," I said.

"Oh, it corroborated you, all right," said the Judge. "And a Hollywood director couldn't have timed it better for effect. Now I really started thumping the table. I told them all they had was suspicion and innuendo, which was a whole lot less than your corroborated diagnosis of amnesia. I said maybe we'd consider paying a fine, if they could show me something more than suspicion and innuendo, and if they could show me in dollar figures how your absence from the second round at Bay Hill damaged the Tour or the tournament.

"Chandler countered by saying no one mentioned a fine. The topic of discussion was your suspension. 'Suspension?' I laughed indignantly. 'Kieran Lenahan is a salt-of-the-earth kind of guy,' I said. 'He's living out the fantasies of every hacker over the age of thirty-five.' Which, I reminded them, fell square in the middle of their advertising demographics. If they suspended you, I told them, I'd raise a bigger public stink than the Tour could afford."

"Jim, I haven't had a reporter come within twenty-five feet of me all day."

"You forget who I flew down with."

"Fisk? He writes for a small chain and gets a column picked up by a national wire service once or twice a year. The Tour won't exactly cringe."

"He'd just be the start," said the Judge. "You know the herd mentality among the press."

"Yeah, but Fisk doesn't run with them." I leaned out of the booth to see beyond the Judge's eclipsing bulk. Several pros were scattered about the room. Half a dozen guys, with the distinctive look of Tour staffers crammed a nearby booth.

"Where's Fisk now?" I said. "You could have invited him to make a public show of courting the press."

"Off interviewing some broken-down old pro for an oral history book about the early Tour," said the Judge. "Nice what we call a book nowadays. Fisk tapes a bunch of interviews, transcribes them into text, the publisher slaps on a cover, and presto."

"Look, Jim, are they planning to drop these . . ." I almost said "charges," but I hadn't been charged with anything

formal, unless you considered being a corporate embarrassment a sanctionable offense.

"Not in so many words," said the Judge. "But I gave them
so much to think about that I'm pretty confident they will.
Now how did you fare?"

I told him about Kenny Palumbo arranging for Hunter to
borrow a car Thursday afternoon.

"What's he, some kind of pimp?" said the Judge.

"More of a panderer. He makes his money selling stolen
equipment and bogus Tour souvenirs."

The Judge puffed hard, considering the obvious implica-
tion that Hunter's actions Thursday were consistent with
driving to Gainesville.

"He does her to keep a lid on his reputation," he said.
"You waltz in, he does you, but doesn't kill you. Friendship?"

"Or carelessness," I said. "Or maybe I'm his only line on
the affidavit."

"Detective McGriff can sort it all out." The Judge pushed
his cellular phone across the table.

"I'll call him from the hotel," I said.

"But you will call," said the Judge. "That was our
agreement."

"Right. You save my ass from suspension, and I hand everything over to McGriff."

I left the Judge perusing the dessert menu and drove back
to the Marriott. I intended to phone McGriff, I truly did. But
not right then, not that second. Instead of heading inside, I
strolled around the hotel grounds. Water hissed, spraying
azaleas and tulips from pinholes in a green hose snaking
alongside the path. A huge tropical bug corkscrewed from
one palm tree to the next and hid among the fronds, clicking

its rear legs. People lounged on balconies, their voices and laughter carrying crisply into the night air.

For three days I'd been fighting to regain memories that ultimately didn't matter a damn. Tommy Garth Hunter, Sharon Paulling, and I had converged for one brief span seven years ago in Tallahassee. Yet that convergence set forces in motion that Cindy Moran, whether by accident or design, had refocused with explosive results. I foresaw McGriff's investigation. Much as I respected him, he'd concentrate on homework and minutiae, while larger issues like greed and morality and values were shunted aside. I foresaw the trial, with Tommy Garth Hunter's defense attorney glibly portraying Sharon Paulling's Eve to Hunter's Adam. I foresaw it all, and I hated it.

I arrived back at the atrium, noticing, but not focusing on, the golf cart with the Tour logo parked beside the door. Inside, the same wise-ass teenager who'd dragged me off the practice range for the first round of the Tour inquisition handed me a note.

"From Mr. Hunter," he said.

Mr. Hunter was it? Maybe only a murderer could earn honorifics from these whacko, modern-day teens. I unfolded the note, which had been scribbled on a napkin I recognized from the buffet.

"We need to talk," it read.

"Does Mr. Hunter have a time and a place?" I said.

"Oh yeah," said the kid.

Hunter was no fool. He must have learned of the inquiries and wanted to clear the air. Fine with me.

We exited the hotel grounds and tooled along TPC Boulevard toward the Players Club, the cart tires rippling on the ribbon-smooth pavement. The kid exuded the same youthful surliness as during our last momentous meeting. I resisted the urge to call him son. We passed through the Players Club gates and turned toward the grass field where spectators parked during the day. Clouds billowed pink and orange over distant downtown Jax. Stars floated in odd patches of violet.

A shadow loomed ahead, gradually resolving into a car. The kid wheeled the cart broadside, about ten yards away.

"Get out," he said, and prodded my shoulder when I didn't react instantly.

The car door opened, and a large, ursine figure unfolded itself from behind the wheel. Another figure followed, and another, until all six stood alongside the car. I recognized three of the others from the slope of their shoulders and the shapes of their heads. Ned Nelson, Sam Young, Chris Jennings. Silhouettes as distinctive as signatures to an old mini-tour buddy.

Fear never occurred to me. Excluding snakes and gators, little danger threatened a Sawgrass night. After all, we were civilized people who earned a living by playing a gentleman's game. And I didn't really believe Hunter killed Cindy Moran to preserve his $30 million endorsement contract. Did I?

"You know what we want," said Hunter.

"Actually not," I said. "My escort didn't tell me."

And I heard my escort in full flight, the cart whining as it sped through the dark toward the clubhouse. The six started moving, and not just closer. They spread out until they formed a wide semicircle.

"We know you're paired with Jason Oliver for the first two rounds," said Hunter.

"We want you to drop out," said Ned Nelson.

"Hey, guys," I said. "Ned, Tommy. Aren't you over-reacting?"

"Not if you tell us you'll drop out," said Hunter.

"And what does that get you?" I said. "Do you think the pairing committee will slip one of you in my place?"

"You leave that to us," said Ned Nelson.

The two figures on the ends advanced, pinching in to cut off any escape.

"Look, guys," I said. "I can understand how you're bent out of shape about that interview."

"No you don't," said Chris Jennings. "You haven't been on Tour long enough."

"Does that mean Oliver spoke the truth?" I said.

The two end figures planted themselves on my wings. The other four—Hunter, Nelson, Young, and Jennings—went very still. Silence deepened, ripped only by the clicking of a huge insect launching itself out of a distant palm. I often wondered how I'd react in a confrontation like this. Alone, outnumbered, unable to run. I expected it to happen on a city street, not on the grounds of a PGA tournament. But the effect was the same. Fear of physical pain was less immediate than the embarrassment of going down like a simpering, whimpering coward. Stiff upper lip, and all that. So I didn't invoke Woody Harrington's name, didn't protest my lack of interest in any of Jason Oliver's crusades. They would know all this, anyway.

Chris Jennings was the one to charge.

"You self-righteous son of a bitch," he screamed, grabbing wads of shirt just beneath my collar.

Jennings was about my height and a good thirty pounds heftier, so I used his momentum against him. I swept my right hand up and under his arms, in one motion breaking the grip of his right hand on my shirt and grasping his forearm. This turned him to his left, and I finished the job by thumping his right shoulder with my left forearm. Jennings crumpled like a blown tire, his right arm locked and helpless beneath my knee. Two of the others rushed me.

"Back off!" I said.

They froze. Jennings yelped in pain.

"Back off, or I end his career!"

I could do it, too. One bounce of my knee, and his elbow would shatter into more pieces than an orthopedist could reassemble. Again, nobody moved. I lowered my knee until it lightly tapped Jennings's elbow. His yelps widened into a full-throated bellow. Everybody jumped.

"Listen to him, goddammit!" screamed Jennings. "Listen to him!"

"All of you get back into the car," I said. "Then you, Tommy, throw me the keys."

"You wouldn't do it," said Hunter.

"Try me," I said.

"Tommy, don't try him," said Jennings. "Please. Just listen to him."

The two end figures retreated first, followed by Ned Nelson and then Sam Young. Hunter jingled the keys.

One day, a client came into the firm and asked the Judge to file a handgun license application for him. The client, a local storekeeper, recently had been robbed at gunpoint while making a night deposit at the bank. A gun, he thought, would even the odds.

"A gun will get you killed," said the Judge, "because you won't be prepared to use yours the way the other guy will be prepared to use his. You show it, and he'll shoot you before you get the safety off."

Right now, I felt like that client. I didn't have the stomach for torturing Jennings much longer. Hunter kept jingling the keys. I was glad for the dark; my bluff would be obvious in the daylight.

"The keys," I said.

The jingling stopped. Hunter took a step backward, his hand slowly withdrawing. He was big as a bear, but quick as a cat. His arm barely twitched, and something stung me in the jaw. I rolled off Jennings, and Hunter was on me in an instant. He straddled my chest, his huge bulk pinning my arms to my sides and crushing my ribs.

"Tommy," Jennings gasped.

"Get in the car!" said Hunter.

"But, Tommy—"

"Get in the goddam car!"

I heard Jennings scramble away. Hunter loomed over me, his hair a wild tangle of curls, his face and head huge and dark against the sky.

"You listen to me, good buddy," he said. His words dripped with hatred, as if the masks had fallen off, as if seven years of supposed friendship had been nothing but an elaborate sham. "You keep your mouth shut about what Sharon told you, eh? You say one word to Oliver, anyone, you'll wish you never came out here."

Purple clouds and gold stars started to swirl. They were in my eyes, not in the sky. I couldn't breathe. My guts flooded my throat. The clouds thickened. The stars faded. So did I.

Then a light snapped on. Hunter blinked, shielded his

face, scrambled off me. Brakes squealed, a spray of dirt and grass rained over me. An engine ignited.

"Get the hell out of here, assholes," someone shouted.

I loosened my eyes. The stars faded and the clouds dissipated, leaving the face of a beautiful dark woman floating above me.

"Not again," I muttered, and let go.

CHAPTER
FOURTEEN

I felt myself jouncing, my tailbone riding the edge of a small seat, my feet tucking up behind me in reverse fetal position. But my head held still, cradled in a kind of cushion yuppie parents buy for their newborns to replicate the womb. I opened my eyes. Up above, light licked her face in a highway rhythm. The cushion became the roundness of her thighs beneath my head, the folds of her stomach against my ear. Somewhere behind her, a motor chugged.

"He's awake," she said, looking down. Her lips broadened into a motherly smile. "How do you feel now?"

There was a Haitian lilt to her words.

"Wife of Bath," I said.

"What?"

"He said, 'Wife of Bath.'" This was a man's voice, coming from opposite that chugging motor. "He means the gap between your teeth. 'She knew muchel of wandring by the waye/ Gat-toothed was she, soothly for to saye.'"

She probed the gap with her tongue.

Better than last time, I thought. At least they understood what I said, however disjointed. I cast back in my mind, remembered the cart ride to the darkened parking field, the six guys surrounding me, Tommy Garth Hunter wringing the air from my lungs. Yes, definitely better than last time, though it didn't take much to knock the consciousness from me.

A tight turn pitched me upright. Two strips of white sand curved into the darkness, past the reach of the headlights. Scrub pine loomed low. Palmetto spines raked the side of the car.

"Jason Oliver, pleased to meet you." A silhouette hand reached over the back of the driver's seat and fluttered until I grasped it in a handshake. "You're a pro, right? Sorry, I don't know your name."

I told him.

"See, Vonnie, I knew he was a pro. Sorry, Kieran, this is Vonnie, the diminutive of Yvonne, even if it carries the same number of syllables."

Yvonne Oliver's hand, degrees warmer than Jason's, lingered in mine before trailing away. The back seat was tight, and I recognized the distinctive curves of an old VW Beetle.

"I'm not great at names," said Jason, "but I remember faces, and I recognized yours from the L.A. Open."

"Where the hell are we?" I said.

"Just a second," said Jason.

He thrust his head over the steering wheel. Enough light reflected back through the windshield to illuminate his Prince Valiant bangs and pixie features. He wrestled the wheel as the Beetle bounced through a series of ruts, hung a hard left, and broke out of the scrub. Across the clearing, flickering torch flames ringed a purple school bus nestled into a wall of palmetto.

"To answer your question in the generic sense, this is home." He eased the Beetle under an awning that dropped from one side of the bus. "In the specific sense, this is a private campground we've come to love. The St. John's River is fifty feet through the brush. Shall we?"

Oliver opened his door, but I grabbed his shoulder before he could slide out.

"Wait a second," I said. "I'm getting my ass kicked in the middle of nowhere, you save me, and you don't even ask what's going on?"

"You lost a bet with those guys and didn't pay up," said Oliver. "It's cool, man. It happens."

"What got you out there?"

"Simple, man. Vonnie told me."

Yvonne Oliver grinned shyly, as if admitting to a harmless prank. Oliver started to get out, but I held fast.

"All right," he said. "We just hit town today. I was checking in with the clubhouse officials. When I got back to the car, Vonnie said she felt something terrible happening nearby. You know her like I know her, you listen when she says she has a feeling. We drove out onto the field. I said, 'Vonnie, this is silly. I don't see anyone out here.' And at that exact moment, I spotted something in the headlights."

"What happened to them?" I said.

"They ran. I didn't get a good look at them because I was more concerned about you. None of my business, but this practice round action can get pretty steep. I know all about it."

"Thanks," I said.

"No problem. Now shall we?" Oliver helped Yvonne squeeze through the small doorway, and then they both helped me.

Fully upright, the first few breaths burned going down. My head lightened, then reasserted itself. The air felt close here, thick and tropical, with the faint scent of a nearby barbecue mixing with the citronella of the torches. Somewhere beneath the riotous chatter of insects, a guitar played carefully, one note at a time.

They climbed into the bus, while I sat on the bench of a foldout metal picnic table. My pants were stained with grass and streaked with grime. I swirled a finger around one ear, and felt sand cascade onto my shoulder. A sudden pain stabbed me in the ribs, then receded into a dull ache.

Oliver clomped down the steps, a ten-pound dumbbell swinging in one hand and a cellular phone in the other. He'd changed into workout clothes that bagged on his skinny but well-defined frame.

"If you don't mind, I'd rather not go back to Sawgrass tonight. You're welcome to stay here, unless you have someone to call." He hunkered down onto the other bench, working his fingers loose.

Given the chance, I'd return to my hotel room, and further down the flow chart, I'd opt for Meg over the Judge. Oliver handed me the cellular and Meg picked up after the third ring. I first secured her promise to come collect me, then parroted directions Oliver gave me between reps of reverse curls.

"Are you at a party?" Meg said.

"Sort of."

I folded the phone and watched Oliver finish another set

of curls with his left hand. He lashed a rubber collar to his forearm, just below the elbow, and pumped his hand four times. A number glowed red on a small L.E.D. readout. Oliver frowned.

"Do any weight work, running, isometrics?" he said.

"Some jogging, when I have the time," I said.

"I do all three, and in precise combination," he said. "The weight work is the hardest to gauge. You want opposing muscles to test at the same tensile strength. Same thing with the analogous muscles on either side of the body's axis."

What the hell was he talking about? Iron pumping for the New Age? No wonder he tripped all over his tongue during that West Coast interview. He seemed genetically incapable of making the simplest statement in fewer than four sentences.

"In other words," he wound up, "I need total concentration during my weight workout, or my axis can shift. You know what happened when the world's axis shifted. We had an Ice Age. People can have Ice Ages, too. Vonnie's inside making you some of her special tea. Do you good until your ride shows."

"I'm a coffee drinker," I said.

"Talk to me after you've had Vonnie's tea."

The bus's interior was remodeled into a railroad apartment, with a galley kitchen hard behind the driver's seat. Yvonne Oliver drew water into a pot, then spooned dried leaves and flowers from a colored tin into an earthen mug shaped vaguely like a human face. Her long, cool Indian print skirt and white cotton blouse with puffed shoulders only added to the effect of her height. She had me by a good two inches, and Oliver, I'd wager, by three or four.

"Make yourself comfortable," she said, a graceful toss of her free hand leading my eye to a lime-green beanbag chair in the living room area.

I hadn't sat in a beanbag chair since college. Purely for nostalgia, I wanted to plunk myself down and feel the little beans reshape themselves around me. But a twinge of pain flared in my ribs, and I decided I'd better stay upright.

A dividing wall doubled as a trophy case built for the hard knocks of life on the road. Screws and garbage bag ties held pictures, magazine covers, and trophies to a corkboard framed with wire mesh rather than glass. Pictures of Jason Oliver posing with counterculture icons, rock stars, and political radicals satirized the usual shots of golf pros flanking ex-Presidents sporting plaid slacks. The magazine covers displayed cartoon renditions of Oliver swinging a golf club in astronaut gear or Buddhist robes. The picture that caught my eye was a photo of Oliver with three elderly black men. They posed as if standing on a tee, when in fact they stood in a cluttered alleyway. Oliver and two of the men leaned casually on their drivers. The fourth squatted deeply to address a golf ball perched on a tee amid broken toys and rusted bedsprings.

The water hissed to a boil. The metallic clinking of Oliver's reps paused briefly as he shifted the dumbbell between hemispheres. Yvonne offered me the mug, which was heavy enough to need both hands. The scent of fresh flowers filled my sinuses.

"Jason rotates the display, but many things never come along." Yvonne pointed to a newspaper photo of Oliver holding a large crystal trophy triumphantly aloft. "That stays in storage. We could redecorate this entire bus for the value of that trophy."

Outside, the clinking stopped again, and didn't resume. I sipped the tea. I didn't so much taste the flavor as see it, the irresistible image being time-lapse film of a huge meadow blooming.

"Wow," I said. "This stuff is legal, I hope."

"Completely," she said. "I gather the flower buds from a field in Kansas each year. Take another sip, but swallow slowly."

The second sip tasted strong, but not as dramatic.

"I named this blend after Jason," she said. "The initial impression differs from the reality. Do you agree?"

"About the tea, anyway." I nodded toward the photo of Oliver and the three men in the alley. "That squat looks familiar. Who is he?"

"Dewey Peek," said Yvonne.

"That's funny," I said. "I never heard of him before Saturday, and now I see him twice within days."

"Where?" said Yvonne.

"Gainesville. Playing at a course named Ironwood. His stance is hard to forget."

"That generation of black golf pros didn't have much equipment to work with growing up." Jason Oliver stood in the galley kitchen, his skin slick with sweat and his face hard from exertion. "Some might have only four or five clubs, so they had to alter their swing or their grip or their stance to turn a six iron into an eight iron, or vice versa.

"That picture was taken back in '88, when I helped Dewey and some of his cohorts teach golf to inner city kids in Jersey City and Newark." He looked at Yvonne as if sharing a bad memory. "I took a lot of ribbing for that project, and I had friends on the Tour back in those days. The Tour intimated

I was wasting my time. What do these kids know about golf, what do they care? They'll never get to play. That was the attitude. Maybe so, I said, but there is more to golf than country clubs and tournaments and money. You learn patience, strategy, the essential unfairness of life."

"How did the project turn out?" I said.

"It died," said Oliver. "But not for lack of effort."

A light flashed outside the window as a car bounced into the clearing. I gulped down the rest of the tea, its sweet warmth soothing my aching ribs from inside. Yvonne bid me good-bye and hung back, while Oliver escorted me down the steps. Meg stared over the steering wheel, her jaw halfway to the floorboards. Hard to tell what appalled her. Oliver, the bus, or the grass stains on my shirt and pants.

"I'm slated for a practice round tomorrow at ten," said Oliver. "Join me and we'll talk."

"Ow! Goddammit, Meg!"

"You said to tighten it."

"Not that tight. You'll puncture my damn lung."

"Then take care of this yourself."

She scrabbled away. The bandage slowly unwound from my chest.

"Sorry, Meg. Let's try it again."

"Only if you promise not to say a word. And no whimpering, either."

I promised. We resumed the position, me sitting on the edge of the bed and Meg kneeling behind me. I held up my arms as she rewrapped the bandage.

"I once dated the captain of a hurling club," said Meg. She tugged hard; I bit my lower lip. "He cared only about his responsibility toward the lads. Broken arm, can't let the lads down. Broken nose, can't let the lads down. Split skull, can't let the lads down. The lads, the lads, the lads. You'd think he led the town militia against armed invaders instead of playing a silly game. You're just like him."

"But, Meg, this is my—"

She yanked hard, and the word *livelihood* disintegrated into a scream of pain.

"There," she said. "Finished."

I walked gingerly to the full length mirror in the bathroom. With the bandage tight as a corset, I looked even slimmer than usual. I turned my head left, then right. Each time, my whole body followed.

Ellis's pills were gone, but I carried a bottle of ibuprofen in my travel case of toiletries. I knocked two caplets into the palm of my hand and tried about six different ways to bend my torso enough to slurp water from the tap. I finally accomplished this by spreading my legs about as wide as my adductor muscles allowed. Great. I wondered how I'd perform other amazing feats today, like crouching to line up a putt.

Playing a practice round with Jason Oliver sounded like a good idea at the time I accepted the invite. About twenty minutes later, it seemed like total idiocy. We weren't halfway back to Sawgrass—and me relating to Meg how Tommy Garth Hunter had danced on my chest—when the dull ache, punctuated by the occasional sharp jab, changed into a constant jab tempered only by the occasional pause for the dull ache. By the time we reached the hotel, sleeping with Meg became exactly that, sleeping with Meg. No euphemism intended. I crawled into bed, contorting into a position that minimized the pain. Meg nuzzled and nestled, with a lot of frontal skin contact that only added to my dire straits. I rode the bed all night, drifting off to sleep and jerking awake whenever a rib nerve fired. I needed a full day's rest to have any chance to heal. But the longer I stared at the ceiling, the more the Olivers bothered me.

The Olivers might turn me into a tea drinker, but they couldn't convince me Yvonne mystically sensed my wrestling match with Hunter five-hundred yards away. And I didn't believe in coincidence. Jason Oliver didn't happen to drive back from whatever planet he inhabited between tournaments and just happen to break up a fight. No, the more I replayed the night—what a luxury to possess the power of memory—the more I believed the Olivers tailed either me or Tommy Garth Hunter. So I strapped myself together, popped some analgesics, and prepared to take Jason Oliver's measure in a round of golf.

CHAPTER
FIFTEEN

I doddered onto the practice range an hour early. After loosening up whatever muscles and ligaments still operated without pain, I performed drastic surgery on my golf swing. I widened my stance, choked down on the grip, shortened the backswing, and reduced tempo to slow motion.

"Not bad," I told my chief doubter.

In reality, I felt like an overstuffed suitcase on the verge of splitting a seam.

It took some fiddling before this swing started to shape decent shots. The balls looked comical in the air, chugging like steam-powered Vernean contraptions, instead of zipping like aerodynamically dimpled orbs. Yet somehow, they managed to stay aloft long enough to deliver quasi-professional results. Meg may have questioned my sanity, but not my resourcefulness.

"I'll corset you everyday if this works," she said.

I had just watched my last drive drift to earth, when Woody

Harrington slammed his electric cart to a stop at the edge of the tee box.

"Kieran, what the hell happened?" He jumped out of the cart and brushed past Meg. She sneered and started assembling my clubs.

"When?" I said.

"Last night."

"I met up with some of the guys," I said. "And our discussion got out of hand."

"It was a fight, Kieran. That's what I've been told. Who was it?"

"I didn't see. It was dark."

"Did you recognize any voices?" he said, tartly.

"Come to think of it, there wasn't much discussion," I said.

"Was it about Jason Oliver?"

I said nothing, trying to slow him down. Woody acted like a man whose responsibilities ganged up on him. Normally laconic to the point of drowsiness, he barked his questions on the heels of my not-so-forthcoming answers. Usually a neat dresser, though not to the razor-sharp corporate lines of other staffers, he seemed a bit unmade. A patch of two-days' growth rode his Adam's apple. Sweat darkened the armpits of his shirt, despite the loosened knot of his tie. Dried mud dotted the inseams of his pants cuffs.

"Goddammit, Kieran," he said. "I don't expect you to defend the guy's honor."

"It won't happen again," I said.

"Better not. I'm up against a real time problem with your suspension."

"I thought that was taken care of."

"Who told you that?" said Woody.

"Judge Inglisi," I said. I related the Judge's take on the meeting, winding up with the prediction I wouldn't be suspended.

"That's not quite accurate."

"The meeting didn't go that well?" I asked.

"The Judge talked, we listened. He made sense to me, but not to everyone else. That's beside the point, anyway, because we're beholden to the Policy Board. They thought the threats were a weak attempt at a very unfunny joke."

"What about the Commissioner?"

"Who the hell knows?" said Woody. "He's due back tomorrow, though I'm certain the Board's already had his ear by now. The hierarchy doesn't make for reasoned decisions. I can't tell you some of the stuff that goes on. It defies belief."

"When will I know?" I said.

"Don't give up yet," said Woody. "I'm dragging my end the best I can. If we get to Thursday, the Commissioner almost has to defer until next week."

"Meanwhile, I'll lay low and not call attention to myself."

"That would help." Woody motioned me around to the other side of the cart. Meg waved, mouthing that she'd meet me on the first tee.

"I get the sense," Woody continued confidentially, "that the Board is less interested in bullying you into a suspension than in learning whatever you forgot."

"The hospital records prove I have amnesia."

"I know, I know," said Woody. "But remembering or not remembering why you were there doesn't change the fact you were there. Why don't you give me something, anything, an innocuously plausible scenario to tell the Board."

"Where does that get me?"

"To Thursday. Maybe to Sunday."

"And you get my pairing with Jason Oliver," I said.

"Don't throw my self-interest in my face. This is the biggest tournament of the year. You do want to play in it."

"What happens if I tell you people one thing, and it turns out I visited Cindy Moran for a different reason. Who saves me from the Board after I've lied to it?"

"What kind of different reason?" said Woody.

"I don't know. Something nonsexual."

A cacophony of shouts rose from the other end of the range. A photographer and a reporter bolted past us, their credentials flying.

"What the hell?" said Woody.

"Jason Oliver," I said, spotting sunlight glistening on the Prince Valiant haircut.

"Shit, when did he get in?"

"Last night," I said.

Woody jumped into the cart, hit the accelerator, and then slammed the brakes.

"How the hell do you know?" he said.

"He saved my ass from the boys."

I watched Woody wade into the crowd, peeling away bodies and finally fashioning a human barricade of marshals between the press and Jason Oliver's tee box. Jason pulled a glove onto his hand, his posture showing total cool, even at a distance. He flashed a wave that told me he wouldn't be long at warm ups. I rotated my body, and started a painful trek to the first tee.

The PGA Tour designed the main golf course at the Sawgrass Players Club as a showcase for the Tour's annual Players

Championship. Stare down the first hole, and you see the Florida golf staples of sand, water, grass, with a lone palm standing apart from the tree line at the start of the fairway. Turn around—slowly, if your ribs are bandaged as severely as mine—and you see something not so common: an amphitheater big enough to hold thousands of spectators rising up on mounds of terraced grass. Golf commentators have described these mounds as "tiered wedding cakes" or "prehistoric burial pyres." Today, with Jason Oliver striding onto the tee, they reminded me of the bleachers of the Roman Colosseum, circa 50 A.D.

"Crazy," said Oliver, staring through orange-tinted aviator glasses at the marshals ringing the tee like a phalanx of centurions. A few feet away, Woody Harrington screamed into a walkie-talkie.

"Send more. I want twenty-five marshals following them the whole round. Make that thirty."

A group of pros filed onto a section of tier opposite the tee markers. They stood as motionless as a military regiment, their arms folded across their chests and their faces grim behind sunglasses and beneath straw hats. A comical sight, really, if they meant to mask their identities. Any golf fan could pick out Ned Nelson's soft paunch and Sam Young's diminutive stature. Chris Jennings wore a bandage on his right elbow, which meant I wasn't the only one scarred from last night's encounter.

Woody Harrington didn't share the humor. He circled Oliver and me into a tight huddle.

"Do you see what I see?" he said.

Oliver cupped a hand over his eyes.

"A poor attempt at grassroots Marxism," he said.

"What?" said Woody.

"They've dressed in an obvious attempt to sublimate their individual identities in a demonstration of group solidarity," said Oliver.

"Don't try to con me, Jason," said Woody. "What I see over there are some of the Tour's best players acting like jerks, and what I see over there are a whole lot of golf fans and sportswriters watching them act like jerks. I also see the manpower I need to expend so you can play a round of golf."

Oliver swung his gaze here, there, and there, taking in each segment of the scene Woody painted.

"I don't see a problem," he said.

"You don't see a problem?" said Woody "You don't see how embarrassing this is to the Tour?"

"The Tour is not immune to folly," said Oliver.

"You take potshots at the Tour, you disappear for a month, and now you come back here and expect all of us to act as if nothing happened."

"I said what I said," said Oliver. "You know the old expression, 'fuck 'em if they can't take a joke.'"

"They aren't joking," said Woody.

"I saw them pummeling Kieran last night all because he drew the short straw to play with me." Oliver brushed past Woody and hoisted the driver from his golf bag. "I know they are serious, but they aren't brave enough to try something in the daylight. That's why we don't have a problem."

Oliver backed up, stuck a tee in the ground, and placed a ball on top. Woody stood directly in front of him, arms akimbo, legs slightly spread. The only movement was the lick of his pants legs flapping in the breeze. Oliver fanned the turf with a couple of practice swings. From my angle, I could see behind his glasses. His eyes focused beyond Woody, on the narrow avenue of safety between the large palm looming left and the shining, sun-dappled lake elbowing in from the right.

"You don't know what you did," said Woody.

"Yes I do," said Oliver. "Believe me, I do."

He lay the big orange persimmon head behind the ball, rubbing its sole plate in the grass. He planted his right foot, then his left.

"Woody," said Oliver. "If you're not going to get out of my way, spread your feet a little wider and give me half a chance to knock this between your legs."

A silence descended. Even the wind died. Oliver waggled the club once, twice. "Kieran," Meg whispered. But I hardly heard. Like everyone else in the amphitheater—the marshals, the press, the fans, the pros—I was mesmerized by this macabre game of chicken.

Time stretched, elongating a single moment. Oliver went completely still. His left arm tensed. His left knee knocked slightly as he began his forward press. Time stretched even longer. He was past volition, I knew, like a missile silo with its fail-safe system shut down. He drew back the club, paused at the top of his backswing, and uncoiled with the same terrible beauty of a python strike.

Woody dove left. The ball jumped off the persimmon with a solid thock, whistling, a white blur that hugged the ground. Woody yelped, reached back to grab his calf. I swear the ball clipped him before climbing into the sky.

"You're nuts, Oliver, nuts!" Woody screamed, as two marshals helped him to his feet. He limped to his cart, and plopped himself behind the wheel. He seethed, his eyes wild with anger and fear. The silence stayed thick until Woody kicked off the footbrake and reversed up the path.

"Damn," Oliver said to his caddie. "I only hit him because he moved."

My tee shot was far less dramatic. Soaring slowly, almost defying gravity, it curved around the lone palm and skipped into the first cut of rough about 240 yards downrange. The pros dispersed, but about a hundred fans and reporters broke from the mounds to follow us. Add our escort of thirty-odd marshals, and we looked like an intimidating force. Oliver settled into step alongside me.

"She your steady?" He nodded toward Meg, who walked twenty yards ahead with Oliver's caddie. "Not bad. Does she know golf?"

"She was an amateur champ in Ireland."

"I had a steady until a couple of years ago," said Oliver. A reporter shouted a question over the gallery rope, and Oliver waved it off. "Couldn't handle the expense anymore. This kid wrote to me a few months back and offered to caddy for me in the Players because he lives nearby. Free, too, because he was a fan. I thought about having Vonnie caddy for me. She doesn't know the game, but she has a good sense when I'm about to make a mistake. Too dangerous for her out here now."

"Especially with you trying to hit a driver right through Tour staffers," I said.

"I was trying to pop it over his head, but I heeled it. Good thing he ducked, otherwise ..." Oliver stopped walking, shuddered powerfully, and picked up the pace. "So what do you want to play for?"

"Play for?" I said. "You mean money?"

"Come on, Kieran, you're not one of those jokers who hits six balls on each hole, are you?"

Six balls on each hole? I'd be lucky to bat one around without my side splitting. We haggled and haggled, agreed that the first hole didn't count, then haggled some more. With some effort, I managed to keep the stakes down to a straight seventeen hole match for fifty dollars. For somebody just scraping by on the Tour, a whole lot of people had been after my money lately. Maybe I should reconsider the voluntary suspension idea.

The game on, Oliver withdrew into an envelope of concentration. No antics, no explications of weird theories, no bodily assaults on members of the Tour hierarchy. No comments to the media or mugging with the fans, who sloughed off gradually in search of better entertainment than a has-been and a rookie squabbling over a Ben Franklin note.

The course is laid out on a grand scale. The huge spectator mounds and thick stands of palms and pines isolate many holes from the rest of the course. But occasionally, another twosome or threesome would come into view, and I could feel their eyes burning across the distance. By the time we reached the sixth green, our gallery had dwindled to only the marshals. We ended that hole dead even and walked around a large, moated spectator mound to the next tee. This was about the farthest point from the clubhouse, and it felt particularly lonely this Tuesday morning.

"Glad to see them," Oliver said as six marshals climbed to post themselves atop the mound. "Someone could shoot you out here and get away easily."

I stayed even with Oliver for one more hole before the length of the course took its toll on my rickety swing. On eight, a long par three, my thinly clipped tee shot augured into a pond well short of the green. On nine, the longest par five on the course, my second shot burrowed into rough as thick as salad. I needed two choppy swings to regain the fairway, and then, from about two hundred yards out, floated an iron shot into a sand trap.

After finishing the ninth hole, Oliver told the captain of our marshal battalion we planned to stop for lunch. The captain sent most of the troops on break and reserved us an escort of six. We crossed a footbridge to an open air restaurant built on an island in a small lake bordering the practice range. Oliver chose a corner table right out on the water. The six marshals milled about fifteen feet away. These were middle-aged men who volunteered their time and laid out cash for uniforms that looked silly anywhere off the golf course. They expected to direct spectators across fairway cross-walks, or to lift *Quiet* signs when a player stood over a putt. They didn't sign on to guard two Tour pariahs.

"Admit it, Kieran, you're surprised," said Oliver after the waitress took our orders.

"About what?"

"About me. Come on, you can say it."

"Say what?"

"Okay, I'll say it for you," he said. "First, you throw out that asshole stunt I pulled on number one tee. I shouldn't have done that to Woody. But throw that out, and forget whatever else you've heard about me, and what do you see?"

"I'd say you're a pretty serious player," I said.

"Thank you. I don't preach, I don't criticize, I don't polemicize."

"Until now."

Oliver smiled. "I can still get into the game I fell in love with as a kid. The physics, the ballistics, the aerodynamics. Making something fly and land where you want it. I don't need to get into the romance of a golf course in the early morning."

"I know all that," I said.

"I'm sure you do," said Oliver. "But I've always been cranky, right from a very young age. I'm given to brooding moods. I take the opposite view from the majority, whether or not I feel passion for the topic. Hear that?"

At that precise moment, the blimp moved in front of the sun. A soft breeze raised a chill on my arms and neck. The blimp engines whirred.

"Not that," said Oliver. "Them."

A few tables away, an elderly couple traded opposing views on artificial cholesterol-free eggs. Neither heard what the other was saying.

"If I'm sitting here alone," Oliver said, "I can't listen without mentally taking a side in their debate. Same thing with Sawgrass. This is our house. This is our tournament. But I can't help taking the opposite side."

"Which is?"

"You really want to know?" he said.

"If you can fit it in during lunch break," I said.

"Crazy, man." He hunched low over the table, his voice descending into a suitably hushed tone. "Golf is the last pure sport. Just you, your equipment, and the golf course. Make the right choice, execute, and you win. Make the wrong choice, make a bad swing, and you lose. No blaming a team-mate or the referees. It's only you.

"Nowadays a corporate ethos dominates. You don't need

to go for broke to win. Second, third, tenth, twentieth place earns you a nice paycheck. You win enough money, you keep your Tour card, and you come back next year."

"I'm out here because of my Tour card," I said.

"So am I," said Oliver. "But I take opposing views, remember? Golf's match with corporate America was made in hell. One day Golf will return to its purest form and be played on vast tracts of barren ground shaped by wind and rain and sheep huddled against the elements. People will look back on these days of automated sprinkler systems and corporate hospitality tents as symbols of a misguided era. If you think I'm talking about a revolution, well, maybe you're right."

"And you want to hurry it along," I said.

"I have no illusion about that. The power belongs to the pampered few, and they won't give it up easily. No, I don't expect to see any of these changes. But I want people a generation from now to look back and say, 'That Jason Oliver was right.'"

"And so you give provocative interviews," I said.

"I stand by my words," he said. "But the sad truth is I've become marginalized. Once upon a time, I was a breath of fresh air out here. Now I open my mouth, and the reaction is, 'Oh, him again.' Sure the players are steamed. You can attest to that. But the Tour won't even dignify that interview with a response. It certainly won't suspend me."

"Wish I had your luck," I said.

"I guess you do," Oliver laughed.

I saw no purpose in explaining Woody Harrington's gymnastics in pairing Oliver with me for the first two rounds, or the subtle irony that Oliver's marginalization might protect me for another week. People like Oliver tended to dismiss any evidence that didn't corroborate their world views. No matter how compelling the evidence and how silly the views.

The waitress brought our food, and we dug in.

"How did you know I was out there last night?" I said.

"I told you. Vonnie sensed trouble."

I gave him my best dubious stare, honed from listening to too many lies coming from the witness stand.

"Okay," said Oliver, "she says she thinks we should be friends. We can help each other."

"How?"

"I'm about to be sued," he said.

"For what?"

"Defamation. A group of players banded together into an association and are threatening to sue me because of that interview."

"I can't represent you," I said. "You wouldn't want me anyway. I'm so rusty."

Oliver waved away the suggestion.

"I have a lawyer. I need a defense."

"You didn't identify anyone in the interview," I said.

"Doesn't matter. My lawyer tells me the association has some esoteric theory about how my words damaged them. A class action, he called it. And since they say it directly affects their livelihood, they don't need to prove as much to win."

In layman's terms, Oliver had described a legal doctrine called defamation per se. In even more layman's terms, defamation per se protected a person's livelihood from false statements. You can't compete in the marketplace by lying about your competitors' products or skills.

I doubted a defamation lawsuit based on that interview stood much chance of succeeding. But I believed a group of

pros mad enough to attack me might file one. During my
years as a lawyer, I'd defended some crazy lawsuits and was
hired to file even crazier ones. Allowing psychotics access to
court is a small down payment on the total cost of a free
society. Or so the theory goes.

"Nobody uses cocaine," said Oliver, "a few players drink,
but more than a few use beta blockers. I just need proof of
one."

"What kind of proof?" I said.

"Something in writing, a bogus prescription, a bottle of
pills. Anything. Because if I'm telling the truth, I can't be
sued."

"Why ask me for help?" I said.

"I think we both know."

"Tell me again."

Oliver lifted his head to check for the nearest set of ears.

"Because I saved your butt last night," he said.

"And what about Vonnie thinking we should be friends?"

"She has her own ideas. You'll have to ask her."

"I'll think about it," I said.

We finished lunch quickly and quietly.

"You know, I almost won the Players one year," Oliver
said as we made our way through the thickening Tuesday
afternoon crowd to the tenth tee. "Came to seventeen need-
ing two pars. I stood over that tee shot and tried to fool myself
into thinking I was one shot back, not one shot up. You're
body acts differently depending on whether you're winning
or losing. It's a hormonal thing, proven by scientists. I almost
fooled myself. But just before I took the club back, for a split
fraction of a second like one frame of a movie, I saw myself
kissing the trophy on the eighteenth green. I chunked that

shot right into the water. Finished with a double bogey and a par to lose by one."

My ribs ached, my concentration was blown to shards. If I had any sense, I would have detoured into the clubhouse and plunked myself down in the sauna. Oliver must have lost his concentration, too. Though every swing felt like my last, and every shot corkscrewed like a misguided missile, I whittled down his lead to a tie by the seventeenth tee.

The seventeenth hole at Sawgrass is golf's Kilroy, finding its way into myriad television commercials and gracing everything from beer cans to credit cards. The image is at once dramatic and serene. A round green shored by a railroad-tie bulkhead seemingly drifts in the middle of a blue lagoon. People call it an island green, which isn't accurate in the strict geographic sense since a spit of grass tethers it to the mainland. But stand on the tee with the spring winds swirling and three clubs in your hands and doubt in your mind, and the strict geographic sense becomes a ludicrous exercise in semantics.

On a calm day, and in trim health, I would use a nine iron to cover the 135 yards from the tee to the pin. But with a stiff wind in my face and my ribs ablaze, I dropped down to a seven iron, and then, in an excess of caution, to a six. Meg looked askance, and I responded with an I-know-what-I'm-doing wave of the hand. Standing over the ball, I blocked out all extraneous thought. Nothing out there but green and calm air. No wind, no water. No shifted axis, no hormonal imbalance. Just take the club back, return it to the ball, and follow through with my hands at the target.

Golf may or may not recapitulate life. I'll leave that question to the philosophers at the major golf publications. But both golf and life are subject to irony. Despite my bum ribs, I made a most perfect swing. The ball zipped off the clubface, flying straight on line to the pin. It was still climbing to the apex of its flight when the stiff wind suddenly calmed. I last saw the ball sailing over the Coca-Cola scoreboard about forty yards beyond the green.

We finished eighteen before a fairly large crowd sunning itself on the surrounding mounds. A buzz filled the air, as if everyone anticipated a reprise of Oliver's first tee antics. He didn't oblige. I peeled fifty bucks off my rapidly dwindling supply of cash. He handed the money directly over to his caddie.

"We'll talk," he said before heading toward the clubhouse. That was the extent of our back nine conversation.

I promised Meg I would return to the hotel and treat my ribs to a heating pad. But when I reached the contestants parking lot, I found my favorite teenager sunbathing on the hood of my car.

"Do you exist?" I said. "Or are you a medieval manifestation of the devil?"

"Huh?"

"Never mind. Who wants a piece of me now?"

"Uncle Dan'l. He's waiting at his house. Here's the directions."

CHAPTER
SIXTEEN

I hung a left out of the Players Club, wondering if the world was about to shift, or if I'd just get my head bashed in again. I stopped at the Marsh Landing gatehouse and showed the guard my I.D. These gated communities are springing up all over the country, but are particularly popular in north Florida. Each one features at least one golf course and, with progress born of one-upsmanship, a steadily escalating package of amenities. Sometime by the middle of the next century, the average gated community will resemble a Renaissance Italian city-state. With wars fought as golf matches.

The guard phoned ahead for clearance, then waved me through. Fifty yards past the gate house, Marsh Landing grabbed me. A few years ago in Milton, a developer tried to shoehorn a country club into a strip of land on the Long Island Sound. Environmentalists cried "land rape," which brought a backlash from feminists but also raised enough of a stir to sink the deal. If building a golf course is land rape, Marsh Landing was land seduction. The developer hardly disturbed the natural beauty of the tall pine forests, the rolling hammocks, the tea-colored lakes, and the lazy streams. Birds wheeled overhead. Turtles regulated their body temperatures on sunny logs. Otters cavorted in roadside ponds. The homes, even the large ones, barely intruded.

My destination was a hacienda-styled airplane hangar backed up to the Intracoastal Waterway. I parked behind a spanking new Lincoln Town Car with a vanity plate that read "Uncle D." The three-tone door chime summoned a maid. I followed her through a marble foyer, a dining room-cum-art gallery, and a gameroom filled with mint-condition pinball machines, before breaking out into a poolside lanai. A ceiling fan beat the air. Stacks of paper on a teak desk fluttered beneath paperweights. Winged golf balls streaked across the screen of a laptop computer, while a fax machine kicked on. The first page to tumble out showed the unmistakable composition of a legal complaint.

The pool was shaped like a pitching wedge, with the shaft three lanes wide and a jacuzzi for the clubhead. Grass sloped down from the pebbled deck to a stand of banana trees lining the banks of the Intracoastal.

Uncle Dan'l lolled in the jacuzzi, his brown knees and brown belly breaking the surface of the foam, a beat-up old golf hat tilted forward on his head to shade the sun from his eyes. One fleshy arm stretched out along the lip of the jacuzzi, its hand curled around a frosted highball glass. The other gripped a paperback, his thumb holding his place in the swollen pages.

We traded the usual pleasantries. I declined a transparently false invite for a dip in the pool. Out on the waterway, a cigarette boat powered down. A couple of pelicans bobbed in the wave running off the hull as the boat chugged through the No Wake zone along Uncle Dan'l's dock.

"What'd you call yourself when you practiced?" he said.

"I don't follow," I said.

"Did you call yourself a lawyer or an attorney? I always suspect a fellow who makes a big show out of calling himself an attorney." Uncle Dan'l closed one eye and cocked his head. "Nah, I'll bet you're like me, and called yourself a lawyer."

I grunted.

"That's good because I just want to set here and pretend we're back in my law office, jawing like a couple of old country lawyers."

He climbed up two steps until most of him was out of the water. Wrinkled and sagging, tanned and wet, he looked like a turtle without a shell. I dragged a chair close, steeling myself for the metaphysical nightmare of two lawyers talking hypotheticals instead of specifics.

"I understand someone's been making inquiries about where a certain golfer may have been last Thursday afternoon," said Uncle Dan'l. "For the benefit of whoever may be making those inquiries, let me explain that golfer's activities.

"Going on about a year now, this golfer's been having an affair with the wife of a certain sporting goods company's CEO. Surprised? Well, this golfer may be a top-shelf talent, but what he does with a golf club can't compare with what he does with his pecker. Or so I've been told. Now the lady, who lives in Clearwater, was at home keeping the fires warm while her hubby preened at the Orlando Golf Expo during week in question. The golfer and she arrange a tryst, but he can't jump in one of those courtesy cars. He might just as

well announce himself with a bullhorn. So he arranges to
borrow a less conspicuous auto, services the lady, and returns
to Bay Hill that night. Innocent enough, except it gets ticklish
if he is ever asked to account for his time. He can't, not
without dislocating a whole bevy of people, including himself.
Now the golfer may know about these inquiries, but he
doesn't understand their full significance."

"He doesn't?" I said. "What about last night?"

"I know nothing about last night," said Uncle Dan'l. "And,
Kieran, you're doing a poor job of playing lawyer by inter-
jecting your personal self into this.

"Now, going back, let's suppose that a few weeks ago, a
different lady, not the one who knows the golfer, contacts a
certain lawyer and says she has a certain document the golfer
might want to keep secret. Discussions ensue via late night
phone calls, all generated by her because she wishes to remain
anonymous. Numbers are bandied about, but no agreement
is reached. The negotiations become sporadic. The lawyer
suspects she is losing interest, perhaps bluffing. Then, last
Wednesday, the calls cease altogether."

"Maybe the lawyer is right," I said. "Maybe it was a bluff
all along, and he's called her on it."

"Maybe," said Uncle Dan'l. "But this lawyer is careful.
He wants to protect this certain golfer from losing a very
valuable asset. He's so careful, he's willing to offer fifty thousand dollars for that document."

"How would he extend that offer if the woman no longer
calls him?" I said.

"He makes his own inquiries. He puts the right words in
the right ears."

Uncle Dan'l pushed through the jacuzzi and breast-stroked

a deliberate lap down the pool's center lane. He knew he'd just put the right words in the right ear, and wanted to give me time to mull the offer. I didn't doubt him for a second. He could drag himself out of the water, unlock a wall safe somewhere in the hacienda, and assemble a few bricks of cash on the coffee table. Made me glad I left the affidavit back at the hotel.

I met him at the end of the pool.

"Is there any truth to the secret that certain pro wants to protect?" I said.

Uncle Dan'l laughed. "You know, every few years somebody claims to see the skunk-ape nosing around Fort Lauderdale. Every few years somebody spots a sea serpent slithering up the St. John's. And every few years somebody accuses a golf pro or two of having artificial nerves of steel. That's about how true it is. But it has the smell of plausibility, which makes it truer than not."

Meg and I met for a late dinner in one of the hotel restaurants. She assumed I spent the hours after the practice round in dutiful R. & R., and I didn't disabuse her of the assumption. Our conversation focused on ribs: my sore ones and the hot slab of baby-backs oozing barbecue sauce on the plate in front of her. Posthumously wrestling with livestock, crustaceans, and other upper links of the food chain didn't intrigue me, no matter what the payoff to the palate. Hence I avoided whole lobsters, whole chickens, clams, trout, and ribs.

While Meg nibbled, I burned with the words Uncle Dan'l put in my ear. He knew I had the affidavit. He knew it before I knew it, which was why he started circling me on the putting green last Friday night. He'd been watching, charting my course, plotting my destination, just as he had back on the mini-tour. The alibi he'd concocted for Tommy Garth Hunter almost too cleverly stitched together strands of information he guessed I already uncovered. Fact number one: Tommy Garth Hunter is having an affair with the wife of his sponsor's CEO. Fact number two: Tommy Garth Hunter borrowed a car Thursday afternoon. The conclusion: Tommy Garth Hunter drove the car west to Clearwater instead of north to Gainesville. But Uncle Dan'l never said that; he just allowed me to draw the inference.

Woody Harrington would want to know this. Hell, McGriff would want to know it, too. But just enough doubt nagged at me. Jason Oliver needed that affidavit as badly as Tommy Garth Hunter. He'd been on the road for a month. Where the hell had he been last Thursday? But Oliver hadn't offered me fifty grand. Maybe the last vestiges of my friendship with Hunter had changed me into a holdout juror clinging to any idiot reason to acquit a defendant.

We met the Judge on our way out. He and Meg exchanged the usual sharp hellos, five seconds of awkward silence ensued, and then Meg allowed she'd go on ahead.

"Ahead to where?" the Judge said after she departed.

"To my suite. The shower in her motel room is on the blink. No hot water."

The Judge thumped my chest with the back of his hand. I gritted my teeth, hoping he would interpret my grimace as a horny leer. He'd spent the day sightseeing and didn't know about the fight. If he did, he'd surmise I hadn't called McGriff. When the shock waves stopped reverberating, I heard the tail end of a critique of my adolescent development.

"Times were tough back then," I said.

"I'm talking present day."

"I'm having a weak stretch."

"You're having a weak year. How will you explain this to Georgina?"

"I'm not, unless I need to."

The Judge shook his head. "I heard what happened on the first tee today. I try to get away for a few hours to take the river air at Jacksonville Landing, and I hear it piped over the local TV feed."

I gave the Judge a less exaggerated account. No, Oliver hadn't actually threaded the tee shot between Woody Harrington's legs. And no, neither of us had lined wedge shots at Woody's rapidly escaping golf cart.

"Thought it was a crock," said the Judge. "What did McGriff say when you told him what we found?"

What *we* found? "He was impressed," I said quickly. "What about my suspension?"

"All quiet, which sounds promising," said the Judge. "Get through tomorrow, and we're home."

No point telling him Woody's take on the meeting. Deflating the Judge's ego was almost as easy as popping a blimp with a sewing needle.

Up in the hotel, I found the door to my room ajar. A snatch of memory overtook me, and I stood at Cindy Moran's apartment. Music played on a distant stereo, a nearby air conditioner rattled. I knocked hard. Unlatched, the door swung back. "It's open," she called from inside. I stepped through, my sun-blind eyes slowly adjusting to the darkened apartment.

"What are you doing here?" said Cindy. She came out of

her bedroom, clutching her purse and dressed in the little bitty skirt and blouse McGriff had described.

"We need to talk," I said. "I know what you're doing, and I want no part of it."

Cindy took in my protest, her face expanding into a sickly sweet smile of triumph. In that instant, the front door creaked as it swung again.

"You want no part of it," she cackled. "Too late. It's already done."

Then her eyes widened. And then—

I snapped back to the present, and pushed open the door.

"Meg?" I called.

No answer. Complete silence. The air inside was slightly closer than in the corridor, laced with a hint of bath fragrance.

"Meg?"

I crossed the tiny foyer, probing with my ears for any sound. Through a doorway, the bedroom opened into view. The drawers were pulled, clothes littered the floor, blankets hung from the bed.

"Meg!"

I flung open the bathroom door. The air was sweet and thick. Steam misted the mirrors. Water dripped from the showerhead. Soggy footprints dimpled the bath mat.

A thud sounded in the bedroom. I rushed out, stopped. No one visible. A breeze lifted the balcony curtain. I edged toward it, careful not to turn my back to the center of the room. I reached the sliding glass. Outside, lights played through the gauze, fuzzy but without shadow or silhouette.

I took a deep breath and swept open the curtain. No one on the balcony.

Another thud sounded, followed by some scraping from a

closet across the room. I padded around the bed, kicking free the strewn clothing that tangled about my feet. More scraping. Another thud. I zeroed in on the direction. Yes, definitely from the closet.

The door was open a crack. A glint, like light reflected in a cat's eye, flashed and faded. I stood to the side, off line from the crack. I cupped my hand over the knob, took a deep breath, braced myself as if addressing my first tee shot of the day. Then I grabbed and pulled.

Meg cowered in a corner of the closet.

She was soaked, trembling, naked except for a damp towel held across her breasts. I lifted her out, and we tumbled back onto the bed. For a brief moment, I thought she played a sex game, erotic hide-and-seek. But there was no passion in her fingers raking my back, in her pelt of slick hair insisting at my jaw, in her legs locked around mine. Her voice made only guttural sounds.

I extricated myself. I sat her upright, wiped a long squiggle of hair from her face, and held her jaw in my hands until her eyes fully focused on mine.

"It was a . . . he was . . . the room."

"Meg, calm down."

"Out there . . . after the shower . . ."

"Meg, it's okay. Take a deep breath."

Her body gave one big shudder, and then relaxed.

"A man came in here," she said. "After my shower."

"Who?"

"I don't know."

I reached across the bed and phoned the reception desk to send hotel security immediately.

"Take it from the beginning, Meg. Slowly." I scooped my

bathrobe from a heap on the floor and helped her into it. She stuck tight against me, no doubt drawing strength and courage from my rock-solid presence.

"After my shower, I went out to the balcony for a puff of night air," she said. The hitch in her voice faded as she spoke. "I heard the door open, and then I heard movement in the bedroom, like the sound of drawers opening and shutting. I naturally thought it was you. Fortunately, I didn't prance in with wild abandon. I peeked through the drapes and saw this stranger rifling through your clothes."

"What did he look like?"

"He was big. Your height, but meatier. He had bushy hair and dark eyebrows shaped funny." She made wave motions with both hands.

"Like ram's horns?" I said.

"That's it."

"Was his hair streaked gray?" I said.

"How did you know?" said Meg.

Before I could answer, the cavalry arrived. The Marriott's version, anyway, which comprised two men wearing gray blazers, blue slacks, and thick-soled black shoes. One inspected the scene, while the other loomed over Meg and me with a notebook at the ready. Meg repeated her account to the point of describing the intruder.

"Did you ever see the man before?" said the detective.

"No, but—"

I squeezed her shoulder enough to derail what I thought she'd say.

"But what?" said the detective.

"Well, many people see us, Kieran and myself, on the golf course."

"Oh, so you're saying this was someone who saw you on the golf course today? That would be the Players Club?" The detective scribbled hastily.

"I meant we are visible, but the people in the galleries are often not," said Meg.

"Did you see the perpetrator before, or didn't you?" said the detective.

"I did not," said Meg.

The detective shook his head in confusion, made a big "X" on his pad, and flipped the page. "Then what?"

"He seemed very angry," said Meg, "the way he tossed Kieran's clothes. I felt he expected to find something, but his expectations were not being met."

"You keep any cash around?" the detective asked me.

"I carry it all with me," I said.

"The man left the room," continued Meg. "I waited until I thought he was gone before coming back inside. But he must only have gone as far as the foyer. I heard him returning and dove into the closet. I was petrified because I thought he saw me."

A commotion interrupted as the other detective tried to bar Woody Harrington from the room. Woody flashed a set of credentials, and the detective went meek.

"Kieran," said Woody, barging in and stopping short in the mess. "What the hell happened?"

"Someone broke in. Gave Meg a scare. What're you doing here?"

"The desk called up to headquarters," said Woody. "We have a relationship with the hotel, and we like to know if something happens to one of our people."

"Can we continue?" said the detective with the notebook.

"Sure. Sorry," said Woody. He arched one eyebrow just enough for me to catch it.

"You were in the closet, ma'am?" said the detective.

"I thought he might see me," said Meg, "because I didn't close the door completely and a sliver of light fell across me at the knees. Fortunately, he didn't look into the closet."

"What did he look like?" said the detective.

Meg described the intruder, using my ram's horn expression when it came to his eyebrows.

"Then what?" said the detective.

"He tore off the bedcovers, lifted the pillows, and then got down on his knees. He found a briefcase Kieran kept between the bed and the nightstand."

"He took it?" said the detective.

"I think so," said Meg. "He moved out of my sight, and I wouldn't risk shifting to keep him in view. But I saw the mattress sink with his weight, and I heard him trying to open the snaps."

The detective stared at me. With the state of the room and the state of Meg, I hadn't given the briefcase a thought.

"Did he?"

"I don't think so," said Meg.

"It's a combination lock," I chimed in.

The detective knelt to peer under the bed, then straightened up and called to his partner. "See a briefcase anywhere out there?"

"That's a negative," said the other detective.

"Looks like that's gone," said the first detective. "I'll need a complete inventory of whatever else is missing. What do you keep in the briefcase?"

"Important papers," I said, and caught Woody's eye. "Like my Tour orientation package."

Woody forced a smile.

"He left straightaway after trying to open the briefcase," said Meg. "I was too petrified to move, even after Kieran came in."

The detective asked her to run through the story one more time. I motioned Woody aside, and we went into the corridor.

"Sorry about what happened on the first tee today," I said, shaking Woody's hand.

"Forget it, Kieran. Nothing you could have done. It's an occupational hazard of dealing with one hundred fifty distinct personalities every week. Some are more distinct than others."

"I'm beginning to wonder whether sticking around this week is worth it," I said.

"You want to get suspended?"

"No."

"Then you'd better stick around," said Woody. "I've devoted much effort to keeping you here. You cut out now, and it's bad for both of us."

"This must be connected to Jason Oliver," I said. "Just like the fight last night."

"So you blame me because I paired you with Oliver?" said Woody. "I seem to remember talking to you about it beforehand. I seem to remember your approval. And I seem to remember a degree of self-interest involved."

"You made your point, Woody."

"Did Oliver talk about the interview today?" he said.

"You didn't ask me to spy."

"Simple question, Kieran."

"Sorry, I'm on edge. I think I still feel the effects of the concussion." I rubbed the back of my head, which was becoming a habit. "He mentioned the interview in passing. I think he regrets it."

"That's nice," said Woody. "Meanwhile, he makes life miserable for the rest of us."

"Do you know anything about a group of the players suing him?"

"About what?"

"Defamation."

"Haven't heard anything about that," said Woody. "I know much about what the players do, and what I don't know surprises me."

I peeked back into the room. Meg still sat on the bed and talked to the detective. Her whole being reeked of fear. Spunky Meg, lovely Meg, the Meg who delivered chastening tongue-lashings on every subject from golf to religion. Seeing her fear nauseated me.

"How about some protection, Woody?"

"From whoever broke in here? We don't know who he is, unless you do."

"I don't," I said. "But you have Meg's description. Ram's-horn eyebrows. Pretty distinctive, I'd say."

"We're not in the bodyguard business." Woody glanced into the room. He must have seen the fear in Meg as well, because he added: "Okay, Kieran, I'll make sure that description goes to every marshal and all security personnel first thing tomorrow. If this guy shows up at the Players Club, we'll grab him."

After Woody left, one of the detectives reminded me to work up an inventory of missing property. I knew only the briefcase was missing, and I knew exactly why, but I made a big show of picking through my scattered belongings, arranging them into logical piles, and screwing up my face in pained concentration as I took inventory. Meg closed herself into the bathroom and emerged fully dressed a few minutes later. She sat tightly wound on the bed, her eyes unfocused.

"The briefcase," I announced. "Nothing else is missing."

"What did it look like?" said the detective with the notebook.

I described it as gray leather, standard size and three inches deep, with two snaps and a locking strap.

"The combination locks were on?" he said.

"Force of habit."

"Could anyone who knows you figure out the combinations?"

"I doubt it." The combinations featured an old girlfriend's birthday and other significant dates. I didn't explain, just gave him the numbers.

"Any idea why someone would steal a briefcase?" he said.

"No."

"But that's the only thing missing."

I shrugged. We all three looked at the only eyewitness, who still stared into infinity.

The two detectives left, unconvinced but obviously unconcerned. I locked up, my ribs starting to ache as the adrenalin rush ebbed. At Meg's request, I looked through every closet, peeked under every piece of furniture, and closed the sliding glass door.

"He was after the affidavit, wasn't he?" she said. "And you know who he is."

"I do and I don't." I told her what Eddie Fort told me about Cindy Moran's sidekick.

"Those detectives know you didn't tell them everything," she said.

"They don't care. If someone targeted me for an unspecified reason, another break-in won't happen. The rest of the clientele is safe, and the case is as good as closed."

"Was the affidavit in the briefcase?" she said.

"No, someplace safe."

This minor triumph didn't impress Meg.

"When he finds it's not in the briefcase, he may return," she said. "I'll not be staying here to invite a repeat performance."

"I'm here now."

"You?" she said. "You can hardly breathe for the bandages on your ribs."

"What do you propose? Your motel?"

"At least that's not here."

"Ah, but when he doesn't find it in the briefcase, he might try there."

"How do you know he knows where I'm staying?"

"That's just it. I don't."

With some effort, I convinced Meg to stay. The conditions weren't cozy. Lights on, Meg fully clothed, me pulling a single eight-hour shift of guard duty. Meg claimed the bed. I kicked two chairs together against the door, and stripped down to my briefs and bandages. For good measure, I lay my practice club at my side.

After my apartment in Milton had been burglarized, I spent a skittish month reacquainting myself with night sounds I once folded seamlessly into my dreams. This break-in hardly fazed me. Maybe I'd have felt differently if I'd actually seen the guy, or if I'd been caught in the shower with my pants down. Or maybe I'd wrestled with so many demons lately, one more hardly mattered.

Tonight's dream returned me to the party again. I followed the woman up the short flight of stairs and down the long corridor to the open room where my putter lay broken on the floor and she stood against the window with her back toward me. Something whirred behind my ear, but this time I kept my eyes fixed on her, steeling myself against the pain about to explode in my head so I could concentrate. She turned this time.

"You are a part of it," Yvonne Oliver hissed through the gap in her teeth.

CHAPTER
SEVENTEEN

Morning came, and with it only slightly less paranoia. Meg refused to shower without me planted in the bathroom doorway, my eyes on the entry door and my mouth engaged in reassuring, if inane, conversation. We changed places, Meg improving security with a chair wedged under the doorknob and my practice club firmly in hand.

I scrubbed down and planned the day. My ribs felt much better, but still hurt enough that I'd need to devise drastic swing alterations. At the same time, I didn't want to overtax my muscles. I figured forty-five minutes to an hour on the practice tee, just enough time to shake out each of my clubs. After that, a practice round, preferably with someone less colorful than Jason Oliver. No betting today. With my current limitations, I couldn't overpower this golf course. I needed to finesse it, so Meg and I would take copious notes in a yardage booklet. After the round, I'd take a sauna, maybe even a massage. The range and the round would loosen the muscles, and I'd need to keep them loose.

In the middle of this preparation, I hoped to find the guy who broke into my room. My current theory—apart from Tommy Garth Hunter and Jason Oliver—was that Cindy Moran and her accomplice fell out. He killed her, and now he was looking for the affidavit to run the rest of the scam and pocket all the loot himself. Theories are great, but, in my experience, an overabundance of theories equals confusion.

Still, I had a plan.

An old Irish saying goes: If you want to make God laugh, tell Him your plans.

Not for nothing, these sayings persist.

We drove to the Players Club together and then separated. Meg went to the ladies' locker room to collect my clubs. I headed for the men's locker room for a shoe change and sundries. The air buzzed with stormy excitement before tomorrow's calm concentration. The practice range would be an unbroken line of clubshafts waving like the legs of a centipede. The entire field would jam the course to cram for tomorrow's test. TV crews would fine-tune camera angles and remote feeds. The blimp's cameras would plot nearby landmarks to give the viewers at home dashes of local color.

I settled in front of my locker. Meg had cinched the bandage so tight I needed to contort myself like a pretzel to wiggle into my golf shoes. Unravelling, I found a Tour staffer behind each shoulder. If the Tour actually had a security arm, these were the guys to hire. Tall, burly, calmly detached behind sunglasses. I thought they came to tell me the intruder was in custody, and that Tour headquarters needed Meg to make a positive I.D., Woody Harrington making it happen.

"Mr. Lenahan," said one.

Uh oh, that formality again.

The other handed me an envelope with the red, white, and blue Tour logo embossed in the left corner. I ripped it open and unfolded the single page inside. The words leaped out at me:

> Effective immediately, you are suspended
> from play in all PGA Tour sanctioned
> events until further notice.

Beneath the terse edict, the ink still glistened on the Commissioner's signature.

"This is a joke, right?" I said.

"No joke," said one.

"Get your things," said the other. "We need to escort you to your car."

I felt stunned. I wanted to slump to the floor, but the bandage kept me rigidly upright in a stupid display of pride. The two staffers didn't budge. A few pros whispered among themselves. None of the six from the other night were in the locker room. Otherwise, I might have heard applause.

I pulled things out of the locker, starting a small avalanche of shoes, socks, boxed golf balls, all manner of complimentary trinkets. I didn't have a duffel bag to carry this stuff. A young valet, sensing this immediate problem, obliged me with a plastic garbage bag liner. Functional, but symbolic. A career in the trash.

I slung the bag over my shoulder. The two staffers flanked me, their hands gripping my elbows in case I bolted toward the forbidden golf course. None of the other pros met my eye as we walked out with my Santa Claus sack of useless junk bouncing off my back.

Outside the clubhouse, they steered me toward the contestants' parking lot.

"What about my caddie?" I said.

"He isn't suspended," said one.

"His caddie's a girl," said the other.

"Oh," said the first. "She can pick up another bag, if she wants."

We reached my car. Following directions, I unlocked the door, tossed in the bag, closed myself inside, and turned the ignition. They stayed in my rearview mirror, watching me all the way to the gate.

Suddenly adrift, I returned to the hotel. I phoned Woody Harrington, only to hear a secretary say he was at a meeting. No estimate when he'd return. Right. He probably hovered behind her with his ear cupped to the phone. I called the Judge's room; no answer. I called his cellular and raised a modem screech. I called the practice range at the Players Club. No sign of Meg.

I paced the room, angry as hell. Jason Oliver defames the Tour in an interview, drops out of sight for a month, then commits civil assault on a Tour official in full view of several hundred spectators. No suspension; not even a reprimand. Tommy Garth Hunter and a small army ambush me. No suspension; no reprimand. The phone rang, and I vaulted across the room to snag it.

"I'm at Tour headquarters," said the Judge. "Your pal Woody called me this morning with the news."

"He calls you and he sends two bouncers to toss me out of the Club."

"I tried heading you off this morning, but you were already

gone," said the Judge. "You got your room burglarized last night?"

"My pal tell you that, too?"

"He mentioned it. He said you've become a great big albatross around his neck."

"Is that why I was suspended?"

"No, and Woody can't figure it out, either. But he did get me an audience with the Policy Board in about ten minutes. I'm going to find out why, and I'm going to get you unsuspended or . . ."

As the Judge ranted, my anger slowly subsided and rational thought asserted itself. Okay, I've been suspended from the Tour. Strip away the emotion, the embarrassment, the disgrace, the injustice, and what's left? The suspension made no sense, unless . . .

I sifted through my memories of last Thursday. Cindy Moran had invited me, but when I knocked on the door she'd expected someone else. Who? The world started shifting again. Not the tiny cogs of a friendship lost but huge cosmic gears.

Someone pounded on the door.

"Hold it, Jim," I said. "I think this is Meg."

I never expected to find Yvonne Oliver in the corridor. She smiled crookedly, as if visiting a strange man in a hotel room unsettled her. Back on the bed, the Judge squawked like an angry mouse.

"This is about Jason, right?" I said.

She nodded.

"Come in," I said. "I'll be just a minute."

"Who the hell's that?" the Judge hissed as I picked up the phone. "Jesus, Kieran, I got about five minutes now. We can't play coy anymore. I'm going to lay it all out to the Board. The scam, the beta blockers, everything."

"Don't say a word."

"But, Kieran, this may be your only chance to get back."

"Maybe I don't want to," I said, and hung up.

Yvonne had followed me into the bedroom. She looked even lovelier than she had the other night. Her hair was pulled back into a single thick braid. Her simple peasant dress tumbled gracefully from shoulders to waist to knees. She seemed equal parts sad and nervous. The sadness dripped from her dark eyes, and the nervousness clung to fingers that worried the beads of her belt.

"I've come to ask your help," she said.

The phone rang.

"My help?" I said. "I've been suspended, I've been beaten up twice, I still suffer from amnesia. My room was burglarized last night. I'm the one who needs help."

"You have something Jason needs," she said.

The phone stopped ringing and immediately started again.

"Won't you answer that?" she said.

"I know who it is. What do you think I have?"

"I don't know."

"But you know I have it. Whatever it is."

Yvonne nodded.

"Is this more of your mystic mumbo jumbo?"

The phone stopped ringing, and a thick silence followed.

"May we sit?" said Yvonne, her voice quaking with an exhaustion I suddenly noticed permeated her whole body. I felt like a boor.

We took chairs on opposite sides of a tiny round table. She

sat Catholic-school proper, ankles and knees pressed together and hands folded.

"What did Jason talk about yesterday?" she said.

"That's a funny question. Jason is a much more serious golfer than I expected. He clipped me for fifty bucks."

"Most people who play with Jason for the first time have the same impression," she said. "Did he speak about his interview?"

"He spoke about lots of things. He spoke about golf returning to a purer, more natural state. He spoke about almost winning the Players Championship a few years ago, until his hormones got in the way. Yeah, he mentioned the interview, too. He says he's about to be sued because of it."

"There is no lawsuit," said Yvonne.

"I didn't think so," I said. "But Jason still needs this."

Yvonne stared through her hands, considering what I'd just said. "You must understand Jason. He's trapped in an image he can't shed. He hates himself for it, yet he continues to act in ways he believes are expected of him."

"Like trying to drive a golf ball between Woody Harrington's legs?" I said.

"What did you think about that?"

"It could have been one of the worst sights ever on a golf course."

"He came home and sank into my arms and started to tell me," she said. "Halfway through, he rushed to the bathroom and vomited. It was as if the real Jason Oliver inside poked through the public Jason Oliver outside and didn't like what he saw."

"He said nothing during the round," I said. "If I didn't

know better, I'd think he and Woody concocted it like a circus stunt."

Yvonne grinned as if to say, I told you so. "Jason believes in his apocalyptic vision of the future. But he wouldn't have given that interview if it weren't for Dewey Peek."

"The Dewey Peek in your trophy case?" I said.

"Jason met Dewey at an inner city golf clinic in New Jersey about ten years ago," she said. "Dewey had been a childhood hero to Jason. Jason admired him for skipping off to Europe after a successful year on the Tour. In Jason's mind, Dewey did what everyone should do. Search for a purer form of the game. But Dewey told Jason he did not leave voluntarily. He had been exiled by the Tour just as his career came into full bloom."

"For what reason?" I said, intrigued by having common ground with Dewey Peek.

"I do not know," said Yvonne. "I was in Dewey's company only long enough to realize I didn't like him. He's a very bitter man."

"Bitter about his exile?"

"I imagine so," she said. "Dewey and Jason stayed in contact over the years. They would speak on the phone late at night, when the rates are low. Jason always hung up very agitated. 'Something's got to be done,' he'd say. But he never elaborated because he knows my feelings about Dewey.

"Dewey is at the root of Jason's problem. They formed a plan, and the interview was a part of it."

"How?"

"I don't know the details. But I can read Jason. Since we arrived here, he's been on an emotional roller coaster. Upbeat, then depressed. I suspect he and Dewey had a falling out, though he tells me nothing. It was only after he connected with you that his hope returned."

"Wait a second," I said. "He's gone through all those changes since Monday night?"

"No, since we arrived here," said Yvonne. "Almost two weeks ago."

"You've been here two weeks? I thought—"

"We checked into the campsite two weeks ago," said Yvonne. "We only first visited Sawgrass Monday night."

"Where was Jason last Thursday afternoon?" I said.

Yvonne closed her eyes and pinched the bridge of her nose.

"With Dewey, I believe," she said. "Jason doesn't know I came here. He'd be very angry if he did."

I stared through my hands, hardly listening to her, as I fit together the possible scenarios.

"This thing you think I have," I finally said. "Turns out other people think I have it, too. The asking price is fifty thousand dollars."

"I understand," said Yvonne.

Two little words, yet Yvonne Oliver managed to shape them into an accusation of everything I hated. I wanted to step outside myself, to shout, "This isn't me. I'm forced to play this hand." But I just stared into her eyes, as poker-faced as I could muster.

"I understand," she said in resignation.

She withdrew her hands from the table, unfolded herself from the chair. I followed her to the door, hoping that her mystic self divined some decency in me.

"There is one more thing," said Yvonne. "Jason has trapped me in my own image: the mystic. It is just as much an act as Jason's. I did not sense your danger the other night. We were following you."

Without my credentials, I stormed the Tour's parapets like any member of the public: trapped in a long line of cars snaking off TPC Boulevard and into the spectators' parking lot. From there, people either climbed aboard a shuttle bus or hiked to the clubhouse admission gate. Neither option thrilled me. I'd been tossed off the premises as well as the Tour and didn't expect a warm welcome if an official spotted me. The Wednesday crowd was the largest so far, but not thick enough to lose myself in. I was planning to ford a small stream near the first fairway, when I heard a familiar voice hawking souvenirs to a knot of people waiting for the shuttle.

Kenny Palumbo executed a perfect cartoon double take at the sight of me.

"What the hell are you doing here?" he said.

"Shut up." I wrapped him in a headlock and dragged him behind a line of cars.

"Hey, that was a captive audience," he said.

I pulled a twenty from my pocket and crushed it into his hand.

"I need to get to the media center. You're going to get me there."

"That's it? That's all you want?" He stroked his generous jowls, calculating the twenty in terms of the time investment and apparently coming up with an acceptable rate. "Follow me."

Kenny tried to pump me for dope on my suspension as we zigzagged through the rows of parked cars. I kept mum, telling him only that "the shit will come down soon enough." I didn't mean anything in particular; it just sounded suitably threatening.

We looped back through the parking lot toward a dusty barnyard surrounded by buildings housing the greenskeeping machinery. During the tournament, the area doubled as the television network's nerve center and satellite uplink. Many signs proclaimed what any idiot could fathom. The area was strictly off limits.

Kenny Palumbo, however, wasn't just any idiot. A temporary fence curved toward a narrow gate where a marshal chatted with a guy wearing network overalls. They greeted Kenny like old pals. Kenny threw them some incomprehensible double-talk, and I was in.

"Got to get back to the store," said Kenny. "Good luck."

Beyond the maintenance barns, a stand of pines separated me from the tent erected as a media center. I circled through the shadows, using the thick trunks for cover. A short sprint across open ground brought me to the tent's door. No one stopped me, the media center being not exactly a hotbed of activity on a Wednesday afternoon.

Randall Fisk pecked at a laptop computer at the end of an empty table. His glasses rode low on his long nose. Sweat in his scalp accentuated the connect-the-dots pattern of his hair plugs.

"This is your professional obituary," he said, without looking up. "Anything you want to add before I blast it into cyberspace? I have my own web site now."

Another great use of technology: Randall Fisk on-line. I bent close to his shoulder and read the account of my suspension for "suspicious, possibly immoral, activities off the golf course that do not reflect well on the high personal standards required of Tour professionals." Except for that quote from an unidentified Tour official, the writing lacked the usual florid Fiskian style. Still, I couldn't resist one keystroke.

"Goddammit, Kieran!" he screamed as the screen blanked. He feverishly clicked a few keys, and the text returned from wherever the hell it goes.

"I need to talk to you," I said.

"Forget it. You're yesterday's news once I finish this," he said. "About what?"

"Ever hear of Dewey Peek?"

"I interviewed him for my book Monday night. What do you care about a broken-down golf pro?"

"He may be the reason the Tour suspended me," I said.

I told him enough for him to fold his laptop, a little more to lead him out of the tent and through the maintenance yard, and a little more to propel him through the parking lot to his car.

"The interview runs about half an hour," said Fisk. "Would have run longer but we got interrupted."

We sat in the media parking lot, the engine idling and the a/c blasting. Fisk slipped the cassette into the tiny recorder and pressed the fast-forward button.

"Most of the early stuff is about him growing up near a golf course and he and his friends fashioning golf clubs out of coat hangers and golf balls out of nuts rolled in oil. The part you should hear is toward the end."

Fisk pressed a button. A breathy voice spoke enough for Fisk to orient himself before zooming forward again.

"He sounds frail," I said.

"Don't let the voice fool you," said Fisk. "Guy's built like a tree trunk. I interviewed him way out the western edge of Duval County. The house is on stilts, and right next door is a field that once was a driving range. Weeds grow up around the yardage markers and through the tee mats. It looks like a motel that gets left behind when a new highway reroutes traffic."

A few more hits on the control buttons, and Fisk found the place.

"I ain't no hero," said Dewey Peek. Birds twittered in the background. "Guys who came up before me, like Chink Stewart and Bill Spiller, they were the real groundbreakers. They were damn good players, better than I ever got, and they had the respect of white pros like Jimmy Demaret and Horton Smith. It was Spiller really got the ball rolling in 'forty-eight, when he and Teddy Rhodes finished low enough in the L.A. Open to qualify for the next PGA tournament up in Oakland, and then got barred because the PGA had a whites-only clause in its bylaws. They sued, and the PGA said it would stop discriminating against us if Bill and Ted and the rest dropped the case.

"Well, they did, and the PGA snookered them because, after that, the tournaments became 'invitationals' and not 'opens,' and no blacks got invites. Wasn't until 'sixty-one when Spiller got the ear of a rich man who got the ear of the California Attorney General who got the PGA to drop the whites-only clause.

"I came out in 'sixty-two. I already been three years playing wherever I could, mostly charity tournaments and opens. Joe Louis had his own tournament back then in Detroit. He was big into golf. But in 'sixty-two I got out there, and if you could put up with the irritations, which I could, there was money to be made by a good player. I kind of flew in under the radar because the Palmer-Nicklaus rivalry was just heating up. There were only a handful of black players back then, just like now, and all the white folks thought we were each Charlie Sifford.

"I had a good year in 'sixty-three. Almost won a couple of tournaments, and just missed top ten on the money list. The few sportswriters who paid me any mind started writing about me being on the Tour, like Dr. King marching on Washington. I didn't want none of that. I was just playing golf, making a living. I didn't see myself like a scout slipping behind enemy lines, playing at all them fancy country clubs. I wanted to match myself against the other pros, white and black, not measure myself against black peoples' hopes and white peoples' prejudice.

"I looked for a big year in 'sixty-four. Started out fine, too, in the West and the South. Things went haywire in the late spring, when we moved north into the border states.

"I was single, and the Tour was a fun ride for a single guy then, like it must be now. I usually stuck to my own kind. But at this one tournament in Maryland, I met this white lady. She was kind of boozy, and kind of tinselly. But nice, see? Lots of those clubs didn't allow us in the bars or the grill rooms. We didn't like that, but we didn't kick because this was 'sixty-four and we knew things would change sooner rather than later. I wasn't much for drinking, anyway, and evenings I liked to practice my putting in the dark because it gave me a better feel.

"The lady came out to the putting green with a little bottle of hootch. Next thing I knew, we were sitting in a golf cart, and she had her big old leg swung over mine and her tongue in my ear, and I was feeling pretty good from the booze. Next thing after that, we were driving out into the dark with her at the wheel. And the next thing after that, we crashed into a pond and she was pinned under the cart and I had to lift it off and drag her out before she drowned.

"Well, the night watchman found us out there. The lady happened to be the wife of the club president. So, before you know it, the club people were there, and the PGA people were there, and the cops were there, and the NAACP was there. Everybody was talking scandal this and scandal that, and the NAACP wanted to keep things quiet because we were perilously close to Washington, and the Civil Rights bill was making its way through Congress, and no one wanted an incident like this in the papers. So they hammered out a deal that sounded more like an ultimatum to me. I had to leave the Tour, go over to play in Europe. If I behaved myself, maybe I'd get let back.

"A week later, I was sailing to France and giving trick shot exhibitions off the deck. I had some success on the European Tour. I became a legend in France. The French called me the Josephine Baker of golf. I met my wife there and we had a daughter, and I kept waiting for the PGA to call me back, but the call never came.

"My game left me, like it does, but I still had an itch to come back here. Around '80 I heard about a Senior Tour being organized, and I actually got a letter from a promoter asking if I'd play. But my wife was too sick to leave France, and by the time she died my hands were too far gone. I need to build up my club grips two, three times normal size to get any feel, and when you do that, you lose the natural power of your wrists.

"So that's what happened. The Tour banished me, and by the time the Senior Tour called me back, my hands were gone. But I came back anyway for my daughter. She wanted to be an American. I once went to Tour headquarters. All those spiffy kids walk around real fast and real important looking. I finally collared one and asked for an explanation why I wasn't called back all those years when I lived up to my end of the bargain. He looked into it, and told me it was an oversight. This is my life, and someone over there just forgot to call me back. Damn."

A commotion interrupted, and Dewey greeted someone who called him "Pop." Fisk stopped the recorder.

"That's the end," he said. "Dewey's son-in-law came to help with some chores Dewey can't handle anymore."

"Run that part back again," I said.

Fisk obliged. I knew that voice.

"Was the son-in-law tall, with glasses and a peach fuzzy beard and acne scars on his neck?"

Fisk nodded. "His name was Curtis."

CHAPTER
EIGHTEEN

A civilian aid led us to the pebbled glass cubicle where McGriff spoke on the phone. The detective sat as erect as a drill sergeant, his free hand doodling a felt-tipped pen on a yellow legal pad. He spoke in monosyllables, his hand occasionally darting to a corner of the page to scratch quick notations. The smile didn't quite break through to the surface of his face when he spotted me over the top of his glasses. But his eyes crinkled with subtle amusement, as if he expected me eventually and knew exactly what would bring me.

"Thanks." He pried the receiver from his ear, but the tiny voice pulled it back. "Right. Thanks again for your courtesy. Good-bye."

He hung up, and now the smile did bloom on his face. It was the same smile DiRienzo often wore back at home. A cat-that-ate-the-canary grin that made me believe all detectives descended from the same East African Eve 100,000 generations ago.

"Hello again, Mr. Fisk," he said.

"Why didn't you tell me about your connection to Dewey Peek?" I said.

"And hello to you, too, Mr. Lenahan," said McGriff. "My, we are agitated, aren't we?"

"Why?" I said.

"Uh uh, Lenahan. I'm still the cops, remember. I ask the questions. Now you tell me why you're all heated up about me and Dewey Peek, and you tell me fast."

This struck me as one of those rare instances when I could learn more by talking than by listening. I quickly spun several alternatives and settled on starting with my original theory: Cindy Moran and accomplice attempt to blackmail Tommy Garth Hunter by threatening to reveal his beta blocker usage. McGriff didn't ask for an explanation. Either he was exceedingly polite, or he understood the import of the charge. Fisk, meanwhile, definitely understood and definitely was not polite. He squirmed in his chair, itching to lay his fingers on his laptop. McGriff noticed, too.

"Mr. Fisk," he said, "if you compromise this investigation with a badly timed story, you'll wish you never met me."

I segued into my second theory: Jason Oliver and Dewey Peek join forces to lay waste to the Tour. Jason wants revolution; Dewey wants revenge. They orchestrate a plan, Jason setting the stage with his interview and Dewey hiring a private investigator to find the proof. But Cindy Moran already has the proof, and she negotiates with two sides, maybe more, to bounce the price higher.

"What's the proof?" said McGriff.

"An affidavit," I said, "attesting to Tommy Garth Hunter's beta blocker usage by the person who supplied him with the pills."

"Dr. Paulling," said McGriff.

"Who?" said Fisk.

"Never mind," I told Fisk, then turned to McGriff. "Cindy Moran roped me into this because she needed my services."

"As a lawyer?"

"More like an escrow agent for the affidavit. She floated it while she negotiated the deals."

"How did she float it?" said McGriff.

"Mailed it to Judge Inglisi."

"Pretty stupid," said McGriff.

"I agree," I said. "Especially for someone otherwise as smart as Cindy."

"Where is it now?"

"My safe deposit box at the hotel."

"Which is why you came back here Monday to see the Doctor," said McGriff.

"The Judge had just arrived with it that morning," I said. "The envelope had no return address. I needed to find out who put the affidavit together. Dr. . . . the Doctor didn't know her name, but she described Cindy Moran perfectly."

McGriff tilted back his head and stared at the ceiling.

"You had the affidavit in hand when I met you Monday," he said. "And you knew it was connected to a murder case. I go to the state attorney right now, I can have you charged with obstruction of justice. Maybe throw in some criminal impersonation to boot."

I said nothing. McGriff lowered his head.

"Any idea who broke into your hotel room last night?" he said.

No point in holding out. I gave him the description Meg

gave me, and tied it to the man Eddie Fort saw in Cindy Moran's apartment the week before the murder.

McGriff lifted a set of keys from his desk and spun them on his finger.

"Damn, Lenahan, now I know why DiRienzo said you're always near a train wreck. You're the damn engineer."

"My daddy and I caddied at Gainesville Country Club," said McGriff. He drove with his left elbow out the Ford's open window and his hand rubbing the fuzz on his jawline. Every now and then, he squinted in the mirror to check for Randall Fisk behind. We were out of Gainesville, out of his jurisdiction. But he had working relationships all over north Florida, he said, so that didn't matter a lick.

"Dewey Peek was a legend with black folk my father's age," he said. "Funny how none of them ever talked about Dewey getting screwed by the Tour. They talked only about the great things Dewey did in France and Europe, and how he returned to his roots after his wife died.

"Some of these same folk, like my daddy, think I was more enamored with the idea of marrying Dewey Peek's daughter than I was with Claudine herself. But the plain truth is, I never liked Dewey much. I still visit him because maybe he might mention me to Claudine at just the right moment and she'll come back. Sometimes I hump things up into the attic or out into the woodshed for him. You know about his hands, right?"

"He said something on the tape about them being too far gone," I said.

"A manicurist in France infected them with a needle. That ruined his game more than anything else."

We swung into a sheriff's station among a no-name gaggle of shacks and storefronts. Beyond a narrow band of marsh grass, the St. John's River spread thick and lazy in the late afternoon sun. The inside of the station smelled like stale coffee. A beefy deputy sat at a desk, thumbing through a hunting magazine while voices hissed on a radio. He gave us a once over, thumbed a few more pages, and only moved to squelch the radio chatter when McGriff flashed his shield.

"Meat locker's down the hall, third door on the right," he said.

The meat locker turned out to be a real meat locker, a stainless steel walk-in with a broken handle jerry-rigged with a can opener.

"This was a convenience store one time." McGriff handed me and Fisk each a lab coat and shrugged into one himself. "The Sheriff's Department took it over and remodelled it into a substation. Cheaper than building one from scratch. The meat locker's a handy feature. Ready?"

He yanked on the door. Cold smoke billowed out and then cleared to reveal a body laid out on a slab. McGriff plucked off the sheet without ceremony. The body looked like something dug from a peat bog. Bloated, broken, the skin stained purple and brown. But I could still see the gray streaks in the black, curly hair and the thick ram's-horn eyebrows that met over the bridge of his nose. The frigid air kept the smell down, but he still stunk awfully bad. Death mixed with river gunk. I choked back the urge to vomit. Fisk unabashedly pinched his nostrils.

"Fisherman found him floating in a cove about a mile upstream this morning," said McGriff. "County medical examiner sent someone over. The preliminary report shows multiple blows to the back of the head, right behind the ear. Lungs had river water in them, which means he didn't hit the water dead. Also, some depressions on the neck and upper back. The thinking is, maybe he was held down unconscious until he drowned."

"He matches Meg's description of the guy who broke into my hotel room," I said. "Any idea who he is?"

"His wallet's gone and no other ID on him." McGriff checked his watch. "But the state police found a car about a quarter mile up river from where his body was found. It's registered to a Leo Tomalini. We ran a computer check on him when the car turned up. Easy pickin's, because he was a private investigator working out of Ocala before he closed his office a few months ago. One more thing. Are you missing a sock?"

"No," I said.

"Tomalini had one clutched in his right hand. A thin black one. Man's size. Let's get outside. The car should be here soon."

It was. We waited outside and drank colas from a vending machine and cleared our lungs with deep breaths of air that smelled great despite the humidity. The tow truck showed up within minutes, dragging an old Pontiac with its blue paint sun-scorched on the hood and roof.

"Look familiar?" said McGriff.

I shook my head.

The deputy came out of hibernation to direct the tow driver where to set down the car. Gears grinded, chains clanked.

"Wait here," McGriff told me and Fisk.

As soon as the hook dropped from the Pontiac's bumper,

McGriff stuck his head in the open window and waved me over.

The briefcase sat on the front seat. One latch had been completely torn off; the other, pulled from the lid, dangled uselessly from the hasp.

"That yours?" said McGriff.

"Looks like it. But I won't know until I look inside."

I reached in to lift the lid, but McGriff grabbed my arm.

"They don't want anything touched yet."

He popped the trunk of the Ford, and returned with a long shiny rod I recognized as a golf shaft.

"One of my temper tantrums," he said, showing me the pinched end where the head had been snapped off. "Comes in handy at crime scenes."

He fed the shaft through the window and wiggled it under the lid.

"There is a stain on the inside where I once spilled coffee," I said. "Shape of a peanut."

McGriff worked the clubshaft deeper beneath the lid, his back arched and his elbows spread so he wouldn't rub any latent prints off the Pontiac's windowsill. When he had enough leverage, he carefully raised the shaft.

The peanut-shaped coffee stain was easy to spot on the gray cowhide lining; the briefcase was completely empty.

Suddenly, something welled up inside me. A disembodied voice spoke through my own.

"It had golf balls in it," I said.

"What are you saying?" said McGriff. "The briefcase had golf balls in it?"

"The sock in Tomalini's hand. It had golf balls in it. Two,

maybe three. Try it sometime. It swings like a blackjack." I
felt the back of my head. "I should know."

Night took forever to fall. Or maybe time ground to a halt.
My senses opened wide, stuck like a broken carburetor firing
images of last Thursday afternoon. The black sock loaded
with golf balls, spinning so fast the dimples showed in the
fabric. The solid thock behind my ear, not unlike the sound
of a persimmon driver at impact. A split second of lucid
consciousness, followed by a thought both quick and stupid:
what the hell happened? And the floor rushing up to meet
me.

In the present, McGriff's Ford sucked hot air from the sky
as we charged across a dry, orange savannah. Randall Fisk,
cool in the a/c of his rental, hung on our tail. I shouted
directions over the rush of wind, trying to backtrack a trail
I'd seen only once.

"Hell of a lot easier if you knew the damn name," said
McGriff.

A whiff of the river filled the car. We'd been running out
of its sight, and now its meandering brought it close enough
for a smell. The savannah abruptly sprouted into a pine forest.
Night crashed as in a Magritte painting, and a sense of déjà
vu flickered inside me.

"There!" I said, pointing to a delta of white sand spewing
from a wall of palmetto.

McGriff hit the brakes. Fisk skidded onto the shoulder.
Both cars reversed, spun into broken U-turns, and bounced
into the forest on the two thin trails of sand. McGriff drove
like a maniac, and Fisk hung right behind. Palmetto spines
swatted at the windshield. Sand sprayed against the wheel

wells, hissing like mariachis. Twice the Ford almost bounded into the trees. Twice Fisk almost slammed into the rear end.

Finally, we broke into the clearing.

"What the hell is that?" said McGriff.

The bus was lit from within. Outside, flames licked atop citronella torches. Oliver sat on the fold-out picnic table, pumping curls with a dumbbell. We crunched to a stop with the Ford's lights trained on Oliver. He didn't look up, just switched the dumbbell from one hand to the other and resumed the curls.

"He has amazing concentration," I said.

McGriff thrust the car into park and left the lights burning while we climbed out. Fisk ran up from behind, and Yvonne descended from the bus with a torch in her hand. Oliver kept pumping, counting each rep with bursts of breath shaped into numbers.

"Mr. Oliver," said McGriff.

Oliver reached twenty and let the dumbbell slide off his fingers. It hit the sandy ground and rolled to McGriff's foot. McGriff introduced himself as a detective on the Gainesville police force.

"We're not in Gainesville, and I don't talk to cops," said Oliver. He hopped to the ground, turned his back to us, and spread his arms to grab the ends of the table in an isometric exercise.

McGriff restated his introduction, very politely and very patiently.

"I told you," said Oliver, without turning around. "We're not in Gainesville, and I don't talk to cops. Yvonne, tell him it's nothing personal."

Yvonne's hands twisted the small torch. I tried to read

her face, and came up with multiple interpretations. Fear, resignation, embarrassment. I supposed I saw whatever I wanted to see. Whatever made me feel better.

McGriff moved in a flash. He spun Oliver from the belly and sat him on the metal bench seat and stuck his face close, saying very coolly that he didn't give a damn who Oliver spoke to or didn't speak to because he had one and possibly two murders on his plate and he was going to get his answers and get them now.

I remembered a segment of TV news footage from my boyhood. One minute, a scraggly haired guy spewed profanity-laced invective at an anti-war rally; the next minute, in unreal edited time, he knelt on the grass, bloodied and sobbing, while police with nightsticks dispersed the demonstrators. Jason Oliver's transformation was just as extreme and, in real time, just as fast. He clutched at Yvonne, gathered her to his side, and broke down. McGriff crouched to eye level, probing for any sign of insincerity. Fisk pawed at the sand with his rubber soles. I climbed into the bus and filled a mug with water. When I stepped back down, Oliver wore the towel draped over his shoulders.

"Dewey had the connection," he was saying. "He knew Tomalini from somewhere. Tomalini worked for Trident Golf, ostensibly as an equipment rep. In reality, he closely watched the players on Trident's advisory staff. If they did anything to impugn the company's good name, he reported them.

"Dewey wanted revenge. He didn't care who got hurt, just as long as the news made a big splash. He hired Tomalini to dig up some dirt. I never met Tomalini, I swear. A few days later, Tomalini reported he had a bead on beta blocker usage.

Dewey didn't know what that meant, and Tomalini was asking for a lot of money. Dewey called me in California to tell me, and I said a beta blocker scandal was big. Real big. I gave that interview to make it bigger.

"We pooled our money to pay Tomalini. Then Tomalini said his source demanded more money and hinted at other bidders. We scraped up more money. But the source went vague, and we felt we were losing out."

"How did Dewey react?" said McGriff.

"He was wild with rage," said Oliver. "He said he wanted to kill Tomalini."

"He said that?" said McGriff.

Oliver nodded and wiped his nose on his wrist. McGriff stood up.

"Are you taking me in?" said Oliver.

"Yeah," said McGriff. "But I don't know what I can charge you with, other than being a jerk."

"Can I change clothes?" said Oliver.

"Make it fast," said McGriff.

Yvonne helped her husband into the bus. McGriff folded a stick of gum into his mouth, considered tossing the wrapper into the palmetto, then stuffed it into his pocket.

"Surprised, Lenahan?" he said.

"Yeah. You?"

He shrugged. "You work a case, you don't know where it takes you. This kept coming up golf, right from the start, with you thinking you got hit by a golf ball. That wasn't far wrong, either.

"He wasn't always bitter, you know. Day I first called for Claudine, he sat me down on his sofa and opened up a bottle of spirits he distilled himself. Cause for celebration, he said, a nice young black man like me courting his daughter. I told him thanks for the whiskey, but next time I couldn't look the other way.

"Thing is, he never got mad about his exile until the Senior Tour became so rich and popular. Then that thing about his hands kicked in. If he wasn't so vain, he wouldn't have gotten that manicure and infected his hands so bad his game went with it. But he didn't see it that way. To him, if he hadn't been kicked out, he'd have never been over in France to get infected."

"That bitterness translates to murder?" I said.

"Never that elegant," said McGriff. "Crime scene unit found some Afro-American hairs where you lay on the floor. When I visited Dewey the other day, I pinched a few off his sofa. They matched."

McGriff leaned into the Ford and spoke into the radio for a long time, coordinating a raid on Dewey's house with the Duval County authorities. Oliver clomped down the bus steps dressed in jeans and a golf shirt. McGriff hooked the microphone onto the dash. He folded Oliver into the cage and locked the back doors.

"Oh well," he said wearily, and to no one in particular. "Not every night you get to arrest your ex-father-in-law."

The Ford backed up in a sweeping arc and peeled away. The pines quickly swallowed the headlights. Fisk tried to elicit a comment from Yvonne, but she withered him with a glance. He ducked into his car and started composing his scoop on a notepad. Yvonne and I stood close. The flames of the citronella torches danced in a sudden breeze.

"I tried to pull the money together by hocking Jason's

crystal trophy," she said. "I would have had the money by tomorrow. But that isn't what you're after."

"No."

"I didn't think so," she said.

CHAPTER NINETEEN

"'Dewey Peek, former touring pro, was arrested in connection with a plan to extort money from the PGA Tour.' No good. We don't know if the cops actually arrested him yet." Fisk jerked the wheel and brought the car back onto the pavement. "How about this? 'Florida police today closed in on arrests in a conspiracy to . . .' No, no. Not immediate enough."

I burrowed deeper into the seat. For torture, listening to Randall Fisk compose sentences rivalled listening to me sing in the shower. In each case, the end product served no public good.

"I never believed it was Hunter," said Fisk, who finally decided writing Pulitzer-winning prose and driving the dark backroads of north Florida didn't mix.

"Why not?" I said. Since Fisk only heard about Hunter's possible connection a few hours ago, his skepticism hardly reached Doubting Thomas proportions.

"Doesn't make sense because of the PGA Tour's plans to revamp its marketing structure. You haven't heard?"

"About what?"

"Player endorsement contracts have been a battleground for years. The Tour wants to fold all player endorsement contracts under a new wing of PGA Tour marketing. Lesser pros who don't have endorsement contracts, like you, would benefit because the Tour would spread its licensing revenue among all the players. Or so it says. But a guy with a big contract, like Hunter, would lose out big time."

"The Tour would subvert individual player contracts?" I said. "That's illegal."

"The Tour wouldn't subvert any contracts, but that would be the effect," said Fisk. "Look, if an equipment company can buy a PGA Tour endorsement for its clubs, why pay a golfer a million bucks a year for the same thing? Golfers complain they don't like certain clubs, they stipulate exceptions, like they won't use the sponsor's putter or the sponsor's driver. And who knows, next year the pro can go into the tank and what's the sponsor bought for its millions? The point is, Hunter isn't going to kill someone to save something he might lose anyway."

Fisk dropped me at the Marriott, and buzzed off to turn his scoop into syndication copy. I only hoped, for Dewey's sake, that his jail cell was beyond the reach of tomorrow's column. Fisk has the ability to turn one man's misfortune into a disaster on the order of mass extinction. Trust me on this; I've seen enough of my indiscretions in ink.

Rather than head directly to the elevator, I crossed the atrium to a bank of pay phones. I felt suddenly dissatisfied with Dewey Peek as prime mover in two murders and my own journey to Lethe.

Uncle Dan'l answered on the first ring.

"Oh that's been in the wind for awhile," he said of the Tour marketing plan. "But no one can get the players to go for it, even though the majority would profit by the deal. Why? Same reason the middle class fights tax increases on the rich. They might get rich someday. Little fish on Tour all hope to become big fish. This is America in a nutshell."

"Is what I heard just another skunk-ape sighting?" I said.

"Nah, there's some truth to it this time," said Uncle Dan'l. "Some of the players think the Tour changed its tack to approach it from the supply side, that is, the sponsors."

"How would that work?"

"Probably try to embarrass one or two stars bad enough that their sponsors would cancel their endorsement contracts for misbehavior. Get all the others thinking maybe Tour endorsements returned more bang for their bucks."

"A star like Tommy Garth Hunter?"

"Yeah, just like Tommy Garth."

"If this is in the works, why would that certain golfer we spoke about pay so much to protect something he may lose anyway?"

"Because he ain't lost it yet," said Uncle Dan'l. "And because he might never lose it."

"Doesn't the Tour usually get what the Tour wants?"

"Not when it crosses swords with me," he said. "A group of players already hired me to file suit for a declaratory judgment. Well, you know I can't file a declaratory judgment suit until the Tour takes some action to violate the players' rights. But I can jawbone people like the Commissioner and Henry

Chandler, and just the threat of a lawsuit can stop them in their tracks. The Tour doesn't have a very good record in court."

I mulled that for a moment.

"You still there, Kieran?"

I grunted, still thinking.

"Kieran, you put those words in the right ear?"

"I did."

"Any result?" said Uncle Dan'l.

"Tell you at the meeting," I said.

"What meeting?"

"Eight o'clock tomorrow morning at Tour headquarters. Be there."

I had one more minor detail to sew up. Seventy-five air miles southwest, at the Downer Dirty Ranch, Nix Downer answered groggily. I had the impression he either drank early or bedded down early, and didn't much care which.

"That private dick I hired?" he said. "Told you already. He gave up, moved on."

"What was his name?"

"Something Italian. Tomalucci, Tomafucci."

"Tomalini?"

"That's it."

"First name Leo?"

"That's the fella. You come across him?"

"Yeah," I said. "He was swimming in the St. John's. I saw him afterward. Big guy, with funny shaped eyebrows, right?"

"Like handlebars. Horns. Think he plucked them that way," said Downer. "He help you with our lady friend?"

"Already has."

"That's good. You see old Leo again, you tell him I got business for him. I don't give a damn about his license."

"I'll tell him," I said. "I'm sure he doesn't, either."

I planned to call Woody Harrington next. But talking to Uncle Dan'l and Nix Downer flushed me with confidence, so I decided to set the ruse in motion by striking higher up the chain of command. Henry Chandler's secretary answered and, after a long hold, shunted me in to her boss. Chandler picked up warily.

"I remember everything," I said.

"This is a tad late, Mr. Lenahan."

"I want you to call a meeting tomorrow. Eight o'clock." I gave him a list of people who should attend.

"All of them?" he said sarcastically.

"As many as you can round up."

"The tournament starts tomorrow. We have other business, and there are procedures for you to follow."

"Screw the procedures, Henry. You call a meeting tomorrow, or you'll have the Commissioner chewing out your ass. I can guarantee that."

Meg didn't rush to greet me. She squirmed uncomfortably in one of the chairs I'd slept in last night, a troubled expression on her face. I decided on the sensitive approach, looking at our new situation from her point of view. Suddenly jobless in a faraway land. Me, her only anchor, missing since morning. She probably spent the entire day worried about herself and about us, with no one to share her misery.

"It isn't that bad," I said.

"Yes it is," said Meg.

"You don't know what happened today."

"Yes I do."

Meg looked to her left, leading my eyes with hers. Dewey Peek stepped out of the bedroom. I'd have focused on his hands anyway, having heard so much about those big, numb meathooks today. But the gun rivetted my attention. It was a pistol, its make and caliber relevant only to the enthusiast. A grimy towel circled the grip and trailed out from the heel of his hand. Just like one of his golf clubs.

"I thought McGriff arrested you," I said.

"That's the trouble with smart boys like you and my daughter's ex-husband. You think everyone else is dumb."

He wore a white, oversized sharkskin sport coat and a straw fedora. He lifted the hat and rubbed sweat from his brow with his sleeve. Furrows ran from his eyebrows clear back to the crown of his bald pate. Thick bags sagged beneath his eyes.

"You know what I want," he said.

"Maybe I don't have it. Tomalini's already been through here." I saw Meg shudder, and thought it a good time to break the tension. "Meg, we must start locking these doors."

"Shut up, wise boy!" Dewey aimed the gun at Meg, who, I now realized, had her wrists lashed to the chair arms with duct tape. "My fingers ain't that steady because of a little accident I had visiting France for twenty years of my life. You want to see how unsteady they can be?"

"Put the gun down, Dewey."

"Where is it?" he said. The gun didn't move.

"It's not here. I can get it. Just put the gun down."

Dewey lowered the gun till it pointed somewhere between me and Meg. Not terribly safe, with his hands and wobbly nerves.

"Move over here real slow," he said, motioning me toward Meg with his other hand. "Now free her up."

I peeled the tape from her wrists, and she clutched at me.

"Now you listen up," said Dewey. "I don't have a thing left to lose, and what I want done I can do from a grave or a jail cell. Makes no difference to me. You remember that before you try something."

He worked the gun into his jacket pocket with his finger still on the trigger.

I told him the affidavit was in the hotel safe deposit box. He laid out our entire trip downstairs. The corridor we would walk, the elevator we would take, the course we would set across the atrium. It sounded like a long trek, and walking it seemed even longer. Amazingly, none of the dozens of people who crossed our path noticed anything amiss. Meg clung to me like a coat of paint, Dewey followed so close behind his shoes twice caught my heel, and I avoided any eye contact that might start a chain reaction.

At the security desk, I dug out my box key and two forms of ID. The clerk returned with the box after an excruciating delay of perhaps twenty seconds. I lifted out the envelope, but Dewey refused to take it.

"It's what you wanted," said Meg, her voice almost pleading.

Dewey mumbled something about privacy, and we all moved into a tiny alcove.

"Open it and hold it so I can read it," he said.

I did. He blinked, rubbed his eyes, adjusted the distance by moving my wrist.

"Just read it to me," he finally said.

When I finished, his eyes were moist. I folded the affidavit and tucked the envelope into his pocket.

"This way." He nodded toward the door.

"You got what you want," I said.

"A little insurance," he said.

Meg sagged against me.

"I'll go," I said. "Leave her out of this."

"A little insurance," said Dewey. "We all go."

We waited outside while the valet brought Dewey's car. A breeze came up, promising a storm with its slight chill. Dewey told me to drive, while he pushed into the back seat beside Meg. I mouthed *help* to the valet. He either didn't understand or flat out ignored me. I cursed the small tips I'd given him, silently promising philanthropic generosity to all service personnel if I survived the night.

The car stank like humus and chugged like a jalopy. The front seat was stuck, so I drove with the steering wheel in my chest and my knees against the underside of the dashboard. Dewey directed me away from the lights of Jacksonville, across the Intracoastal, and into the dark savannahs of north Florida. He'd pulled the gun out of his pocket. If I raised my head, I could see the glint of metal in Meg's ribs.

The minutes and miles dragged. Traffic thinned to the rare set of headlights curving out of the distance. An armadillo froze on the pavement and ducked under the bumper.

"Dewey, this is crazy," I said. "Whatever you got planned, this is crazy."

"Not crazy."

"Why don't you just drop us here. You'll be in Georgia before the cops find us."

"Ain't going to Georgia. Ain't going anywhere else no more.

Curtis already got one murder pinned on me. Two more won't matter."

Meg choked off a scream. I lifted my head enough to see her shoulders shaking. My stomach went hollow, my thoughts splayed into barbs of raw terror. I fought for concentration, knowing that engaging Dewey in conversation was our only hope.

"One murder? What about Tomalini?" I watched for his reaction. He swallowed hard, and held my eye in the mirror.

"Like I said. Two more make no never mind."

The savannah gave way to pine forests. I'd heard about the pine forests of north Florida and south Georgia, tracts so vast that loggers still discovered shells of private planes that crashed decades earlier.

Dewey told me to slow down, and then to turn onto a sandy path shooting off the highway. For one giddy moment, I thought we headed into Jason Oliver's campsite. But the road dropped into a long, sweeping descent that leveled off at a lake. Several battered canoes leaned against tree trunks. Tire tracks dug deep ruts into a dirt boat slip.

"Cut the engine," said Dewey.

A silence followed, with faint sounds rising as if from the depths of a well. Insects buzzed in the distance. Water lapped among the upthrust roots of cypress trees. Light fell faintly and evenly, diffused by a cloud ring surrounding the moon.

"Get out," said Dewey.

Meg, sobbing, refused to move. Dewey reached the gun over her head, and fired out the open window. A sharp crack resounded. The echo took forever to return. Meg screamed for help.

"Yell your damn-fool head off," said Dewey. "No one can hear you out here."

He kicked open the door, and shoved her to the sand. I jumped out, and picked her up.

"What's he going to do, Kieran?" she blubbered into my chest.

"Dewey, this is crazy," I said. "You have what you need. You don't need us. You stop right now, drive away, and let us walk. We won't say anything to anyone."

"That a promise?" he said.

"Yes."

"People made me promises thirty-five years ago. They weren't worth nothing then. They sure ain't now."

He grabbed a wad of my shirt, and pulled me and Meg toward the canoes.

"This one," he said, kicking one over. "Drag it down there."

I pretended not to understand, though I knew exactly what he meant. He grabbed my wrist and slapped my hand against the gunwale.

"Take the canoe down to the water," he said.

I hooked my hand under the prow. The light aluminum hull whooshed across the sand and pine needles and bounced across the tire ruts. I dropped it at the edge of the water. Dewey kicked one end afloat while the other prow clung to the slip.

"Tie her hands behind her back," he said, nudging a roll of duct tape into my hand.

"Dewey, this is a big mistake," I said.

He grabbed my shirt, yanked me down until our faces were inches apart in the gray light.

"Tell me how it's a mistake," he said.

I felt it, literally felt it. And just as Dr. Ellis had explained, it felt like a bunch of little balls, jammed in a tube, suddenly lining up and rolling again.

I lay on the floor in Cindy Moran's apartment. My head throbbed. Salty sludge filled my mouth, slowly enveloping a thin shaft of air.

"Who this?" said a voice high above me.

"I know him. He's on Tour," said another voice. "It's not anywhere here. Let's get out."

"But he's breathing, he's still alive." The voice sounded closer now. A thumb peeled up an eyelid. Dewey Peek stared at me.

"Let's get the hell out of here," said the other voice.

"Can't do that. This one's living," said Dewey. He worked a finger into my mouth. Blood drained out and the air shaft thickened.

"Tie her hands," Dewey said in the present. He stuck the gun in my ribs, the hard round barrel igniting as much pain as if he fired.

"Sorry, Meg," I said.

She must have passed into some form of dissociative state because she stopped sobbing and allowed me to gather her wrists behind her back.

"Tight," said Dewey.

He tested the wrap, and then prodded her into the canoe. She climbed over the gunwale like a zombie, but resisted lying down until he kicked the backs of her knees. She crashed hard and loud. I rushed toward Dewey, but he quickly swung the gun on me. I froze, and somehow he didn't squeeze the trigger.

"Your turn," he said, and wrapped my wrists behind me, while pressing the gun barrel against my chin.

"Dewey, I remember it now," I said.

"Remember what?"

"You and Jason at the apartment. You didn't kill her. You didn't hit me. You came afterward. You cleaned out the blood in my mouth."

"Don't mean nothing no more."

"Dewey, I'm a witness. I can testify."

"You didn't see nothing. You were out. I don't give a damn what you testify because no one's going to testify. I came back here to do something, and now's the time. Now you get in and lie down. Uh uh, head up that way."

He meant for me to lie with my head opposite Meg's. He wrapped our legs together with duct tape so we couldn't squirm beside each other and work at loosening our bonds. Finished, he stepped out of the canoe, and leaned close to me.

"Used to fish here when I got back from France," he said. "Decent place, till the gators took over."

He put the gun next to my ear and fired through the bottom of the hull. Then he shoved the canoe into the lake.

My ears rang with the gunshot. Water bubbled through the bullet hole, spraying my face with a fountain of tepid slime. I kicked my legs. Meg responded weakly, as if tossing in her sleep. She either had passed out or was paralyzed with fear.

I couldn't swim a stroke under normal circumstances; I didn't know about Meg. Once the canoe sank from under us, Dewey's configuration gave us a diabolical choice. We could keep only one of our heads above the water.

I wormed my way across the bottom of the hull. A sharp edge of aluminum cut into my pants at about groin latitude.

"Meg, you got to move."

No response; I kicked hard.

"Meg, I got to move toward you."

A groan. A slight twitch in her legs. The water rose quickly now, licking around my face. I took a breath, tucked my head against the roughened bottom of the hull for leverage, and pushed with all the strength of my neck and chest.

We moved an inch, maybe two.

I lifted my head, sucked air, held my breath again.

Another inch. I could feel that sharp edge with the tips of my fingers.

Once more. Two inches this time, and the tape binding my wrists reached the edge. The water circled my neck, crawled up toward my chin. Panting, spitting water, I pumped my arms like crazy. The water closed over my nose, splashed into my eyes. I sawed the duct tape on the sharp edge, not caring if I slit my wrists in the process.

The tape split. I wrenched my arms apart and bolted up with an explosive gasp. Water swamped the hull halfway up the gunwale. Luckily, I'd pushed us so far Meg's head curled up under the prow. Frantically, I unwrapped the tape from our legs. We were twenty-five, maybe thirty yards from the slip and drifting slowly away. I could make out Dewey's shape in the darkness, standing by the front of his car.

I kicked off my sneakers and rolled over the side, gripping the gunwale. My feet touched nothing, not even mud. Goddammit. I needed to flip the canoe while I could still trap enough air to keep it afloat. I kicked myself up, grabbed Meg's wrists, somehow found the strength to rip the duct tape apart. She flailed, coming out of her trance.

"Meg, come on. You got to get out."

She locked her arm around my neck. "Kieran, what's happening?"

"We need to flip the canoe. Can you swim?"

"Uh huh."

"Good, because I can't."

Rain started to fall, fine droplets that hissed on the lake like sand. Meg slipped over the gunwale and treaded water beside me. I was kicking like mad to stay up, probably using twice the energy of a more proficient swimmer. We bobbed to opposite ends of the canoe and flipped it.

That's when Dewey switched on the headlights.

The beam cut a wide swath on the water. Ripples from the canoe rolled lazily across a surface fuzzy with raindrops. Halfway to shore, the ripples broke around a jagged, roughly triangular piece of driftwood. The driftwood slowly rotated, revealing a single glistening eyeball staring into mine.

"Oh shit," I said, "a gator."

Meg rose slightly out of the water, as she kicked her legs faster.

"Where? Oh God."

Our years on golf courses made us experts at judging distances and estimating lengths. The gator's head floated twelve yards away. Its stubbled body broke the surface for fourteen feet from the tip of its snout to the end of its tail. It slowly wagged its head from side to side, using one eye then the other.

"Can he see us?" said Meg.

"I don't know."

"Can he hear us?"

"I don't know."

"Can he—"

"Meg, I don't know a damn thing about gators," I said.

"Well, what do we do?"

"Keep the canoe between him and us. Try to stroke toward shore."

"Which way?"

"Any damn way," I said.

We'd already started kicking like mad, propelled by our fear. The canoe didn't move, but the ripples spread faster.

"It's coming closer," said Meg.

"No," I said. "That's just the ripples."

The gator's tail stroked a single powerful beat, instantly halving the distance between us.

"Oh Christ," I said.

"That's not the ripples," said Meg.

We pulled ourselves amidships.

"Keep the canoe between us," I said.

The gator stroked again, stopping a few feet short. It raised its snout out of the water as if studying us and the canoe. Its head looked about three feet long and two feet wide in the fish-eye perspective you get staring death in the face. We stopped kicking and clung to the canoe, as if mesmerized. The last of the ripples rolled past the gator, leaving the surface flat and smooth, except for the dapples of rain. The head sank out of sight. The entire jagged body line dissolved into the blurry lake.

"Where did it go, Kieran?"

"I don't know," I said, though my mind's eye saw the image of a bull lowering its head to charge.

The rain shut off like a faucet, leaving the night dead silent. Meg and I tried to pull ourselves atop the upended hull. But the canoe bobbed like a cork, and huge burbles of air escaped.

"Oh God," said Meg. "Something just slid past me."

"Don't move," I said. Great advice. I didn't know whether we were on the regular menu, or whether gators mistook human limbs for lake trout the way sharks mistook surfers for sea turtles.

Then I felt something rub my knee. Was it the gator? Or was something else bumping around in the dark water?

A loud bang cracked the silence, and suddenly the wildlife didn't matter. Dewey was shooting. One bullet pinged off the hull. The next zipped into the water.

"What now?" said Meg.

"Stay low behind the canoe," I said. "He can't have too much ammunition."

"And then what?"

Good question. Dewey kept firing, and the rain came up hard again, and I couldn't tell the raindrops from the bullets.

The water between Meg and me began to boil. Meg screamed and flailed toward her end of the canoe. I felt myself rising, as if borne up by some powerful eruption beneath the lake.

Suddenly, the huge head of the gator shot past me with the sound of a thunderclap. It rose out of the water, froze momentarily, and crashed down onto the canoe. Its jaws yawned, and then snapped shut out of joint. Black blood pulsed out of an eye socket. A foreleg spasmed.

Dewey's last bullet slammed into the hide with a solid thud. The gator slowly slipped off the hull and floated sideways.

A parade of headlights and blue gumballs burst into view. Men rushed out of cars and surrounded Dewey's silhouette.

"Out here," I yelled. "Out here."

A spotlight found us. Four men jumped into two canoes and swiftly paddled out. They hauled me into one canoe, Meg into the other.

"Well, look at that," said a deputy.

Out in the beam of the spotlight, a dozen sets of gator eyes watched the dead gator turn slowly in an eddy.

I leaned over the side of the canoe and spat a mouthful of bile.

CHAPTER TWENTY

Wrapped in blankets, we huddled in the back of a police van. The rain had turned serious, pounding the roof like fistfuls of gravel and swirling ankle deep around the task force McGriff had assembled.

"Freezing," said Meg.

Another argument erupted among the gaggle of flapping ponchoes. I reached an arm out into the cold, gathered Meg close for whatever spark of body heat I afforded, and listened to three different law enforcement authorities debate how many Dewey Peeks could dance on the head of a pin.

Two of the group broke away and splashed to a cruiser. They opened the back door, pulled Dewey out, and hustled him into another cruiser. This was the third transfer in the last twenty minutes and, from the increased volume of the voices, promised not to be the last. McGriff had explained that they sniffed out Dewey on the off chance he holed up at his favorite fishing spot. I wondered how many arguments preceded their timely entrance.

They moved Dewey one more time before two men headed our way. I'd lost track of which authority had Dewey in its clutches—state, county, or Gainesville P.D.—but I recognized one ponchoed figure as McGriff.

"Follow my lead," I told Meg, "no matter how nuts it sounds."

McGriff climbed in, slapped back his hood, and rubbed his glasses on a corner of my blanket.

"This is Hawkins, Assistant State Attorney," he said.

Hawkins looked barely old enough to have graduated law school. Short hair receded from a prominent forehead, and a rectangular smile opened above a cleft chin. His eyes twinkled with happy expectation, as if people loved him all his short life, and he saw no reason to doubt we'd think his mere presence set the world right. In other words, a typical young lawyer.

"We want to run through what happened," he said. He worked his arms, spraying water from his poncho like a dog drying itself. A power tie poked out of his collar.

They didn't ask questions so much as recite what we'd just been through, in all the sterile language of law enforcement. McGriff authored most of this, beginning with the perpetrator accosting Meg as she returned to the hotel room after dinner. Then Hawkins interpreted every act in light of the Florida penal code. So far he could charge Dewey with attempted murder, assault with a deadly weapon, kidnapping, and reckless endangerment.

"And that's just off the top of my head," he said, joking by the look of his right-angled grin.

"Does it matter if we don't press charges?" I said.

Hawkins's grin closed a notch. McGriff, more acclimated to me, leaned closer.

"What did you say?" he said.

I repeated myself.

"He's joshing us, right?" said Hawkins.

"Joshing?" said McGriff, as if wondering what Western reruns Hawkins watched on late night TV. " 'Fraid not."

Hawkins looked at me hard. I'd seen his type in law school, the eager young man who saw the world in black and white, who learned trial strategy on the state payroll and then cashed in big time helping insurance companies hold on to their premiums.

"You're not going to press charges?" he said. "Are you crazy?"

I shrugged.

"Lenahan's crazy like a fox," said McGriff.

"We don't need him, we don't need her," said Hawkins. "We saw what we saw, and that's enough."

"What did you see?" I said. "Dewey shooting into the dark? You find that gator floating out there with the bullet in its brain, and you'll see he saved our lives. What else? Dewey didn't accost Meg."

I elbowed Meg into a kind of assent that was long on comedy and short on credibility.

"She knew he was looking for me and invited him to wait," I said. "When I finally arrived, I thought Dewey would be interested in seeing an affidavit I received in the mail."

"That affidavit is what all this is about?" said Hawkins. "It's not even a good affidavit. It wouldn't stand up in court for a second against the rules of evidence."

"Those words have a pretty powerful effect in some circles," I said.

Hawkins turned to McGriff with the same exasperated look the Judge often wore.

"What were you doing on the lake, smartass?" he said. "And what about the duct tape we pulled off ya'll's wrists and ankles?"

I winked at Meg, who didn't enjoy the show, but gamely played along by keeping quiet.

"That's our private affair," I said.

"Hawkins," said McGriff, "maybe you best let me talk to Lenahan."

"Be my guest. I think I'll take a dip in the lake." Hawkins pulled up his hood and jumped out into the rain.

"Dewey didn't kill Cindy Moran," I told McGriff.

"He was in the apartment, Lenahan. That's been confirmed."

"I know he was there, but he didn't attack me or Cindy Moran."

"You saying you remember what happened?"

"It fell back into place while I was out on the lake."

"That doesn't cut a whole lot of ice with me," said McGriff. "You say you remember something now, you may say you remember something else later."

"This is what happened," I said. "I went up to Cindy Moran's apartment because I figured out her scam and wanted out. She laughed me off and told me I was too late. She'd already sent the affidavit through the mail, which is probably all she wanted me for, anyway. While we talked, the killer showed up. He was one of the parties she was negotiating with. But it wasn't Dewey. He came later."

"That's a pretty way-out story," said McGriff.

"It's what happened, generally," I said. "I'm serious. I won't press charges against Dewey because Dewey didn't kill anyone. You try playing hardball with me, you'll hear the rest of the story first time from the witness stand."

"What's the point, Lenahan? If your story holds, we can squeeze Dewey easier than we can squeeze you."

"I got used and abused and dragged into this," I said. "I need to set this right."

"Law enforcement isn't your personal tool," said McGriff.

"It's not yours, either," I said.

McGriff's head snapped back, as if he'd told me about Claudine and Dewey in a buddy-to-buddy confidence and I threw it back at him at the first opportune moment. He whipped up his hood and jumped into the rain, his big feet splashing puddles dry as he stalked off in search of Hawkins.

"They don't actually need us," said Meg.

"I know."

"Then I expect they will arrest Dewey despite you."

"They won't," I said. "There's just enough doubt in their minds about what I know. A lawyer like Hawkins needs all the answers before he starts asking any questions."

I heard shouting above the beat of the rain and saw McGriff and Hawkins jaw to jaw behind the cruiser, where Dewey's silhouette sat motionless in the splattered glass. McGriff returned after ten minutes of solid arguing. He didn't bother to climb into the van, just leaned in far enough for the water to run off onto my blanket.

"We keep him in custody," he said.

"I never asked otherwise."

"Well, what the hell do you ask?"

"Two things," I said. "First, you keep Dewey's arrest a secret. Second, I have an eight o'clock meeting at Tour headquarters tomorrow. That gives you and Hawkins about ten hours to line up your ducks."

Despite the early hour, traffic backed up out of the Players Club and onto TPC Boulevard. Tournament marshals lined the road, scanning for players mired in the public bottleneck. Whenever they spotted one, they'd wave him into a clear lane marked by fluorescent cones. Chris Jennings sped past in this fashion; Ned Nelson, too. Meanwhile, Meg feathered the gas pedal to inch us along. Another perk lost. Simple, yet emblematic of how far I'd fallen in a week.

I used the time productively, drumming my fingers on my knees and mentally rehearsing my speech. In my mind, it sounded like one of my old trial summations, the way it built toward a climax I hoped would smooth the wobble in a very small part of the world. Not exactly polished Ciceronian rhetoric, but then I wasn't addressing the Senate and people of Rome.

We finally pulled into Tour headquarters. The parking lot bespoke the intense interest in the meeting Henry Chandler called. Jason Oliver's Beetle, Uncle Dan'l's Lincoln, a courtesy car with a bear claw towel spread on the driver's seat, and four other late models fittingly upscale for high-ranking Tour staffers. I opened the gray leatherette briefcase I'd picked up at one of those all-night superstores selling everything from toiletries to jet engines. After a quick look over my arsenal, I snapped it shut.

"Ready," I told Meg.

As we headed toward the entrance, McGriff stepped out

from behind a palm tree. Hawkins, looking like a typical spectator in bermudas and sunglasses, read a newspaper on a bench. Two other plainclothed agents of the law revealed themselves in strategic locations. McGriff and I reconfirmed our signals.

"This better work," he said.

I avoided the bravado of a prediction.

The conference room was quiet as a church, but the table where Chandler, Haswell, Lang, and Woody Harrington sat seemed less imposing than an altar. Funny how your perspective changes when you hold an advantage. Chandler, wearing his best bulldog face, tapped a pencil on the table. Haswell and Lang stopped whispering long enough to sneer at me. Woody, leaning back as usual, shot me that same knowing grin as last week.

In front of the table, Tommy Garth Hunter and Uncle Dan'l sat opposite Jason Oliver. Hunter, resplendent in bear claw finery, plainly itched to get out onto the golf course. Uncle Dan'l, perched on the verge of amusement, waved languidly. Oliver reposed in perfect symmetry, upturned hands resting on each knee.

I dragged a chair into the aisle to underscore my impartiality; I hated them all.

"Sorry I'm late," I said, opening the briefcase. "Traffic."

"Yes," said Chandler. "In addition to this meeting, the Tour is holding a golf tournament today. We'd very much like to attend it, sooner than later."

"Then I'll curtail my opening remarks," I said.

"You do that," said Chandler.

To my left, Uncle Dan'l grinned and Tommy Garth Hunter

rearranged his bulk. To my right, Jason Oliver remained sym-metrical, but unhooded his eyes.

I held up the affidavit, sealed in a clear plastic Sheriff's department evidence baggie.

"This is an affidavit," I said. "I have to admit, as affidavits go, it doesn't score very highly on what lawyers call probative value. But we're not in a court of law. We're in a never-never land where the writing on these sheets of paper is worth more money than is decent even to talk about. You want proof? Two people already died because of the words on these pages, and two more almost died last night."

I unsealed the baggie, and let the pages wave free in the air.

"It's easy to understand why so many people are after this. One person wants to use it as a catalyst to return the Tour to a pristine former state. Never mind that state never existed. Another wants to use it as a tool to exact revenge for a wrong that may be more real than imagined. A third wants to deep-six it to protect a valuable asset. Quite a lot of freight for a few pieces of paper.

"I've been through hell the last few days because of this affidavit. I'd like to return to my own pristine state as I existed before the Tour came to Florida. I'd like to exact my own revenge for some wrongs. And I'd like to protect my own asset. Unfortunately, I don't think any of that is possible anymore. But I have earned the right to do this."

I flicked a cigarette lighter. The paper burned slowly at first, then speeded up, the ashes curling black and spiralling away as the line of flame climbed toward my fingers. I blew out the flame, and let the last bits of paper drift to the floor.

"Some of you are happy now, and some of you aren't. Sorry,

I can't please everyone. Now for the small matter of my
suspension. You people don't like me, which is fair enough.
But I couldn't figure out why you would suspend me because
I didn't believe I'd done anything worthy of a suspension.
Hell, guys did lots worse than me. Look at Jason the other
day, practically killing Woody. Now if you were a paying
spectator, Woody, instead of just an expendable Tour staffer,
then Jason would have been suspended."

"You're suspended because the Commissioner says you're
suspended," said Chandler. "Get to the point."

"The point is, when I got suspended, the situation became
clear. I wasn't suspended for what I couldn't remember or
wouldn't admit or for potentially embarrassing the Tour or
its all-important sponsors. I was suspended because the Tour
knew more about Cindy Moran than I did."

Chandler slammed his fist, shattering his pencil on the
table top. "That's a damn serious charge."

"But I can prove it," I said, "because now I remember
why I was there, and who got there right after me."

Back into the briefcase, this time for a new pair of black
Banlon socks and a three-box of golf balls. The balls were
department store caliber, not the kind a pro would use in
competition, but just as rock-hard when placed in opposition
to the human skull. I separated the socks, dropped the golf
balls into one, and knotted it closed.

Chandler leaned forward. Lang squinted, elbowing Haswell
in the ribs. Woody shifted in his chair.

I rose slowly. My ribs ached. Blood pulsed close to the skin
where the duct tape had bound my wrists. The cold of the
lake water still chilled my toes. My head began to throb again,
probably from the power of suggestion.

I rapped the sock against my hand. The balls clicked together, filling the irregular surface with brute kinetic energy softened only by the meat of my palm. One rap clipped the funny bone at the base of my wrist. I bit my lip to keep from yelping.

I saw everyone as though they had high beams inside their eyes. Oliver stared at Hunter; Hunter at Oliver. Uncle Dan'l divided his attention between the two of them, as if he'd lay odds on one but also might take a long shot bet on the other. The four staffers stared at me. Three of them, anyway. Chandler, Haswell, and Lang thought I was nuts; Woody knew I wasn't.

I gave my hand one more rap, just in case anyone didn't understand golf balls in a sock equalled a blackjack. A deadly weapon in the Florida Penal Code so dear to Hawkins' heart, even though he never felt those balls wrapping around the curve of his skull, looking for a place to crash.

One step, another step. Time stretched, as it had when I first drove a car down Poningo Point Road in Milton, as it had when Jason Oliver lined up his tee shot straight at Woody's heart, as it had whenever my world shifted. Tommy Garth Hunter. The mini-tour gambling ring. The world was about to shift again. But this time, that world wasn't mine.

I stopped in front of the conference table.

"How many of you know Leo Tomalini?" I said. "Come on, let's see a show of hands."

One by one, they reached hands into the air. Chandler, Lang, Haswell, Woody. I turned around. Oliver and Uncle Dan'l lifted hands aloft. Uncle Dan'l nudged Hunter, and he did as well. The scene almost struck me as comical.

"So we all know Tomalini, Mr. Lenahan," said Chandler. "I could have told you that."

"My point precisely," I said. "Everyone who was on Tour five or six years ago knows Leo Tomalini. Let me be the first to tell you that Tomalini's dead. The state police fished his body out of the St. John's River yesterday morning. He was clutching a black Banlon sock just like this one here. The sock held golf balls at one time, just like this one. The police know that, because Tomalini had a crack at the base of his skull."

"We're all sorry about Tomalini, but he's been away from the Tour for several years," said Chandler. "You had better start explaining what this means to us."

I waved a hand behind my back, and paused to take a breath. In the silence, Meg's sneakers squeaked across the carpet. The conference door whispered open and closed. The countdown began. Five minutes.

"It all started," I said, "when Dewey Peek and Jason Oliver, each for his own reasons, hatched a plan to embarrass the Tour. Dewey hired Tomalini, who was by now scraping by as a private investigator outside Ocala. Tomalini quickly dug up information about a certain Tour star who used beta blockers during tournaments. But he didn't turn the information over to Dewey and Jason right away. Why? Because a few years ago, an Ocala rancher hired Detective Tomalini to investigate the past of a woman he'd married on impulse. That woman, who changed her name as often as a Gypsy, is the woman we know as Cindy Moran.

"She'd run scams in Ohio and Pennsylvania, and who knows where else. And the info Tomalini developed led to a quickie divorce. Now Tomalini knew the beta blocker scoop was a hot commodity. So he contacted Cindy Moran to put together a scam that would bring in more money than Jason and Dewey were able to pay. First, they turned the info into something tangible. The affidavit. Then they decided to offer it to other interested parties to see who was willing to pay the most. Cindy Moran got me involved late in the game. She presented it to me as a dispute with a business partner. In reality, she and Tomalini fell out during the critical phase of the negotiations. She mailed the affidavit to me as a means of safeguarding it.

"To be fair, I don't think the Tour star knew about the blackmail. His agent, manager, whatever, tried to negotiate a price. But the negotiations broke down, as they already had broken down with Jason and Dewey. Why? Because Cindy Moran and Leo Tomalini aimed at a bigger target."

"If you mean the Tour, Lenahan," said Chandler, "you're nuttier than I thought. If the charges in that affidavit were true, we would have known long ago, and that player would have been suspended immediately."

"Immediately after you ran your cost-benefit analysis, Henry," I said. "And immediately after you discovered— if you discovered, that the Tour stood to gain more from suspending one of its top draws than not."

"Do you believe we are that shortsighted?" said Chandler.

"Just the opposite," I said. "Tomalini knew about the Tour's long-range plan to create its own product marketing wing that would essentially do away with direct individual endorsement contracts between players and equipment companies. He knew that embarrassing the parties to one of golf's most lucrative endorsement contracts would pave the way. Equipment companies would shy away from relying on unpredictable celebrities, and turn to the Tour for marketing endorsements.

"If Tomalini had approached you, or maybe Sally, he might have pulled it off. Instead, he picked the players' best friend."

I dropped the sock in front of Woody.

"Want to finish the job?" I said.

"I don't know what you're talking about," said Woody.

"Come on, Woody, one more shot." I bent down, exposing the back of my head. "Shouldn't take much more effort than a chip shot with the state of my skull."

Woody slapped the blackjack off the table. One of the balls bounded out of the sock and rolled across the carpet.

"Woody?" said Chandler.

"He's gone crazy, Henry," said Woody. "It's the suspension. It's affected him."

"I went up to Gainesville because I'd pieced together enough of the scam to know I wanted no part of it," I said. "Cindy laughed. Said I was already in too deep. That's when you showed up, Woody. You took care of me first, then tried to get the affidavit out of Cindy, free of charge."

"Woody?" said Chandler.

"He's gone insane, Henry," said Woody. "You can't believe him."

"Believe me, Henry," I said.

Woody's midwestern jock facade collapsed in an instant. He turned frantically from side to side as McGriff and his men fanned out behind me.

"You son of a bitch!" screamed Woody. "I should have killed you when I had the chance."

"But you couldn't," I said. "You weren't sure if I saw you. When you couldn't find the affidavit, you figured it would turn up with me some time. But I had amnesia. So you dangled the suspension over my head, hoping I'd crack and cooperate with the Tour through you. But you blew it with Tomalini. Anyone who knew Tomalini would have recognized him from Meg's description of the guy who broke into my hotel room. See, Tomalini wanted to finish the deal himself, and he knew Cindy had mailed me the affidavit."

Woody didn't resist. He allowed one officer to handcuff him while McGriff read him his rights. No one else said a word. Henry Chandler lowered his head to the table. A sick smile froze on Peter Haswell's face. Sally Lang nervously twisted a lock of hair, as if scared I might have more allegations up my sleeve.

I dropped the blackjack into the briefcase, took Meg's arm, and followed McGriff's retinue. Jason Oliver's chest heaved like a bellows. I remembered Yvonne's story about the aftermath of the practice round, and hoped Jason kept breakfast down until I exited. Tommy Garth Hunter bit his lip, while a twinkle gleamed in Uncle Dan'l's eye. They both knew Tommy Garth dodged disaster when that affidavit went up in smoke.

Outside, cars crawled toward the spectators' parking lots. A white haze filled the sky, promising unseasonable heat for the end of March. Woody walked between McGriff and one of the plainclothes cops. Their hands held his elbows.

McGriff later blamed miscommunication. Each assumed he would open the back door of the unmarked cruiser; both released their grip on Woody at the same time. Woody bolted, running across the parking lot with surprising speed for a big man with his hands cuffed behind his back. McGriff hesitated for only a moment, giving Woody the lead he needed.

Back on TPC Boulevard, a marshal waved a pro into the empty lane. The pro later said he had cut his arrival time too fine. He was late, in danger of starting the tournament with a two-stroke penalty for missing his starting time. His eyes locked on the small digital clock on the courtesy car's dashboard as he gunned the accelerator.

Woody never gave any sign of seeing the speeding car. As he loped across the road, the car hit him dead square on the hood ornament. Woody cartwheeled over the top, pounding the hood, shattering the windshield, and thumping the rear deck before slamming to the pavement with a thud that still resounds in my ears.

The courtesy car flew out of control, knifing through a stand of pines and plunging into a shallow lagoon. Woody's shoes lay on the pavement, marking the point of impact.

We huddled around him. He lay crumpled on his side. A thin stream of blood trickled from the corner of his mouth. One eye opened enough to find me.

"Kieran," he muttered.

I leaned closer.

"Kieran . . . sorry about Gainesville . . . Did it for them . . . the players. . . . The Tour . . . too powerful. . . . Own momentum now."

"Save it, Woody," I said.

"No . . . you said it inside. . . . 'Players' best friend' . . . I like that . . ."

He collapsed into himself.

The line of cars had stopped completely. Spectators who came to see a golf tournament milled outside their cars, telling each other what they'd witnessed. A marshal yelled into a walkie-talkie. A siren wailed in the distance. The pro who'd driven the courtesy car waded out of the lagoon, saw Woody's body, and fainted. He would later withdraw from the tournament.

The Tour revoked my suspension by midafternoon. Too late for me to regain my berth in the Players, too late in other ways as well. In the evening of my hotel room, I tried to compose a few lines in response. The letter burgeoned beneath my pen, filling pages and pages of hotel stationery. In the end, I tore the paper to shreds and substituted two words.

Friday afternoon, we boarded a plane. Our last-minute booking allowed only three seats together, with the fourth several rows back. I took the single seat. Near dusk, the plane banked around a huge thunderstorm brewing over the Carolinas. I watched lightning flash from cloud to cloud until the storm moved astern.

Seven years later proved to be seven years too late for the Tour. I was not popular enough to be forgiven my sins, not weird enough to generate my own protective force field, not consumed enough to sacrifice my life to a game I no longer recognized. If I felt a kinship to anyone in this whole sordid affair, it was Dewey Peek. He'd been wronged and had waited for years to right that wrong, only to find himself mixing with people he couldn't possibly fathom. I saw myself heading on that same course, and so I cut myself loose. My two word response to the Tour's invitation: No thanks.

Now I winged back to Milton, where I could reclaim my pro shop with a minimum of slick talking, where I would be an insider again, not the outside agency of other people's agendas.

A few rows forward, Meg and Fisk roared while the Judge regaled them with a story. The Judge would start carping in a few days, portraying my little job at Milton Country Club as a no-man's land between the Tour and a renewed law career. Fisk would crucify me in his columns again, as he tried to wring mythic themes out of the stupid local golf tournaments. Meg and Georgina would face off against each other, possibly over my dead body.

Damn, it's great to know where the gators are.